PLAYING
WITH
FIRE

RACHAEL WAECHTER

DEFIANCE PRESS
& PUBLISHING

PLAYING WITH FIRE

ISBN-13: 978-1-963102-00-0 (Paperback)
ISBN-13: 978-1-959677-99-4 (eBook)

Photo credit for back cover is Madeline Barry

Published by Defiance Press & Publishing, LLC

Bulk orders of this book may be obtained by contacting Defiance Press & Publishing, LLC. www.defiancepress.com.

Public Relations Dept. – Defiance Press & Publishing, LLC
281-581-9300
pr@defiancepress.com

Defiance Press & Publishing, LLC
281-581-9300
info@defiancepress.com

Dedicated to Joshua

CHAPTER ONE

The only thing I knew for sure: *I wasn't dead.*

Somewhere in my subconscious, I realized this and suddenly jerked to life, gasping for air. My head screamed out in pain, temples thumping in tandem with my heart. I could barely open my eyes; the light stung them and caused my head to ache even more. I felt the hard asphalt under me, crumbled and broken, and the thick, dusty air was impossible to breathe.

Sitting up a little and leaning back on my hands, I glanced around. I was in the middle of the road. On both sides of me, cars had flipped over, some were on fire. The road had been destroyed.

What the heck happened? Where am I? How did I get here?

My body was numb, my senses weakened. All I could feel was the throbbing pain of the worst headache imaginable, the crumbled road under my hands, and a rhythmical pulsing in my left ankle.

I looked around and saw people running in the distance. They were panicked and running in different directions. Women were sprinting and sobbing with their children scooped up in their arms. Pathetic, scared people wore torn, dirty clothing. While I knew they were screaming, I couldn't hear their cries. In fact, I couldn't hear anything but dull ringing. Focusing on it made my head hurt more.

What caused this? Was there an earthquake?

And if there was an earthquake, why was I lying in the middle of the road? Why was I in so much pain? And above all, why was no one helping me?

I tried to push myself up, but my ankle couldn't bear the weight. I wasn't strong enough to hoist myself off the ground. On hands and knees, I panted into the hot asphalt.

Then it hit me: *I might die here.*

How? How do I deserve this?

I had no memory of any events; my mind was blank, so truthfully, I didn't know whether or not I deserved to die in the middle of that road. The only thing I could remember was my name.

I tried pushing up again, but this time, my arms gave out, and I collapsed onto my stomach. The air grew hotter. The fire was getting closer. I was going to die.

Fighting to stay conscious, but to no avail, I started slipping away: I was going. Suddenly, out of nowhere, I heard a voice. I had no idea where it was coming from, but beyond it, I could finally hear screaming in the distance. The voice spoke again; this time it was shouting.

"Keep breathing! Focus on breathing! We've got you!"

Without warning, someone rolled me over and scooped me into a cradled position. My eyes were barely open, but I saw a second person staring at me—a young man. I could make out brown eyes and a calm face.

"Miss Bianca Williams? We're here to help you. You're safe now."

And then everything went black again.

CHAPTER TWO

I woke up in a twin bed in a small room, no bigger than what you'd find in a college dormitory. It didn't appear to be a hospital room. I couldn't see the typical equipment, and the floor was carpeted. The space was fairly empty, containing only the bed, a dresser, and what I assumed was a closet. Opposite the door, was a window, on my right. A little light streamed in through the blinds, but I couldn't tell if the sun was coming up or going down. On the dresser a fishbowl contained a single goldfish. There was no other sign of the room being lived in.

I pushed back the comforter and swung my legs around so I could sit on the edge of the bed and look down at myself. I wasn't wearing shoes, but my left ankle was wrapped and carefully bandaged. I wore a white 'Disneyland Christmas 2016' T-shirt and pajama shorts with tiny elephants printed on them. I couldn't remember if I was in these clothes back on the road, or if someone had put them on me. I wasn't even sure they were mine, nor if I had been to Disneyland in 2016. Everything was blurry.

I heard rustling and whispering outside the door. My first sign of company. Curious, I put a little weight on my feet, testing to make sure my bad ankle wasn't going to give out if I stood. Luckily, the pain was not severe, not enough of a problem to prevent me from standing, especially if I put most of my weight on my other leg. I hobbled the few short feet over to the door and hesitated.

I didn't know who was out there or where I was. I considered getting back in bed or escaping out the window on the chance malicious people beyond the door had brought me here. But before I could make that decision, the door swung open.

I stood face to face with a girl who looked a year or two younger than I. She had pale, blonde hair, almost white, that barely reached her shoulders. She wore a floral, midi skirt and a light pink cardigan, straight out of the 1950s.

Her bright eyes looked shocked to see me standing there, almost as shocked as I felt.

"Um, she's up," the girl said softly.

Immediately and from what seemed out of nowhere, a young man rushed over and gently maneuvered past her. He was tall and broadly built, almost an exact contrast to the girl he moved aside. He grabbed my arms, slowly pulling me out the bedroom door and into a larger room.

"Here, come sit down," he said, pulling me toward the ugliest couch I'd ever seen. Although I could walk and function perfectly fine on my own, he helped lower me onto that couch, and I sank in comfortably. He told the small blonde girl to get me some water, and she rushed off through a doorway behind the couch.

The man hovered, stood in front of me, staring, but saying nothing. Maybe he didn't know what to say. He looked concerned as he brushed his hands through his short, dark hair. I took this opportunity to size him up. This guy was clearly an athlete of some sort, or at least he was built to be one. The circumference of his arms appeared larger than my head, and he had to have been about 6'3" and over 200 pounds. Taking this into consideration, I was 95 percent sure he was the person who picked me up and carried me here.

Since he wasn't speaking, and I wasn't sure exactly what to say, I sat up slightly and looked around the room. Much like the bedroom, it was fairly empty. From the couch, I could see a cabinet that held a television, a vase with rather fresh-looking flowers, and a few framed pictures. I sat too far away to see what sort of pictures the frames held. On each side of the cabinet were two doors, the one I came out of on the right and an identical one on the left. The left-hand door hung slightly open, allowing me to see what appeared to be a second bedroom.

The blonde girl came running back, handed me a glass of water, and sat down on the couch next to me. "Hopefully this helps," she said. "You've been asleep for a long time, so you haven't had anything to eat or drink. Actually, you slept so long that we were starting to get concerned that you were dead." She laughed awkwardly.

"Earlier I thought I was dead and then I woke up in that bed," I told her, hearing my own voice for the first time in a long while. I took a sip of water and let a million questions race through my head. I didn't know where to begin. I thought it best to start with a simple, "Where am I?"

"This is our house," the blonde girl said. "It's about a five-minute bike ride from the Beckworth College campus."

I hadn't heard of Beckworth College. I didn't know where that was.

"So, you're both college students?" That seemed to make sense. The girl certainly looked like a college student.

"Well yes and no. I'm the only one still in school. Four of us live here, actually. I still go to Beckworth, finishing up my final year. But everyone else graduated either last year or the year before. Well not from this college exactly, but another college somewhere."

She laughed awkwardly and continued, "Except Theo. He graduated from Beckworth this last Spring." I was still confused. Before I could interject, she continued. "We aren't far from where we found you, in Victory. That's the city you were in, in case you didn't know. We're currently in the suburbs, about a five-minute drive away from downtown. It's a very convenient location out here, close enough to get into town quickly but quiet enough to breathe a little. That's why we picked it. Especially when the others showed up, it made sense to stick together. They came all the way here because they heard there would be a place for them—we couldn't ignore their expectations. So, we got the house!"

I heard a sudden rattle behind me and jumped out of my seat. My foot stung from the sudden jolt. Directly behind the couch and on the right wall, I saw the front door. A key fiddled at the lock, causing my heart to pound. The door opened and another two people came in.

First was a girl, about my age, with a tan and stunning, long, dark hair. She was taller than me, certainly taller than the other girl. Next to her was a male with light brown hair and dark brown eyes. I recognized those eyes immediately.

"Hey, she's awake! We were getting worried," he said, throwing a backpack on the floor and closing the door, locking and securing the dead bolt behind him.

"Yeah, she just woke up. Trying to catch her up a little, but we've barely gotten started. You didn't miss much," the other guy said. I was pretty sure his name was Theo.

"Well, we're happy that you're ok," the new guy started. "Theo was convinced you were dead the entire drive back here. And when you didn't wake up right away, well …"

"How long have I been out?"

"We got back here yesterday evening. So about twenty-four hours," he said. He gestured for me to sit down, and I resumed my spot on the couch. He came over and sat on the floor by my feet and the dark-haired girl joined him.

"So how much do you remember?" she asked. Her tone indicated concern—for what, I wasn't sure. But she didn't smile as she spoke. She raised her eyebrows and waited for my answer.

"I remember waking up on the ground in the middle of the road. I remember thinking I was dying, and I remember being lifted. Nothing immediately before that and nothing afterward until about fifteen minutes ago."

I struggled to continue. My mind searched for any detail that could explain my identity or how I came to be here. Taking a deep breath, I started at the beginning with what I knew for sure: my name.

"I know my name is Bianca Williams, and I'm twenty years old. But I don't know how I got to that city. In fact, I've never even heard of Victory. I was born and raised in the middle of the country—Indiana, actually. I know I'm a college student, and I graduate this year. I know all of these details. But there's an empty gap in time between my being at school and being in the city on the ground. And at some point, I ended up wearing this," I said, gesturing to my ridiculous outfit. The room remained silent.

"What do you think is today's date? If you had to guess," the jittery blonde girl asked, biting her lip, and tapping her foot.

"The second week of April 2017," I replied, confidently. "Like I said, I'm graduating in a few weeks."

No one said anything in return. The brown-eyed boy stood and began pacing around the room. My body reacted before my mind did. My pulse raced, and my brain struggled to catch up, as if my body knew what was coming, but my mind wasn't ready to believe it.

"Bianca," he said, looking at the floor, "it's 2019; you're actually twenty-two years old, and you've already graduated from college. In fact, you've done a lot since graduating two years ago. Like, a lot."

Dizziness seized my body. The dark-haired girl took the water glass from my hand and set it on the floor. Then, she knelt, grabbed both of my hands in hers and looked directly into my eyes. "Shhhh," she said. "It's all going to be fine. We are going to explain everything."

Shivers ran down my spine and cooled my nerves. All at once, I felt calm. I nodded in agreement to everything she said. It was as if I believed anything she told me. Her eyes seemed to speak the truth. If she said it would be alright, it would be alright. She smiled, and that made me smile in return. I had no idea why, without knowing her at all, but I inherently trusted her so much.

Wait! What was I thinking? I didn't know her. I snapped out of the trance. "How are you doing that? Why am I so relaxed all of a sudden?"

She broke eye contact, let go of my hands, and looked down. All my worries flooded back. I panicked again.

"Seriously, who are you people? I need answers. Now."

"Well, I tried my best," the girl said, rolling her eyes.

Ignoring her, the blonde girl replied. "My name is Penny Anderson. This is Theodore Martin, but we call him Theo," she pointed to the guy I believed was Theo. At least having predicted that correctly meant I knew *something*.

"The pouting one is Jasmine Kahale, and Sebastian Caswell is the lunatic who is currently stress-pacing."

Jasmine made a huffing noise, got up, and went to the kitchen. Sebastian continued to pace, looking at the floor. Penny continued, "As I said before, I go to school here at Beckworth, but that's a cover, since we need to be on the edge of Victory."

"Why?"

The boys looked stunned, glancing at Penny as if she'd said something she wasn't supposed to. After a long series of glances and shrugs, Sebastian finally sighed and mumbled, "I guess we have to tell her eventually."

My heart started beating rapidly again.

"Don't you dare," Jasmine yelled from the other room. "Sebastian, I mean it. Don't you say a word."

"Ignore her; the rest of us are in agreement," said Theo, quietly. He smirked, glancing up toward the kitchen to see if the coast was clear. "Go on, Pen."

"Because," Penny said, hesitating a little, "we need to protect Victory."

CHAPTER THREE

efore I could get her to explain further, Theo cut in, "I ran into Penny years ago. We both grew up in a fairly small town, not too far from here. You know how news spreads fast in those kinds of places. Well, one day I heard a rumor from some friends at my high school that a weird girl was taking a ballet class downtown."

Penny's head whipped around to look at him.

"Hey," he said, "that's just the word my friend used. His sister was in the class, so he didn't know you personally."

"Ok, ok, continue," Penny said, smiling a little at his backtracking.

"So anyway, I found out this girl's name was Penelope Anderson and that she'd seriously injured another dancer during a rehearsal. She accidentally kicked her during a routine. The thing is, a small kick shouldn't have left a bruise. But it did, and more. When her foot hit the girl, it blasted her into the wall." I looked over at Penny and stared at her accused feet.

"So the next day, I went over to the dance studio to see for myself and waited until she was out of class. It really wasn't that hard to pick her out; the girl looked pretty damn rejected, having been socially shunned because of the incident and what-not. She was the last one out of the building that day. Without thinking, I grabbed her and introduced myself. I told her—"

Penny cut him off, saying, "He told me I wasn't the only one. That is, I was not the only person who wasn't quite normal. Initially it freaked me out—I thought he was crazy. But he said he could prove it, which honestly, made me curious. He asked me to wait outside as he made his way up to the roof. At first, I thought he was pranking me or making a fool of me, like everyone else did after the ballet class incident.

"A few minutes later, I heard him call my name. I looked up and he was waving at me from the roof. And then … and then he unexpectedly jumped off."

My mouth dropped open as Penny continued, "But instead of dropping like a bag of rocks, he somehow floated down like a feather, practically weightless. He became part of the air, floating along with the wind. For the first time in my life, I realized I wasn't alone," Penny said sniffing and tearing up a little. So Theo jumped back in.

"Obviously, since we realized *we* were both the weirdest people to ever walk the earth, we quickly became friends and met up all the time. We stretched the limits of our skills, testing and practicing them. We started going into Victory on weekends, finding convenience store robbers and bike thieves to take down. Almost overnight, we became Victory's neighborhood superheroes.

"Then I graduated high school and applied to Beckworth College in order to stay close to Penny and to Victory. After a year, Penny graduated and came here too. We both continued school and more importantly, continued fighting for Victory. And then last year, after hearing on TV about the mystery 'defenders of Victory,' Sebastian and Jasmine appeared, looking to help. Seb came out from Texas in March and Jasmine came out in August, all the way from Oregon. They were just like us, needing a place to live where they didn't have to hide their skills. Where they could help people. So, we welcomed them into our world. Since I no longer had a dorm room and since Seb and Jasmine didn't have anywhere to live, the four of us decided to buy a house, giving ourselves a communal space to live without worry."

"And since then, we've been keeping Victory safe," Sebastian said. "Kinda as a team. We're like the mini-Avengers or something. But our powers are much less cool."

"Like your friendly neighborhood Spiderman, before he joined the Avengers and got the real fancy suit. That's us," Penny sniffed and smiled.

I was in awe. Either I was still in a coma or dead, because this certainly couldn't be real.

"You're lying," I said. "You're telling me that you're superheroes? That you can fly and stuff?"

It just wasn't believable!

"There's no way. You're making up some story, so I won't report you to the cops for abducting me. You don't have to do that. Please, I only want answers."

The heaviness of what had happened weighed me down, and the stress of the aberrant situation was breaking me. I closed my eyes and took a deep breath.

"Please," I whispered, "I deserve answers. Please."

"Well first of all, I ride air currents, I don't fly," Theo said, breaking the silence. "Which is super stupid, but I deal with it. And what the hell would four twenty-somethings get out of abducting someone? That's *also* stupid, and you know it. Finally, yes this is real, and I can prove it." He went over to the door, unlocked it, turned the knob on the dead bolt, and walked outside.

We all got up to follow. Jasmine yelled something incomprehensible from the other room, presumably telling him that he shouldn't do whatever he was about to do. We stopped on the porch, but he continued out to the middle of the lawn. There, he closed his eyes and felt the air around him. Sebastian whispered in my ear that this was Theo's way of searching for a breeze. He must have felt it because suddenly, he opened his eyes, looked at me, smirked a little, and jumped into the air. The wind swept him up with the leaves, and to my surprise, he flew. As long as the little breeze was willing to keep him suspended, he remained in the air, floating around. When he landed, my jaw dropped. Once again, I stood speechless.

"If you like that, watch this," Penny said, running down to the side of the road. Dragging up the rolling trash bin, she set it near where Theo landed and smiled. She backed up across the yard and then proceeded to perform a few running leaps towards it. When she reached the bin, she executed a turning kick to its side, and it flew—not just across the lawn, but all the way down the road. She annihilated it. I couldn't comprehend what I was seeing.

They were superheroes. Real life superheroes.

Rather than jumping back to the assumption that I was actually in a coma, I suspended my disbelief for another moment and without hesitation, turned to Sebastian and asked, "What do *you* do?"

"Well, I can be handed any weapon and automatically know how to use it. For example, you could toss me a knife, and I'm a knife thrower, a bow and I'm an archer, that kind of thing. Better yet, you could throw me something that isn't a weapon, and I can make it one. I've taken someone out with a hair dryer, so you really don't want to mess with me," he said, laughing. I couldn't help but smile.

"What does Jasmine do?" I asked.

"I have the lamest skills," I heard from behind me. Turning to look,

I saw Jasmine coming back out of the house. I guessed she decided to join us after all.

"They aren't physical per se, but I've gotten pretty good, if I do say so myself. I'm a master of persuasion. I can essentially hypnotize anyone if I can get them to listen to me long enough. I usually have to make eye contact, but I'm getting better at doing it with only my voice. I practice on telemarketers." She smirked, so I couldn't tell if she was serious.

"It's handy. I often used it on my parents as a kid. I also used it to get this house for practically nothing. Plus, it calmed you down earlier. Or at least, it did briefly before you decided to panic again."

"So *that's* what that was!" I replied. I was floored. I'd been under her spell!

"Guys, this is incredible," I said a little too loudly as I ran my hands through my hair. "You're all amazing; why didn't you tell me this the second I woke up?"

Sebastian laughed, "Because it's not the easiest thing to explain. I'm not even sure we did it justice if I'm being honest." I didn't know what to say, or think, or do. I quickly came down off my emotional high and remembered how this all began.

"So wait," I asked, "what does all this have to do with me? If I was someone you rescued, how did you know my name, and why did you bring me back here?"

Once again, glances were exchanged among the four of them. Jasmine shot a death glare at Sebastian who shrugged at Theo. Theo gave Penny an unsure look. And with hesitation, Penny finally spoke up.

"Bianca, I know you don't remember this because the last two years of your life are missing from your memory for some reason, but you're one of us."

CHAPTER FOUR

While I couldn't remember anything from the last two years or so, I knew for a fact that Penny was wrong. I wasn't like them. I had no powers. I could barely microwave popcorn without burning it.

"No. No. No. You have the wrong person. There must be some other Bianca Williams, some other person with powers you're searching for. It's a very common last name, so you've definitely got the wrong Williams."

"Oh, we aren't wrong," Penny exclaimed. "We've been keeping an eye on you for a while, so when you came to Victory, we knew …"

"Guys," Jasmine said, grabbing Penny by the arm and dragging her towards the house, "Haven't you said enough already?"

We all made our way back inside, following a sullen Jasmine and a dragged-along Penny. Sebastian crossed his arms and looked at the ground while he walked, as if calculating something in his head. Theo appeared annoyed, but gave in to Jasmine's wishes, fully aware that she would sulk again if he opposed her. Once inside, Penny climbed the metal, spiral staircase in the kitchen, and Theo disappeared into the neighboring room to the one I woke up in, closing the door behind him. Jasmine locked the front door and looked at me.

"I'm going to run up to the loft and get some towels and stuff ready for you. You can sleep up there with us tonight. And tomorrow we can get you in new clothes—I don't want you to wear my pajamas forever."

I opened my mouth, but before I could speak, she cut in, "We found you in other clothes, but they were really dirty, so Penny and I changed you into these. That way, you could sleep without getting asphalt all over Seb's sheets."

After a slight pause, she added, "Don't worry; the boys saw nothing." She winked and went up the stairs.

This left Sebastian and me alone. He fiddled silently with something on the TV stand, not realizing that I stood behind him. I was unsure of where to go. "Hey," I said, causing him to jump. "Um, thanks for letting me have your room. I didn't know it was yours."

"Oh no problem. You needed a bed, and I had one, so I really didn't mind. Plus, the couch made a fairly comfortable replacement bed." He went over and sat on it. "Really, you should try it now that you're more awake. It may be ugly, but it's like heaven to sit on." He patted the spot next to him. I hesitated a moment before joining him.

"See? Pretty great," he said and smiled at me. He was right. I sank into the cushions, appreciating how comfortable the couch was. I felt strangely calm, and Jasmine wasn't around to force me into it. But even in this relaxed state, something significant still tugged at my mind, and my gut. I didn't know how or why, but I knew if anyone would give me what I needed, it was Sebastian.

"I won't be able to sleep tonight, you know, without an explanation," I said, taking a deep breath. I felt nervous to ask such a favor, especially on my first night here. But it seemed necessary to try. "I need an explanation of who I am and why you all brought me here."

He didn't seem irritated or even shocked that I brought up the elephant in the room.

"I know," he said, "you deserve it." He sighed and shifted uncomfortably in his seat. Closing his eyes, he thought for a moment. Opening them, he said, "Have you ever been so angry that you felt like the world around you was burning?"

What should I say to this? He didn't even answer my question. Despite my immediate irritation, I tried my best to answer him as calmly as possible. "Well, of course. I don't know if I made myself clear before, but I've been angry all evening because none of you will give me the answers I deserve. You'd be angry too, I imagine."

"No, you haven't been angry. You've been frustrated and perhaps a little mad, but you haven't been truly angry. There's a difference. Mad is when you're simply unhappy about a particular thing. Anger, real anger, is a pure emotion. It overtakes your entire body. You can 'be' mad, but you *feel* angry. In your case, you've been too distracted by your quest for answers to feel pure emotion." Sebastian looked into my eyes, "What I'm trying to say is that you aren't *actually* angry. You're too curious to be."

"What do you mean?" I felt warm, and my pulse was a drumbeat echoing across the Sahara.

"You're too distracted," he replied. "You can't focus on one emotion at a time; your anger is clouded by something else. I don't know if it's fear or anxiety or something else entirely."

He sat for a second in silence, considering his words carefully, before continuing. "Maybe it's a secret bit of pleasure, like you're enjoying the unknown world. I have no idea, but I am quite positive that what you're feeling is *not* anger."

"And how do you know that?"

"I just do." He shrugged. "I'm one hundred percent certain."

Now this made me angry. Not mad, as he said before, but actually angry. Who was he to tell me what I was feeling? I scowled directly at him, feeling the heat rising in me. He sat still and stared at the floor with his hands folded in his lap; he was cool and relaxed.

"You don't know me. You don't know my emotions or how I express them," I said, a little louder than either of us probably expected. "You have no business poking fun at me for my state of confusion. It's not my fault that I'm here—you are the ones who did this to me, who dragged me here. So cut it out and give me answers."

He smirked. He glanced up, and his eyes finally met mine.

"Not until you come to grips with the fact that you aren't really angry." He casually picked up his glass of water from the floor next to the couch and took a sip, never losing eye contact.

"Face it," he said, shrugging, "You can't feel pure, undistracted emotion. You're incapable …" He leaned back even more. "… of feeling."

That was it.

I sprang to my feet and let him have it. "You complete and utter … ugh! You sit around all evening, keeping your mouth shut and pretending to be earnest, but clearly, you've had some sort of agenda to kidnap me, drag me here, and torture me. I don't know who you are, but I despise you. In fact, I may even hate you."

The world around me flared in a hot, red haze; my vision turned scarlet. Rage burned through my body like it was on fire. The flames engulfed me as my haphazard hands moved with my words, my emotions. I hated him with the deepest hatred my body could muster. I wanted him to burn.

"Now," I seethed, "you're going to give back the clothes you found me in, and I will be leaving. Immediately. And honestly, you can burn in—"

But before I could finish my sentence, I swung my right arm down, angled out a little from my side. And as that happened, in a direct line from my right hand, the carpet caught on fire.

The flames of rage in my heart were snuffed out the second the flames on the rug ignited. I couldn't believe what I was seeing. My eyes shot from the rug to Sebastian's face.

Without hesitation, as though he'd seen this kind of thing every day, Sebastian maintained eye contact and poured his glass of water over the flames, leaving me to stare at the little wisps of smoke with my mouth ajar.

"Alright, that's enough for tonight. You should get up to bed."

I turned my attention back to Sebastian, who was giving me an, "I-told-you-so" smile. He said nothing. Just gave me a prolonged look, one I wouldn't shake off for some time. His taunting … it wasn't to hurt me after all.

Now, I didn't want him to burn. Not anymore.

I wanted to tell him this, but I couldn't piece together the words. My mind felt numb, and my mouth fell silent. Instead, I picked up my glass, put it in the kitchen sink, and climbed the winding, metal staircase to the loft, unable to move my hands or understand how in the world I caught the carpet on fire.

"Goodnight, Bianca," Sebastian yelled after me. I could imagine the smirk on his face, but this time I wasn't mad; I was stunned.

I was being chased. Heart pounding, I ran down an alley. Although I couldn't see him, I could sense him following me. Dodging dumpsters, boxes, and crates, like a scene from a comic book. I ran.

I tried to feel the heat, tried to force something into my hands. I tried to focus on the feeling of burning, of light and flames.

Nothing.

I kept running, trying to stay in the shadows the best I could. He had to be closing in on me. I hooked a sharp left and ran down the dark side of a building. I briefly considered climbing a fire escape but shook that idea from my head, realizing almost immediately that he would still be able to find me. And when he did, I would be trapped. Done.

Anger. Why couldn't I feel anger?

Because of the fear. It was all fear.

I panted and shook uncontrollably. I felt like a deer the moment it locks eyes with the hunter. And like that deer, understanding its fate, yet still clinging to that small, impossible hope of survival, I ran.

CHAPTER FIVE

Between the four local superheroes, there was only one car, if you could even call it that. They took turns driving a beat-up, tan minivan that Theo had purchased back in high school.

On my first journey out in said van, only the girls piled in, leaving plenty of extra space. Jasmine drove and let me sit shotgun with Penny in the back. The planned destination was a mall about an hour and a half west of Beckworth, the opposite direction of Victory.

"Isn't there a mall in Victory? And isn't that significantly closer? I mean, not that I even know this area. I've never seen it before. But I feel like a big city would have shops," I questioned, staring out the window, taking in the rolling hills and scattered trees. It took everything in me to keep calm and to pretend this new life was normal—like I hadn't discovered life-altering secrets about these people, or about myself.

Beckworth sat on the East Coast where the terrain actually changed as you drove along. Growing up and spending my whole life in middle America, I wasn't used to this new world. It fascinated me. How did I get here? Why did I come here? Was I lured to the coast for its beauty? Had my home not satisfied me?

"Oh, this one is really nice, I promise," Penny quipped from the backseat, pulling me out of my head. I wasn't sold on her reply, fully believing they intentionally planned this trip to keep me from the city where they'd found me. However, with my exhaustion and general shock still in play, I recognized that now wasn't the time to complain or question. It was a time to buy pants.

"How are we paying for this? I don't have any money."

Without taking her eyes off of the lonely, winding road, Jasmine reached in her purse and pulled out a blue zipper wallet. Tossing it on my lap, she replied, "Yes you do. We found this on you, inside of a fanny-pack type thing. Super funny if I'm being honest. You've got a good amount of cash in there."

Penny added, "And whatever you can't cover, we can. All four of us work; we can pitch in. Besides, it's not like you're on a shopping spree. We are getting you essentials—stuff that's your own. In fact, I think Seb is running to Walgreens to get you a toothbrush and other toiletry stuff, so you'll be set on that front."

I reasoned and wrestled with my situation since waking up in Sebastian's bed, but my natural, trusting state continued to win out. I logically knew that I shouldn't trust strangers, especially those with supernatural powers that could kill me, but at the same time, my mind kept populating the same thoughts: They saved my life. And furthermore, they had revealed themselves to me. In fact, Sebastian revealed *myself* to me. Surely, they wouldn't have done these things as part of a long-form, torture scheme? Regardless, I struggled to imagine Sebastian trying to buy me a toothbrush and deodorant. Part of me felt grateful, and the other part felt embarrassed.

I unzipped the little pouch and pulled out $300 in cash. Oh, that would do. Also in the wallet was a punch card to a frozen yogurt shop, a Barnes & Noble gift card, and my driver's license. My actual driver's license. Bianca Jane Williams, DOB 06/12/1997. Issued April 2017. Two years ago.

I looked at the picture. My hair barely fell to my shoulders. Instinctively, I reached up and ran my hand through my hair. It was pretty much the same color, but now it was long, halfway down my back. I'd forgotten that it wasn't always like that. In the photo I smiled brightly. I looked a little like Penny: young and carefree.

"What'd you find?" Jasmine asked as she glanced over.

"My license. Just staring at the picture. I don't remember looking this young and happy."

"Let me see." Penny reached up around my seat as I handed it to her. "You look so cute, my goodness. Oh, and it's not expired! That's convenient!"

"Yeah, but I don't look like that anymore; I probably need to get a new one."

"You don't look that different, just older, which everyone does two years after their license photo. You can still use it!" I had only known her for about twenty-four hours, but this felt like a typical moment for Penny, making the best of any situation.

Passing the license back to me, she asked, "Are you going to keep the long hair, or do you think you want to cut it to the length in the photo? I like it both ways."

I ran my hand through my hair again. Did I want to try to replicate my life before forgetting; was I hoping to magically sink back into that person I used to be? Or was I ready to accept who I had become, regardless of how much I knew about myself?

On the one hand, old Bianca seemed happier, surer, and more hopeful. The current Bianca felt worried, confused, and overwhelmed. I was incredibly torn, trying to decide the best path forward without the knowledge of how I came to be at this particular place.

"I don't know," I said. "In regard to the big picture of what person I want to be, I don't know what to do. But in terms of my hair, I think I like it long. While I want to remember who I was two years ago, I like being able to start fresh with something. Plus, the more recent Bianca seemed to be growing it out, since she didn't cut it. Maybe there was a reason for that."

"Good choice," Jasmine said. "Fresh starts are always nice. I had one when I moved out here, and it's the best thing that ever happened to me."

"Yeah, what's your story?" I asked Jasmine. "Penny said you moved out here from Oregon, right?"

Jasmine kept her eyes on the road and smiled. She didn't seem to mind the prying today, which was good news for me since I had spent all of yesterday digging for answers in a mine that refused to produce.

"I grew up in Hawaii with my parents and little brother until I was about ten, when we moved to rural Oregon. I wasn't happy about that. I didn't like being torn away from my friends and my school. I liked being where my culture felt alive. My mother is from a line of native Hawaiians, and my father is Japanese American. It was important for me to celebrate that. Also, even as a child, I liked routine. Having that suddenly ripped away was hard. So, I started to take it out on the other kids at my new school. Hitting them, taking their things, you know? Your classic childish bullying."

"My goodness you were a school bully! That's hilarious!" I laughed.

Honestly, it wasn't that hard to picture. Since the moment I met her, I was terrified that Jasmine was going to pummel me. I wasn't as terrified of Penny, whose skills, could pummel and *obliterate* me. As evidenced by my first night, Jasmine had certain energy that said, "Watch yourself, or I'll make you suffer."

"Yeah, kind of," she laughed. "But it didn't take me long to find a different way to mess with people and get what I wanted."

"Your powers," I said.

"Yep. There was a day when I got busted for stealing a kid's dessert during lunch period and when the principal sat me down. I focused on the lie I was going to tell her. I didn't know it would be a mystical lie or anything of the sort. I desperately wanted to sell it. I told her it was another kid's fault, made up some evidence, and honestly, she should have questioned it. But instead, she stared blankly at me, as if she were hypnotized. She said I was right, and she would punish the other kid. And she did.

"I quickly realized that it shouldn't have been that easy. I clearly had a knack for this. So, I tried it on the other kids. Instead of stealing, why not merely lock eyes with them and ask them for their twinkie? You can't get in trouble if they give it to you on their own accord! So, starting then, I pretty much got whatever I wanted, and no one was any wiser. I started using it on my parents, my brother, everyone. I continued to do this though high school, and then I got three years into a four-year college degree before I realized that I had to stop. I was becoming a person I hated."

"You woke up one day and wanted to change?" I was shocked that someone could have so much self-control.

"I didn't want to go through life knowing I was only thriving because I hypnotized people into letting me. Getting ready to finish college, I realized I didn't know what to do. I felt like I had wasted my life. I vowed to finish my degree. To finally complete something on my own, and then use my talents for good. Not my powers. I tried not to use them anymore. Nope, my degree in biology. I would do … something with it."

"And you didn't."

Jasmine flashed me a glare.

"No, no, not in a bad way. But you obviously changed your mind during that last year. I mean, you're here and not doing biology," I reasoned.

"I graduated and had a job lined up in San Diego at a lab, doing research on different kinds of bacteria. Honestly, fascinating stuff. Things were great until about a week before I moved. While packing, I turned on the TV for some background noise. I tuned in to the news, wanting noise and not distraction, but then a story came on that I couldn't help but overhear."

"It was Penny and Theo. Saving someone in the city, wasn't it?" I didn't know why, but I felt so strongly that I could see that news story too, if I tried hard enough.

Jasmine looked surprised.

"Yes, it was. I knew that's where I had to be. So, I packed my bags and got on a plane to Victory, without telling my parents why. I told them that things had changed, and a better opportunity had come up."

"Just like that?"

"Just like that."

APRIL 12, 2017

I sat alone on the living room couch in my pajamas. It was a Saturday night in April, the night before I had to return to school from my college's spring break.

My dad yelled something from the kitchen that I couldn't quite hear. I was supposed to be finding something for us to watch on TV. My mother and sister could be heard upstairs, rushing to get their pajamas on before joining us for family night. These nights were pretty rare; they were special occasions. Since I was going back to school the next day, I insisted.

I flipped through the channels, scanning for a movie. As I whizzed through, I saw a flash of what looked like someone flying. A superhero movie … that could work. I went back and watched.

A young guy, no older than me, jumped from a building and floated to the ground, landing in front of three guys in ski masks. The film was shaky—probably filmed with a phone camera. Suddenly, a younger girl came up behind one of the masked men and kicked him to the ground.

As they fought, the camera dropped to the ground and the video cut out. A newscaster appeared on the screen and explained that a bystander took the footage while the robbers came out of a 7/11. The caption across the screen read, "Victory Supers? Two Mysterious Defenders Stop 7/11 Robbery.

"Who these defenders are, we do not know. Have superheroes been discovered in Victory? Or is this some hokey set up? We will closely follow this story and bring you the latest."

Then a story about a local school debate team came on. This wasn't a movie! This was the news channel! My heart started pounding as I hit rewind and paused on the anchor and the caption. I ran to where I kept my backpack, grabbed a pen, and tore a page from a notebook. Rushing back to the couch, I started scribbling.

"I hope you picked a good movie," my dad said as he walked in. I hit, "Live TV."

"Not yet. Still looking," I replied. I shoved the piece of paper into the waistband of my pants. Written on it were two words: *Victory City.*

CHAPTER SIX

I t was a few days after the mall run, and my time in the house had become routine. Every morning, Penny walked to campus for class, and Theo accompanied her. Jasmine drove the van to the local vet clinic where she worked.

I asked Jasmine about her job and how she qualified to be a vet. She said, "I work at the front desk, which is pretty sad, but I 'persuaded' them to pay me double the normal rate. I should feel bad, but we need it. Plus, we keep their city safe so they can chill."

Sebastian biked to an office near the Beckwith campus where he served as a research assistant for a professor who was writing a book on some Greek mathematician's greatest works.

Everyone spent the morning either making money or finishing their last year of college while I wandered around the house. I felt pathetic being the only one in the house who couldn't use their powers. What was worse was that it was depressing to wander around the house alone every morning, accomplishing nothing of true value.

Well, I guess I wasn't entirely alone. I discovered that the house had a frequent visitor, a small, gray cat who could meow louder than any cat I'd ever encountered. While it wasn't another human, it truly made a difference having another living creature around. Stroking the cat grounded me, drew me out of myself and allowed me to focus on something other than my torturous worries.

The house had a little garden out back where Jasmine and Penny grew produce and flowers. Each morning, I took it upon myself to go out and pick anything that looked ripe, making sure that the garden was being put to good use, and that I was being put to good use. After my first dinner at the house, I noticed that Jasmine had used the bell peppers and green beans from the garden to make dinner, so I continued to pick vegetables each following day. At least I could be useful in some little way.

Besides wandering, petting the cat, and picking vegetables, I also spent my mornings snooping around and trying to catch things on fire. To be fair, I only snooped because they wouldn't give me answers. I could at least try to find answers for myself. That felt productive.

I only searched common places and the open, more public areas of the upstairs girls' bedroom. I especially didn't feel comfortable going into Theo's and Sebastian's rooms, digging around in their messes. Besides, it felt wrong to dig through the rooms of two men, in any circumstance. For privacy reasons, I also didn't dig through Jasmine and Penny's drawers and closets.

My search proved to be a waste of time. I couldn't find anything related to me or my past. To be frank, I couldn't find anything related to their secret powers either. If a random person were to wander in with no knowledge of the powers held inside this home, they would leave with that same lack of knowledge. This seemed to be a normal house full of college-aged kids. A little messy, pretty darn small, and nothing out of the ordinary. Very inconvenient for the curious side of me, but very comforting as a whole. They were safer this way, and therefore,

I was safer too. I may have been worried about trying to remember my past and grow my powers, but at least I didn't have to worry about being attacked in this house while everyone was away. Probably.

In the realm of catching things on fire, I also wasn't having any luck. Most of the time I sat out in the backyard, but only when the neighbors were gone. Otherwise, if neighbors were out and about, I sat on the kitchen floor, figuring that the linoleum was the least flammable spot inside the house. I raised my hand and concentrated on creating a flame. I tried to remember the exact phrases Sebastian used the other night and how my brain processed them. I tried to work myself up to getting stressed out, and I pushed that stress and frustration down into my hands. Nothing. I tried thinking of warmth and heat and picturing my hand on fire. Nothing there either.

But "hand on fire" wasn't a bad idea, or so my Tuesday-self thought. I stood at the stove and turned one of the gas burners on high. Was I crazy to think that someone who had fire powers could avoid being burned? Especially when that same someone was very prone to things like sunburn?

Turns out I *was* crazy, and less than a second after I stuck my left hand into the flame, I doubled over the sink, running it under cold water, spitting out words I never thought would leave my mouth.

So I wasn't fire-proof. But I still felt confident that the flames emitted from my hand a few nights prior were real and that I could make them appear again. Every morning, I sat and concentrated, never producing anything, but also never stooping so low as to stick my hand in a burner again.

In the afternoons, Penny came home first and studied for a bit in the living room. Then, she went out again, this time to the dance studio for an hour or two. Jasmine came home in the early evening to make dinner. By the time dinner was ready, Penny and the boys would finally return. The boys taught a self-defense class at the gym.

"Isn't that incredibly suspicious? Two guys with super powers teaching a self-defense class," I asked them at dinner a few days after the burnt hand incident.

"I don't think so," Theo said. "Anyone and everyone can use self-defense."

"Yeah, but two superheroes," I reiterated, "Teaching self-defense? While also trying not to let anyone find out that they have powers? I don't think Clark Kent taught kickboxing after work."

"It's only suspicious to you because you know about it. To everyone else, it's two young men teaching a class because they need money. And they're certified, which is why they're so good. No one asks questions if you're certified." Theo buttered a piece of bread and passed the butter dish to Jasmine.

"Besides," he continued, "neither your powers or mine are being put to use. We teach defense and hand combat. Seb needs something to use as a weapon, and I need to be able to float around, so neither is a problem in this scenario."

"Plus, it sharpens our combat skills," Sebastian said, between bites. "In actual combat situations, I don't always have something to use as a weapon, so this comes in handy in a fight. You should come to class one night. It might be good for you too."

Jasmine choked on something and glared at Sebastian. "I don't think that's a good idea," she said between coughs.

"I don't see a problem with it," Sebastian replied, nonchalantly taking a drink of water, and then offering his glass to her. She refused it and coughed a little more.

"Of course you don't," Jasmine said after she stopped coughing. She pushed out her chair, picked up her plate and glass, and headed towards the kitchen. She mumbled under her breath as she left, but right after exiting, she purposefully raised her voice loud enough that we could hear, "You're the one who got her to catch the carpet on fire."

Sebastian pushed his chair back, disregarded his unfinished dinner, and followed her.

"She could be useful! Have you thought of that? What's your plan? Keep her here until she regains her memory and then throw her out? Why can't we help her start over? Why can't we help her hone her skills?"

Jasmine made a grumbling noise, jetted past us to the stairs, and started climbing. Over her shoulder, she said, "You just see her as a pet you can train. You don't actually have any interest in her otherwise. She fascinates you. You want to use her. Grow up, Sebastian! She's not a toy!"

Sebastian followed her up the stairs, and the conversation became muted. I heard thumping, which made me think Jasmine was slamming drawers shut. Sebastian kept yelling, "Don't you dare think about using your Voice! I'm not that stupid, and it's not going to work." And then there was more muted arguing.

Penny collected dishes left by her and Sebastian and walked to the kitchen. Theo and I collected ours and followed, helping her clean up. "Do they fight a lot?" I asked, running the water while scrubbing a pan in the sink.

"They bicker. We all fall into that trap occasionally," Penny replied. She dried the dishes as I handed them to her. "It's really hard to stay sane sometimes, seeing that we are each other's only friends and each other's only family. We can be incredibly close friends, but also squabbling siblings.

"Jas and Sebastian tend to have the most sibling-like banter. Both of them have the tendency to think big, just in different ways. That usually leads each of them to believe that they are correct and the other isn't. This causes a lot of tension. They both want what's best, and they'll see that eventually and calm down. Might take a few days for it to disappear entirely."

"I think it's usually best to let the dust settle," Theo added. "Penny and I try not to pick sides. We don't want to lengthen the recovery period."

"Even when we have strong opinions on who's right," Penny smirked. I suddenly wondered who she agreed with in this particular circumstance. Who did Theo agree with? Did they think I should be trained, or did they think Jasmine was right?

"And you never speak up? Wouldn't your opinion potentially heal the situation?"

"I mean, maybe. We occasionally chip in if we really see the need. But most of the time, it's a stupid little fight. Like the time that Seb was unemployed and tried to do everyone's laundry for them. He didn't sort it out and it ruined several people's clothes. Jas went insane. Or when Jasmine used Seb's bike without his knowledge and blew a tire. Seb was really mad. Stupid little stuff like that."

Theo laughed, reminiscing, "We just let these kinds of situations play out. If we don't act like it's a huge deal, even if I have to go and buy an unstained white dress shirt and new underwear, they quickly realize they're overreacting." He put the last of the plates away and shut the cupboard.

"So, this current fight, about me—is it them overreacting? Is it really not that big a deal?" My future was on the line, whether Jasmine liked it or not. I continued,

"I mean, I feel like this is something you two should weigh in on. I want to be trained, and I don't think we should let time decide whether I sit in this house alone forever or if I can actually be of use and master my powers."

"That's the thing," Penny said as we left the kitchen and made our way into the living room. "It's not anyone else's place to decide whether or not you choose to pursue mastery of your powers. You're the one in control, not either of them. You're an adult; they aren't your parents."

"So essentially, when this is all over and you finally get the nerve to ask Seb to train you, Jasmine will see she was wrong," Theo said and smiled. Then he and Penny left the room.

As Penny went upstairs, she passed Sebastian coming down.

"Women," he said, "I'll never understand them." He smiled at Penny, who returned a laugh and disappeared upstairs to console Jasmine. Sebastian crossed to the front door and grabbed the keys to the van. "I need to get out for a bit. You up for a drive, Bianca?"

CHAPTER SEVEN

It was a little after two in the morning as we drove around a town that was long asleep. Not a person in sight, not a car to be seen; we could run as many stop signs as we wanted, and no one would ever know. But we didn't.

"We have to keep order," Sebastian explained. "Sometimes, when I want to be rebellious or break the rules a little, I remember that it's my duty to uphold the rules for the protection of others."

"I'm not one to go around disregarding rules either, or at least I don't think I am. In all honesty, I don't really know anything about myself. While I don't think I seem to be a rule breaker; my gut says that life needs a little edge sometimes. I mean, what's life without a little risk?" I said.

I turned my head slightly to see how Sebastian would react. He didn't seem to catch where I was going. Or if he did, he sure wasn't showing it.

"I mean," I continued, "I think there are certain times to take risks. Especially when those risks don't break rules per se. In fact, I believe that good can potentially come from taking risks, even when others question whether it's a good idea. One might go so far as to say that breaking rules may even be necessary sometimes, if it's for the good."

"So, by that you mean it would be potentially advantageous for me to help you learn to use your powers, regardless of the pushback I'm getting from Jasmine. I know where you're going with this, Bianca. I'm not sure that it's a good idea."

"You don't think it's a good idea, or Jasmine doesn't? Because you seemed to think it was a good idea when you followed her upstairs yelling. Did she use her Voice and change your mind, or did you willingly give in to her arguments? You don't seem easily persuadable, Sebastian."

He took a left and began another lap around Beckworth campus. "No, she didn't use her Voice; I was listening and trying to understand her argument. And honestly, Jasmine has some concerns that I can't disregard."

We sat in silence for a moment, and he started again, "Also, you assume I *can* train you. But I can't. I can't train you. I'm not an all-knowing, force-driven Obi-Wan Kenobi. Heck, I'm not even Mr. Miyagi. I teach basic self-defense; that's it. I've never trained someone in their powers, and I'm pretty sure I couldn't even if I wanted to. I don't know the extent of your powers or entirely how they work. You can't train someone in something that you don't understand. It's that simple."

"But you knew how they worked enough to make me catch the carpet on fire the other night! You could give me advice on how to get to that point again! Maybe I don't need full training. Maybe I need some guidance to get back to the place I was the other night. And maybe teach me some self-defense as well! So what if you've never trained someone? I could be your first!"

"Bianca, that's not a good idea. I don't want to be responsible if something bad happens."

I saw a park up ahead. Leaning across Sebastian, I got a, "Hey stop that," and I flicked his turn signal on.

"Pull over," I said. "See that park? Pull over."

I didn't think he would listen, especially after he grumbled a sigh. But miraculously, he gave in and pulled over. I hopped out and stood staring at him through the window until he got out as well. He followed me over to a picnic table where we sat on the table and propped our feet on the bench.

We sat there in silence for a bit, looking around, breathing the cold night air. I didn't know what I wanted to say. I knew that Sebastian could give me something I needed, whether that be specific answers or general clarity. I tried to find the words to beg him to give me a chance, to teach me how to start my fire again. Before I could get the words, Sebastian started talking.

"Do you ever think about how there's a sort of beauty in this time of night? The stillness of it all?" Sebastian laid back on the table and looked at the sky. I laid back too, trying to see what he was seeing. He continued, "There's this peace that comes at the end of a chaotic day. No matter how bad the day was, how long it felt, how loud and soul crushing it seemed to be at times; there's this quiet at the end of it. And realizing that—I mean really actively thinking about it—well that feels like the whole world slows down for a moment, and you're the only one in it.

"Like standing in the eye of a hurricane or in that pause after an orchestra builds, and builds, and builds, and then suddenly hits a peak and stops completely. Then, after a few moments, it begins to play again, softer than before.

"There's a stillness to that moment of silence, like holding your breath. You know that you're going to have to take another breath. You know the orchestra is going to start playing again. You know that tomorrow is another unpredictable day, and you can't hide in that moment of silence forever. But while you're in it, it's pure bliss."

He lay there for a minute or so, saying nothing. Finally, he spoke again, "I can't teach you how to use your powers. I don't have them, so I don't have the experience to teach you. More importantly, I can't teach you how to control them, which is why I'm not going to try. It's too dangerous; we'd be playing with fire. Literally and figuratively. However, what I do know, and what I can tell you is that your powers are connected to your emotions.

"The other night, I attempted to get you angry, but that wasn't enough. From what I observed, you had too much going on in your head. You were sputtering, upset. You needed *pure* emotion to make something happen, pure anger in your case. I figured if you could isolate that anger, make it void of any other emotional influence, you could possibly cause a physical reaction. And it worked. That's how you made the fire.

"I don't know how to get you to that point again, I can only make you angry. But separating your emotions, really making them clear and focused—that was all your doing. I suggest, if you want to do it again, that's what you need to focus on. You need to get angry, and only angry, nothing else. And then lock your focus on that."

I had a million questions, all of which I wanted to ask at once. However, his talk of stillness shrouded them, and instead I lay in stunned silence.

"How did you know?" I asked.

"How did I know what?" He turned and locked eyes with me. "How did I know that you had fire powers? Or that anger caused them?"

"Both."

My stomach flipped at the thought. I knew what his answer would be.

"I saw you do it. That day that we found you. I saw that you were yelling in anger, and you threw flames. It set an empty, abandoned car on fire. Shortly afterward, something knocked you out. That's when we got you out of there. That's how I knew that you had fire powers."

"Do you know why I was angry or why I caught a car on fire? Did I do it on purpose?"

Sebastian paused for a moment and looked back at the sky. "I don't know. I assume you were caught in the middle of a battle between us and someone we were fighting, and you got angry about it. You probably saw something that made you mad. I wasn't in your head. I don't know what your motives were. I just know that you seemed angry, and you suddenly had fire in your hands."

We lay in silence. Eventually, he sat up and I mirrored him. I stood and gestured for Sebastian to follow.

"Come on. We should get going. It's late."

Sebastian stayed seated. "Come here," he said.

I moved to stand in front of him. He took my hands and turned them so both palms were up, and he kept his palms—radiating a soft warmth—under mine.

"What makes you truly angry? Right now."

Jumbled thoughts ran through my head. I couldn't distinguish what made me angry and what simply annoyed me.

"Jasmine doesn't want me to master my powers," I said, staring at my hands, as if a magic flame would suddenly pop out of them.

"No," he replied, squeezing my hands a little. "Not what makes you annoyed. *What makes you angry?* Close your eyes."

I looked up at him, and he stared back in all seriousness. His voice was stern, and his eyes felt sharp and commanding.

"Close your eyes," he said again, and reluctantly, I obeyed.

"Concentrate. What makes you angry? What fills you with rage?

Take whatever it is and focus on it. Brush aside any ounce of 'upset' or 'stress.' Focus on the anger and the fire that it's lighting within you."

I tried to focus on anger, but I felt a lot of things. I felt stressed, and nervous and cold all at the same time. But my hands felt warm. Was that the flame, or Sebastian's hands? Also, I liked that he was holding my hands. How could I possibly be angry when he was finally helping me? How could I be mad that he was holding me and showing me that I could trust him? That I finally had someone listening and being there for me?

In the dark, feeling nothing physical around me except the soft, spring breeze and Sebastian's hands touching the back of mine, I tried to shift my thinking. I moved my focus away from his hands, and suddenly I became increasingly aware of my heartbeat. Yes, that was good.

The fire that's lighting within you.

I imagined a small flame inside my chest, flickering and growing with my heartbeat. Immediately, I locked in on something, and my heart rate doubled.

Yes, I'm angry. This makes me angry. Not anxious, not scared, not bothered. Angry.

As my heart beat faster, the inner flame grew. My hands began to warm, not from Sebastian's body heat but from inside me.

I kept my focus, and I knew the fire was coming.

"Yes, that's it," Sebastian said. I felt him lower his hands, likely wanting to get out of the way, just in case. "How do you feel, Bianca?"

My rage broke through the floodgate and poured out: "I feel like I want to set something on fire!" And suddenly, a gush of heat poured into my hands. I opened my eyes to see two flames, each about the size of a baseball. Shocked, I laughed a little. The flames flickered.

"Control it, don't lose it! Keep focusing," Sebastian cut in.

"Whatever you do, don't throw them. I don't have water this time. Just keep them alive."

He coached me as I kept them alive for another ten seconds or so, and then they went out.

"That was incredible! I did it!" I yelled, still in disbelief. I jumped forward to hug Sebastian, and accidently knocked him backwards a little.

"Thank you," I said. "Really. Thank you so much." He smiled and hugged me back. It was the best I had felt since waking up with amnesia, realizing that I wasn't dead. He held me there for a moment, his breath warmed my hair, and I never wanted to let go. I finally felt calm, in control. I felt truly safe.

We made our way back to the car, and as he started it, he asked, "What were you focusing on, by the way? What sparked it?"

"The fact that my whole life is a mystery. I'm angry that I can't remember. I'm angry at myself and at the situation and honestly at whoever or whatever did this to me."

"Makes sense. The good part about that specific trigger is that so long as you don't have your memory, you can continue to use it!"

He laughed awkwardly. That should have made me mad, but it didn't. He was right; this could be a good thing to use for now. I planned to use it as much as I could before getting my memory back and having to find a new motivator.

After a little more silence, he caught me looking out the window and up at the sky.

"What?" he asked, smirking at me.

"Have you ever thought about how the moon seems like it's just an object in the sky, but we know that men have walked on it?"

Sebastian replied, "No, because it *is* just an object in the sky. The moon landing was a hoax."

"Sebastian, you can't be serious!"

"I doubt that actually happened. Come on; there's so much proof to the claim that it was staged."

"Ok, you need to stop that right now before you make me start a fire in this car."

"Oh yeah?" Sebastian was laughing too. "*That* is going to make you angry enough to start a fire?"

"Yes! So shut up and drive!"

We laughed the entire way back to the house, and nothing in that still moment of bliss could get me to spark another flame.

I had fire in my hands. I felt a deep calmness, my heart practically beating in slow motion. I walked down an alley, not at all stirred by the darkness or the quiet. I had no fear, just fire. The anger inside me was evident but not overexpressed. I remained stable and held the whisps of light between my fingers. I didn't have to think very hard; it just came to me. I had mastered the fire.

I heard a noise around the corner. It surprised me, and jumped causing the flame to flicker. I concentrated, and it stabilized again.

"Reveal yourself," I yelled. "Come on out." Despite my nerves, this wasn't a defensive call. I followed the noise, hunting the source. I wasn't being chased; I was chasing.

Suddenly, a shadowy figure stepped out and I smiled. Immediately, I attacked. I threw balls of fire from my hands and charged the figure who came at me with a crowbar. I kept moving forward and releasing flames. A fireball brushed the arm of the figure. A cry of pain rang out. I didn't stop. I couldn't show weakness.

I kept approaching, fireball in hand planning to finish my mission. As I pulled my arm back to throw a flame at my victim … I suddenly woke up …

I was on the couch, back at the house, shaking. It was another bad dream. It wasn't real. I was ok. Through the door, I could hear Theodore snoring in his room. Holding up my hand, I tried to spark a flame. Nothing. It was definitely a dream—I didn't have the ability to do the things that the 'dreaming me' did. Not yet anyway. Whatever made 'dream me' so angry—so powerful—was simply a nightmare. Relieved, I fell back asleep.

CHAPTER EIGHT

T he next morning, the routine I had gotten used to disappeared. While Penny sat in the living room writing a paper, and I lay on the kitchen floor trying to get my hand to light on fire. The front door flung open, and Theo ran in, yelling for Penny to change clothes. With no further instruction, Penny knew exactly what he meant. She slammed her laptop shut and ran upstairs. Meanwhile, Theo shut his bedroom door, presumably changing as well.

Within minutes, Jasmine and Sebastian also came running through the front door and went to their respective rooms. Sebastian shouted that everyone was to meet in the van in five minutes.

I assumed this included me, so I ran upstairs. Penny was already changed into what seemed to be a black wet suit and black sneakers. I didn't even know they made all black sneakers. Jasmine emerged from the bathroom, putting her hair up. Her outfit was exactly like Penny's.

"What should I wear?" I asked. Both of them continued getting ready and ignored me and my question.

"No, seriously guys. Should I change? Do you have an extra suit?"

They took off down the stairs and I chased them.

"So I guess I'll go like this. I'll grab my shoes!" I ran to the door and started putting on my sneakers. I wasn't dressed for the occasion, but apparently, this would have to do.

Theo opened his door and came out in his black wet suit. He looked pretty ridiculous, but I held back my laughter. The moment he saw me, he stopped and asked Jasmine and Penny, "Wait! She's coming?"

"No," Jasmine replied flippantly. "She's not. She's staying here."

"Are you serious?" I asked, tying my shoes. "No, I'm definitely coming. I can stay in the car! I'll be out of the way! I feel like I should at least get to come watch."

Sebastian left his room and went straight for the door. Grabbing the car keys, he said "I'm going to start the van. Bianca, we'll see you when we get back tonight."

I followed him outside, yelling profusely as he pulled out his cell phone to make a call.

"You've got to be kidding, Sebastian! You can't expect me to—"

"Hello?" Sebastian said into the phone, "Hi, we will be there as soon as possible. We're leaving right now. Yes—Bianca, stop it. Go inside. Sorry, go ahead. Yes, we're about five minutes out."

He got in the driver's seat and continued his call. I could hear the others locking up the house. I was pretty sure, or at least hoping, that because of the chaos, they thought I was inside.

While Sebastian was distracted, thinking I was heading back in the house, and before the others could round the corner, I popped the trunk enough to slip inside and lie down. I held the trunk almost shut but waited to latch it until Theo shut one of the doors, aiming to avoid making a recognizable noise. I was in and no one noticed We were finally going back to Victory City.

The trunk was downright uncomfortable—so much so that I considered letting them know I was in the van, hoping they would accept it and keep driving, maybe even let me help upon arrival. Yet, knowing Jasmine's adamant desire for me to stay out of the way, I figured that my dream scenario was a long shot. It was much more likely that she would pull over to the side of the road and hand me some cash to get dinner, claiming they would be back for me in a bit. The best option was silence. Besides, I didn't want them distracted once they got there; they had a mission, and I wanted to observe. They didn't need to know I was there until they got back to the van.

They spent the car ride in silence. It wasn't until we were almost there that Sebastian let the others know that he planned to park "by the bank on Fifth Street," and they could "walk from there." I gathered that the van would be away from the action, and in order to get a good look, I would have to get out and walk. So, as Sebastian parked, and they all got out, I gave it about three minutes before poking my head up to look out the window. They were gone.

I put on a big, black sweatshirt that I found by my feet. I pulled the hood up. It was far too large, most definitely Theo's, but it would do. The black would help me hide. I climbed over the backseat and exited the sliding door, latching it behind me.

Now the real question: How do I find the action without knowing what action I am looking for. Not only that, but how do I find literally anything in an unfamiliar city. Luckily, I heard a distant *bang* and took off running down the street in the direction of the sound.

I didn't know what I planned to do when I reached the scene. Probably find a place to hide and watch? I guess I had just expected to sit in the van and watch out the window while they absolutely destroyed the bank robber or whatever. Regardless, I was sure I could find a bush or a car or something to hide behind.

As I ran around a corner, I saw smoke (ok, not a bank robbery) in the distance. Another loud *bang* and some screaming echoed through the street. Rounding corners, I kept running towards the noise. Suddenly, something different came into view. It was Theo, *flying* across an opening between two buildings. I ran along the road, inched my way towards the corner, and pressed up against the wall. Reaching the corner, the whole perpendicular street came into view. I crouched down, but stayed around the corner and against the wall. I wanted to be able to peek around and watch but not be seen.

About 200 yards away, Penny and Sebastian engaged in hand-to-hand combat with a tall man, dressed in a suit much like my friends wore. While their black, slender suits were simple, his was a deep purple color, shifting between maroon and black as he moved. He held a tall staff and used it to block and counter Penny's powerful kicks. Sebastian wielded an interesting weapon, the blue mail flap from a post office pickup box. I had no idea how he had gotten it, but I could only assume there was a destroyed mailbox somewhere on this street.

As a result of Penny's intensity combined with Sebastian's ability to use this piece of metal as a weapon *and* a shield; the man in purple struggled to fend off both of them.

The man got in a few good hits, but then he took a few good blows. I hung onto every punch, every kick, every swing of his staff with fascination. Abruptly, he took a step back from both of them and clapped once before disappearing.

Sebastian shouted and ran down the road with Penny following. I could only assume that his shouting was not because he was surprised, but rather because he was annoyed. He seemed to already be aware that this man could suddenly disappear by clapping his hands.

I quickly followed, ducking behind cars. Up in the distance I saw what Sebastian and Penny were running towards: Theo was now fighting the same man on the second story balcony of a large hotel. Below him, Jasmine helped people evacuate the building.

Did this man mysteriously disappear and then reappear down the road in a different spot? This wasn't a typical bank robber; he was superhuman. A supervillain, perhaps.

Theo knocked the man down and leapt off the balcony, floating down to meet up with the others. The man stood up, unfazed, and knocked the base of his staff on the ground twice. The top of it, which had previously been a blue, orb-like ball, caught on fire. He looked down at Penny, Sebastian, and Theo for a brief moment, and then turned around, used the bottom of his staff to break the window behind him, and threw a flame inside. Smoke began to pour out of the room. The man tapped his staff twice again and the flame went out. He then clapped once and disappeared.

Penny yelled, "Where'd he go?"

"He probably went inside to get whatever he's after," Theo replied. "I don't know why he's attacking this hotel, but there must be something inside that he really wants."

"I'll go in after him," Sebastian said. "Penny, you come with me. Theo, you work on putting out the fire. Jasmine, you keep getting people as far away from the building as possible." He and Penny ran toward the building, and Theo felt the air briefly and jumped into the breeze.

"Everyone, listen to my voice! Stay calm and listen to me! Walk to Seventh Street in an orderly manner," Jasmine yelled and directed people away from the building. They followed her every instruction like sheep.

I wanted to help. There had to be something I could do without being seen. I looked toward the hotel, seeing the fire spreading quickly. Theo couldn't put it out alone, and the fire department hadn't arrived yet. Or maybe they weren't coming at all. Theo needed backup. I saw him doing something inside the window, presumably trying to smother the fire with bedsheets or water from the bathroom. That was it: *water.*

The smoke detectors hadn't gone off, so neither had the sprinklers. Either they were broken, or someone had tampered with them. To the best of my knowledge, modern smoke detectors were usually connected via a control box. *How did I know this?* I assumed the control box could be found in the lobby or the basement. If I could get to the box and turn the sprinklers on, it would help extinguish the fire. Simple enough.

I came out from behind the car and made my way towards the hotel, directing the panicked crowds along the way. I continued reminding them to keep running until they were far enough away. They barely listened to me. Most simply screamed louder and ran faster.

I knew going inside risked being seen by the others, but someone had to get to the sprinkler system. I ran through the revolving door and entered the lobby as it started to get truly smoky.

Where the hell would they put the sprinkler control system?

I ran behind the concierge's desk and scoured the wall. Nothing. There was, however, a closet behind the desk. I swung the door open and shoved aside some hanging concierge coats. Then I saw it. *Bingo.* I opened the flap and examined the buttons and switches. *Which one?* Before I could decide, or at least start hitting random buttons, I heard a whooshing noise and then a voice.

"Hello there," it said. I whipped around to see the man in purple, standing tall with his staff, blocking the doorway. "I would get out of there if I were you. In case you hadn't heard, the building's on fire."

CHAPTER NINE

My body froze in place, but my heart didn't. It flipped uncontrollably, immediately bringing a wave of queasy, fight-or-flight fear over my entire body. I had become trapped in the back closet of a hotel lobby with an actual supervillain blocking the only exit. I kept my head down, so he couldn't see my face under the hood, and I concentrated on my hands.

I needed the flame, but I couldn't keep my heart rate down. I tried thinking about my missing memory and how no one would tell me anything about my past. I focused on anger, but I couldn't get any feeling to rise to the surface except fear.

He swung and hit me with his staff, knocking me to the floor and the hood off my head. I looked up and locked eyes with him for the first time, completely panicked and wondering what was about to happen to me. But instead of advancing further, he stood, stunned.

"You," he said under his breath. He tapped his staff twice, and the fireball returned in place of the orb. It was ironic, really. He conjured exactly what I desired to conjure myself. And not only that; he did it with such ease. But I didn't have time to be envious. He pulled his arm back to throw the flame, like a serpent before the strike. I cowered and covered my head.

But the fire never came. Instead, I heard a crash. Sebastian had come running and tackled him from the side. Sebastian and Penny stood between me and the man. With every bone in my body shaking, I pushed myself to my feet and stepped up to the box on the wall. I flipped every switch and hit every button. Suddenly, a loud, beeping noise began; the fire alarm lights started flashing; and water rained from the ceiling.

I stepped back into the lobby where, in the middle of combat, the man froze in shock and clapped once, disappearing.

"He's outside!" Penny yelled, pointing out the window. The man smiled at us and ran—clapping as he ran—and he disappeared. Almost simultaneously, a fire truck pulled up in front of the building.

We ran out front, Penny and Sebastian kept running, not in the direction the man ran, but instead toward the parked van, a few blocks over. I followed, confused.

"Why aren't we going after him?" I questioned, trying to keep up. "Seriously! We need to get him! Come on!"

"Because he teleported, we don't know where he went. The building has been emptied, and the fire department has taken control. It's no longer our duty," Sebastian yelled back.

"Where the hell did you come from and why?" he continued. This was the angriest I'd ever heard him. Why could everyone conjure pure anger except me?

"I hid in the trunk because I knew I could help, and I did. The building would still be on fire if it weren't for me."

Neither Penny nor Sebastian challenged me, but neither verbally agreed with me either. Still, they didn't seem too happy. We reached the van where Jasmine and Theo were already waiting inside. Jasmine cursed when she saw me. Theo asked where I got his sweatshirt.

"We found her getting knocked down by S," Sebastian explained as Theo started the engine. "He was about to kill her. We stopped him, Bianca set off the fire alarms and sprinklers, and he escaped down an alley and teleported away. The good news is that I don't think he got whatever it is he went in there for. Penny managed to stop him upstairs, and he retreated to the lobby, where he found Bianca."

"I'm sorry," I said. Words spilled out explaining my guilt-ridden panic. "I wanted to help, and I thought that maybe under pressure, well, I could perform."

"I'm happy you're ok," Penny said, reaching across the seat, grabbing and squeezing my hand.

Penny was kind, but blunt. "Honestly," she said, "it was brave of you to try, but it was also very stupid of you."

"I know," I replied. "I'm sorry. I'm sorry he got away; it's all my fault."

"No, it's not," Sebastian said. "He always gets away. Which is why we keep having to go back."

"Important question," Jasmine said, obviously still fuming. "Did he see your face?"

"Yes," I said, "he did. And he seemed to recognize it. I don't know why. I've never seen him before."

Everyone rode in silence. I wondered if they was always this quiet after a mission. Probably so if there was always this sense that the story isn't over, and the world still isn't safe. After a bit, Theo laughed. He smiled and glanced back at me.

"Knocked on your ass, huh? Yeah, if you're going out again, we need to give you some self-defense lessons. It sounds like your performance was pretty pathetic."

CHAPTER TEN

I sincerely thought Sebastian would be mad at me for what happened in the hotel. Anyone who knew anything about his personality would have guessed that, and he could hold a grudge.

Compared to my other male housemate, Sebastian's serious nature dominated his personality. When looking at Theo, the first things you saw were a strong sense of humor and endless charm. Sebastian's strengths were his intellect, his wit, and his drive. While he was capable of joking around, a level of seriousness always lingered. Sebastian was simply a serious man who cared about serious things. And I liked that about him.

But despite all of this, Sebastian wasn't one to hold grudges. In fact, the opposite could be said. That evening, he asked me to accompany him on a walk. While I initially thought this would be a chance for him to chew me out for my stupidity, I quickly realized that he wanted to check in on me.

"I've been thinking about you for the last few hours," Sebastian said as we rounded the corner onto Jackson Lane, "Truthfully, I've been a bit worried."

"Honestly, it's been a hard day. I didn't wake up thinking I'd be cornered by a supervillain. I can't stop thinking about the look on his face as he stood over me. That evil smile. I don't know why, but it really shakes me to my core, you know?"

Sebastian kept his hands in his pockets as he looked up at the sky. Always so fascinated with the sky, this boy. Without looking over at me, he replied, "S is a true villain. That's for certain. He's done terrible things, and we can never seem to stop him."

"But maybe you could with me," I said, causing him to snap his head in my direction.

"You know that's not going to happen," he replied matter-of-factly.

"I still don't understand why you won't give me a chance."

"I *am* giving you a chance. I told Theo he could train you in self-defense. If you get good enough, maybe you could help Jasmine evacuate civilians."

"But you know I can do more than that! I proved it today!"

"All you proved today is that you're still unable to make your fire come on command. And you look absolutely helpless when a supervillain is hovering over you."

His words, though true, stung. I felt heat rising to my face.

"You're mad at me for stowing away in the van today! This is backlash for my lapse in judgment."

"It's absolutely not. I don't let my emotions linger."

His voice remained calm. His posture never changed. While I had prepared for an argument, he planned to continue rational conversation. He might have been the most level-headed person I'd ever met.

"I am not mad at you, Bianca. I completely understand why you made the decisions you did. And I don't blame you for being easily beaten. You simply don't have the tools to take on an attacker, especially him."

I opened my mouth, but he cut me off, and continued: "And I know that this is your moment to say, 'That's why you should train me.' But we've already established that I can't. I hope that maybe with time, you can figure it out yourself. And in the meantime, maybe Theo can get you trained enough in self-defense … What am I trying to say?"

"What *are* you trying to say?" I asked, surprised he even considered letting me go out again. He sighed, stopped in his tracks and moved his hands to his hips. He tapped his foot and thought for a moment about how he would continue.

"I can't train you."

"Yes, we've established that."

"But I'm not opposed to you going with us if you can properly defend yourself. In fact, if you do get your powers to cooperate, maybe you could fight with us, too. Maybe."

My heart leapt in my chest. My mouth dropped open.

"But you have to be able to control your powers. And I mean really control them. I don't want any chance of you getting hurt. I don't want to see you like I saw you today. I don't think I can handle seeing that again."

Now my heart leapt in a different way. This time it felt suspiciously like butterflies. Sebastian worried about me. I was more than a number on his team. I wanted him to keep talking, to keep telling me why he wanted me safe. But something in me panicked and changed the subject.

"I want to apologize for something," I said. He laughed a little at the tone shift and started walking again.

"You better not be giving me your millionth apology for sneaking into the van earlier." He smiled as he spoke. There was that soft side again, the side that broke through the logic. The side I couldn't stop thinking about.

"No, I want to apologize for screaming at you that first night and for being so mean to you. You were trying to help me, but I let my anger take over. It was inappropriate and selfish."

"You didn't know any better. You were in a scary situation; you had no memory of the last two years, and I was a stranger poking you with a verbal stick, trying to make you react. I'd freak out if I were in your shoes."

"I didn't know if I could trust you."

"But do you know now? Do you trust me?"

We stopped again. Our bodies stood only a few feet apart. He looked at my hands. I wondered if he wanted to reach out and hold them. I wondered why I wanted him to hold them. I still barely knew him. In the grand scheme of things, he was still a stranger, and yet I knew the answer to his question.

"Yes," I whispered. "I do. For some reason."

"Good." He smiled.

Neither of us moved. He still stared at my hands. My eyes moved up to his face. His eyes rose to meet mine, and I instinctively looked away in a panic, starting to walk again.

"We should get back to the house. Gotta get some rest if I'm going to start self-defense lessons with Professor Martin tomorrow."

What was I doing?

"Bianca," he said, stopping me again. My heart raced.

"I really do hope you'll be able to join us on missions. I hope you can get your fire back."

"It never will if you all keep being so nice to me. How on earth will I feel angry enough to make it appear?"

"Guess I'll have to start revealing my true self to you. You trust me? Well joke's on you, I'm actually the jerk you thought I was on the first night. Boy, don't you feel foolish now!"

He grinned as I laughed and bumped him off the sidewalk. I wanted to reply with some clever quip, but I couldn't think of one.

CHAPTER ELEVEN

Two weeks after the hotel incident, I was getting the hang of punching people. Penny blocked my hits but didn't fight back at full strength, giving me a challenge but thankfully not a concussion. Theo assisted me with all my physical training, showing me how to stand, how to hit, and most importantly, how to take hits. In those first few practices, I realized that Theo both looked and hit like a professional boxer.

Additionally, his teaching skills matched his physical ones. He always remained calm and patient, which turned out great for me since I wasn't very good at anything physical. However terrible I performed, though, he insisted I keep pushing, giving it everything I had in me. He wanted me to execute each and every movement with maximum power and intent. He let me punch him as hard as I could, which did absolutely nothing to him, but allowed me to see what I had to work with. Well, everything I had to work with except for the fire, which still refused to cooperate.

Once or twice I got a spark, but nothing big came from it. Time and time again, Theo told me not to worry about it, to focus more on the hand-to-hand combat. He said the fire was a distraction anyway, and I needed to prepare my body for those moments when fire wasn't an option—essentially, every moment I would potentially be in combat, since the fire situation wasn't looking very promising.

My new friends dedicated much of their time to my training. I spent a few hours a day in the backyard or the gym practicing. While Theo acted as my dedicated fighting coach, he often brought Penny along to square off against me. No matter how many times the others encouraged her to join us and learn combat skills herself, Jasmine, however, refused to participate. She constantly made it known that she was displeased with everyone for encouraging me. Regarding her own training, she insisted that hand-to-hand combat wasn't necessary for her to learn, since she never found herself in the midst of a fight, but rather on the side directing people out of the area. I frequently tried reasoning with her, but she remained stubborn. After about three days of trying, I stopped asking her.

Sebastian, on the other hand, did occasionally join us. But he didn't fight. He sat and watched me fight Theo and Penny, occasionally yelling things like, "Bend your knees," and "Watch your left arm." He knew how to stay in his lane, letting Theo coach me and give me corrections. But he provided another set of eyes and constructive encouragement. It felt odd having a spectator, but it made me better. I wanted to impress my audience.

One day in June, as Theo helped me take some warmup hits, I decided to strike up a conversation with the two of them. Penny and Jasmine stayed home. Penny insisted she had a "special project" to work on and Jasmine was being the usual curmudgeon.

"That day at the hotel," I said, taking a swing at Theo's chest. He blocked it and told me to go again. I continued my thought, "Sebastian referred to the man with the staff as 'S.' Is that his name? Or what he goes by? Seems too short to be a real name, don't you think?"

"We gave him that name. S stands for staff," Sebastian laughed, "We don't know his real name. Sometimes he's S. Sometimes he's the man with the staff. It really depends on the context. S is easy. It's ominous. I don't know that it's better than Mr. Staff. We considered that one for a bit."

"Keep your eyes up," Theo said, dragging my attention back into what I was supposed to be doing. He began circling me in the boxing ring, and I rotated, trying to keep him in front of me.

"Don't take your eyes off my face; use your peripheral vision to see what my arms and legs are doing. If you look away from my face, you'll miss what my eyes are doing, where they're looking."

"He wants you to see how pretty his big brown eyes are; don't be fooled," Sebastian shouted from the sideline. Instead of using it to watch Theo's face, as he told me to, I used my peripheral vision to see Sebastian casually leaning back in a folding chair with his feet up on the edge of the ring. He had a smirk on his face. No surprise.

"One thing Sebastian neglected to mention was that I myself have never said that my eyes are pretty, so that must be what *he* thinks," Theo swung at my head, and I ducked just in time.

"Good," he said to me, switching direction.

"He's lying!" Sebastian yelled again. "He goes around all the time bragging about how good he looks. First, he locks eyes with you, and then he tries to lock lips with you. Just wait. He's a womanizer." I could hear the smile in Sebastian's voice. I don't know why, but I laughed.

"You're trying to make me lose my focus! You two are the worst!"

Theo smiled slightly and recognizing a potential moment of weakness, I tried to sweep his leg, but he remained standing.

"That was a good try, but unfortunately you *are* losing your focus, and we *are* indeed the worst, thank you," Theo went for my gut, but I blocked his arm. "You were doing really well too." Then he swept *my* leg and knocked me down.

Panting, I doubled over, resting my forearms on my thighs. I turned and looked over at Sebastian.

"This is your fault you know. I was going to win that one. Also, it's a bold claim to call Theo a womanizer, especially to a woman."

"Oh, because it's true," Sebastian said as Theo reached down to pull me to my feet. "He's a womanizer. Women take one look into those eyes, and they can't resist. As I said before, never lock eyes with Theodore Martin. He takes pride in it."

I gasped, mockingly asking, "Theo! Is this true?"

"Oh yeah. They know I'm an absolute prize. Plus, it definitely fires Penny up. And I love keeping that girl on her toes." Theo smirked and helped me under the ropes.

I saw the way Theo looked at Penny when we were around the house. He was a smooth guy; it was hard to read much from his actions or emotions. I knew Sebastian joked about his being a womanizer, but it seemed plausible that Theo knew women swooned over him. He was handsome and strong, a very impressive male specimen to be sure.

But Penny … Theo occasionally looked at Penny like she was the most beautiful girl in the world. And he was right in doing so. Penny looked like an angel with her soft, blonde hair and rosy cheeks. She was small and thin. A perfect contrast to Theo's strong build. And her bubbly personality—icing on the cake. No reason in the world why Theo wouldn't fall for a girl like Penny, and vice versa. But for some unknown reason, they continued as friends, seemingly pretending that they had no interest whatsoever in a romantic connection. But still, I saw the looks. And those spoke a thousand words.

"You guys are ridiculous, you know," I said, pulling on my jacket.

"Having seen the way you fight, I would never have expected the antics. You always come across as being so serious. I don't know, seeing the antics … it's sort of endearing."

Sebastian checked his phone and laughed. "Speaking of antics," he said, "Penny's waiting for us at home."

Within seconds of stepping inside the front door, we were ambushed by a bouncing ball of energy. Penny rushed up to us and whispered something to Theo, who smiled and gently shushed her.

Sebastian hung the keys on the wall hook and laughed, "Wow, Pen, we barely made it in the door. Can you calm down just a little?"

Sebastian didn't seem too shocked by this "bouncy Penny" behavior, and at this point, I had started to get used to it myself. It's a bit weird how things change so quickly when you only know four people. Plus a super villain, but I wasn't too enthusiastic about counting him.

Penny smiled at us, "I'm really excited."

"Rightfully so," Sebastian said, untying his shoes. There was definitely something happening—something I didn't know about, but everyone else did.

"Theo?" Penny made a waving hand gesture I didn't understand and skipped over to the stairs. I looked at Jasmine who was reading on the couch with her feet propped up. She looked at me, irritated.

"Don't look at me. I'm not involved," she said, and went back to reading.

"Ok," Theo said. "We got you a little something, so I'd love it if you'd come with me. Oh, and if you haven't figured it out yet, it's a surprise."

I didn't like the idea of any sort of surprise, not after what I had been through, but unfortunately, it didn't look like I had much of a choice in the matter. I started to realize that I didn't have a choice in a lot of matters while under this roof. I followed along and hoped I wouldn't die in some altercation in Victory.

Theo asked me to close my eyes, and then gently positioned himself behind me, putting one hand on my shoulder and the other over my eyes.

"This is stupid; you know that, right?" I said as he pushed and maneuvered me across the living room and kitchen. My heart rate quickened. I had only known these people for a little over a month; we still weren't officially past the point of them murdering me, were we? Once again, reason clashed with emotion, and I let my housemates take control. Especially since Jasmine wasn't involved, I figured I was probably safe.

"Yeah, but Penny insisted that this is the proper way to do the whole surprise thing. So we are just going to roll with it because we don't know any better," Theo replied, moving me slowly across the room. I waited with bated breath for him to run me into a wall or knock me into some furniture.

"That's because it *is* the proper way to do a surprise," Penny said from up ahead of me. "It's dramatic and makes the reveal so much more satisfying."

"Please don't trip when we get to the stairs; that would be bad," Theo said to me as we slowed down. "Can someone grab her hands? These stairs are the worst."

Someone immediately reached out and grabbed my hands, pulling me up the stairs. Somehow, I knew Sebastian's hands when I felt them.

Goodness gracious.

I could hear Penny bounding up the metal stairs ahead of us. She cared far too much about whatever she was about to reveal. The matter of trusting strangers and the metal stairs themselves, felt incredibly unsafe. In the case of the stairs, I was 90 percent sure this particular staircase wasn't stable, especially with so many of us on it at once.

As Sebastian slowly pulled me up the dangerous, winding staircase, and Theo continued to hold onto me as support, I finally heard Jasmine sigh and follow behind us.

"Fine, I'm coming. But I still stand by the fact that this is dumb."

Upon reaching the top, Sebastian let go of my hands, Theo squared my shoulders to the left, and I waited for a second. My heart thumped at record speed. If only it beat heavily from anger; then maybe I would have had a good defense assuming this was a trick to attack me at a weak point.

"Ok, you can look," Penny said.

Theo removed his hand, and I blinked at the bright light. Up against the wall, where the dresser used to be there was now a twin bed, already made, with my pajamas lying across it. The dresser was shoved in the corner, making it very obvious that the room was maxed out on furniture space before the bed was added. This addition would be a clear inconvenience to the girls. But it meant the world to me. I instantly teared up.

"Is this mine?" I could barely get the words out. I didn't even need to hear the answer because I knew it was mine. I had a bed. I had my own bed. It was mine. Not only that. A bed symbolizes home. I had a home.

"It's not huge, but we thought it would be better than the couch," Sebastian said.

"Yeah, the couch is great and all, but you needed a real bed," Theo chipped in.

"And it only made sense for you to sleep upstairs with us," Penny said. "We thought it would make you feel a little more at home."

That word again. *Home.*

I looked at Jasmine, "And you're ok with this?" Everyone looked at her, causing her to blush and seem ill at ease.

"I'm not a monster! Yeah, sleeping on the couch isn't great, so you should definitely have a bed. You are living here after all."

I was. I lived in a small house with people I considered to be my friends—my closest friends. Not much of a competition since these were the only people I knew, but still. They had started to feel like family, and this place had started to feel like home. *Home.*

"Thank you all," I said in tears. "Truly, you don't know how much this means to me."

Without thinking, I jumped forward and hugged Theo. He gave me a big hug back.

"I figure you're the one who had to carry this upstairs, so thank you for that," I said. He laughed.

"You're welcome. I'm just happy that now you won't be able to hear me snore. Truly embarrassing."

I hugged Penny and Sebastian too. Penny still bounced a little. Sebastian's hug ran chills down my spine. Not the fluttering again—what on earth did that mean?

"I'm so happy you like it," Penny said, snapping me out of it.

When I turned to Jasmine, she held up a hand, "Please don't hug me."

For my own satisfaction, I hugged her anyway and thanked her once more. Suddenly, everyone joined in, and we squashed Jasmine in the middle of a group hug. While she yelled for us to get off, we laughed, knowing that she liked it, and all of us, far more than she admitted.

CHAPTER TWELVE

MAY 11, 2017

I'd been driving on a flat tire, and I knew it. I had finally reached southern Pennsylvania on my way to Victory City, and at some point in the last few miles, I had run over a nail or something. Thankfully, the timing wasn't too terrible. The sun had already set, and I needed to pull off to grab dinner anyway.

I took the next exit and began scanning the signs for an auto shop. Lucky for me, there happened to be one. However, as I pulled into the lot, the sign on the door indicated the shop had closed for the night and would open at seven the next morning. That wasn't ideal, but I would have to make it work. I parked and got out of the car. Knowing that my tire would be totally flat by morning, it made sense to leave it at the shop and walk down the road to look for a restaurant and hotel. In the morning, I would walk back, get a new tire, and be on my way. I could still reach Victory by early afternoon, and I could use the rest of tomorrow to find a place to stay.

My legs ached from all the driving. I had gone about six hours without stopping, and my body definitely felt it. I felt physically tired, extremely hungry, and emotionally exhausted. I had graduated from college that afternoon and had not slept the night before.

The days leading up to graduation, I transported all my belongings except for two suitcases and a duffel bag full of my bedding to a local storage unit. I purchased the unit the day I returned to campus from spring break, the day after I saw the news story about Victory. I spent the night before my graduation packing up everything I had left, and before the ceremony, I piled it in my car.

I explained to my family and friends that I needed to leave immediately after the ceremony because I would start a new job on the East Coast early the next morning. It wasn't exactly true, but I needed to get on the road as quickly as possible. I needed to get to Victory before those people—those "Victory defenders" disappeared. I had been waiting weeks to head east, and now that I had finished my degree, I finally had a valid excuse to run without anyone knowing the reason why. The ceremony ended at 3:00. By 3:30, I had changed into jeans and a T-shirt and hit the road.

Now, at about 9:30, I wandered down the cracked sidewalk, pulling a suitcase behind me. My phone died hours earlier, so I had no map. I didn't even know what remote town this was. I saw very few buildings and even fewer signs of life. I hadn't encountered another person since arriving. Fortunately, after a few minutes of walking, I found a twenty-four-hour diner. Finally, the first sign of life. A middle-aged waitress named Rhonda sat me at a small table by the window. After a few minutes, I ordered a burger, fries, and a Coke, and stared out the window at the small town.

I had no idea where I would sleep. Hopefully there was a hotel within walking distance. If not, I'd have to sleep in the car, which didn't sound pleasant.

Besides myself, there were only two other patrons in the diner. A man sat at the counter laughing through the window with one of the cooks. At the table next to me sat a woman, probably in her late twenties. She sat alone, sipping a cup of coffee and reading the menu. She never looked up to acknowledge me, or anyone. I ate in silence, wondering where on earth I was going to sleep.

A little while later, when Rhonda came to bring me the check, I asked her about lodging. I explained that my phone had died and that I hadn't had the opportunity to charge it. She kindly told me that about half a mile down, there was a small roadside motel. I thanked her and handed her my bill and card.

As she walked away, the woman at the next table turned and asked, "Do you have a car, or did you take the bus?"

Confused, I replied. "Excuse me?"

"I'm also traveling, and I happen to be staying at that motel, the one the waitress told you about. I didn't drive here; I took the bus. However, it doesn't come until morning. I wondered if I could possibly catch a ride with you to the motel, since, well …" She gestured to her suitcase.

"Oh, I'm sorry. I'm in a similar situation. My car got a flat, so I left it at the auto repair place. I won't be able to do anything about it until tomorrow. I'd be willing to walk with you since it's dark and neither of us should be walking alone this late."

Young women in diners weren't sketchy or dangerous, right? Besides, it really was late, and I wasn't comfortable walking half a mile alone in the dark.

"That's so kind, thank you," she said, collecting her belongings and pulling her suitcase to my table. Rhonda returned with my card and wished us both a good night. As we left the diner, the woman introduced herself as Alexandra Oliver. She had been working in a small town in Texas, but her job relocated out east. She, like me, was moving. "I worked out in a small town called Durango for a couple of years but accomplished all the work we needed to do out there, so my boss moved to a town on the East Coast. He's slowly been moving people out there to join him. I'm the final transfer, so now we'll all officially be out in Victory."

I jumped. "Wait, did you say Victory? As in Victory City?"

"Yes, Victory City. I'm surprised you've heard of it! It's pretty small as far as cities go."

"I'm actually on my way to Victory. I have … family out there," I lied. I didn't want her to know why I was headed to Victory, but it was pretty clear by my shock that this place held significance.

"I'm moving there to be closer to them," I continued.

"Do you have work out there?" she asked as we approached what appeared to be the motel.

"Not yet, but I'm hoping my aunt and uncle may know of some places."

"Well here then, take my card," Alexandra said, pulling a small business card out of her purse. "We will be doing some charity-type work there. Look us up at this address. If you're interested in our organization, you should reach out. We're always looking for interns and entry level staff. I would be happy to put in a good word for you."

"Thank you so much. I really appreciate it." I took the card and slipped it into my pocket.

"Anytime, Bianca," she said. "Have a great night and a safe rest of your drive. Maybe I'll see you in Victory." Alexandra turned and went up to her room.

I stood for a second trying to remember if I had told her my name. Unable to recall, I went into the lobby and asked for a room for the night.

CHAPTER THIRTEEN

Theo needed to complete some errands one afternoon, so for the first time, Sebastian and I went to the gym to train without him. When he told me that morning that he couldn't go, I asked him if it was smart to continue on alone. He assured me that Sebastian would be more than helpful. Then he made a joke about Sebastian and I using this time to finally, "explore physicality together." I felt myself blush and had to walk away.

At the gym, Sebastian and I spent the first half of the training going over some of the things that Theo taught me. I worked on tucking and rolling as well as kicking. I insisted on kicking the bag rather than having Sebastian hold something for me, like Theo usually did. Theo's joke that morning really stuck with me, bringing to mind a multitude of questions, and causing me to avoid physical contact with Sebastian.

First and foremost: Did I feel anything, anything at all, towards Sebastian? I didn't think so. I just thought he was sweet. And the tiniest bit attractive. And my gut always seemed to react to any nice thing he said to me.

However, I hadn't been around long enough to have feelings like that. Right?

But then again, if I didn't have feelings, what made Theo's joke bother me so much? I felt called out. If I didn't like him at all, why would I feel called out?

Second: Did Theo see something in Sebastian's and my friendship that I didn't?

Now I was definitely overthinking. I became anxious thinking about it, which was ridiculous. I was a college graduate superhero who could catch things on fire (or at least *had* caught things on fire at one point). I didn't need to think about stupid, petty things like crushes. I needed to focus on destroying this bag.

I kicked it a few more times before Sebastian suggested I take a break from that exercise. He decided that it was time to take things in a different direction, a direction I was hoping to avoid.

"Punch me," Sebastian said.

"No, I'm not going to punch you," I laughed uncomfortably. I did not, under any circumstances, want to punch him.

"No really, punch me."

"I only punch people who attack me, sorry," I said, heading away from him, towards the benches to get some water.

Suddenly and silently, he came up behind me and wrapped his arms around me in a tight hold. He leaned back, lifting my feet off the ground. He pinned my arms to my side at the elbows and I kicked my legs wildly.

"Sebastian, stop! Put me down!"

He dropped me and—immediately—before I could recover, he transitioned into gripping my wrists. I pulled away to get out of the hold, but he twisted my arms, so my fists ended up in front of my face, with my forearms making a wall between us. I laughed awkwardly, unsure of what to do.

"Sebastian, what are you doing?"

"I'm attacking you," he said. "You have to get out of it and fight back."

"Why?"

"You said you fight people who attack you. Prove it."

I steadied my breath, trying to remember what Theo had taught me about holds like this. Recalling the action, I flipped my wrists out towards his thumbs and pulled down, falling out of his grip.

"Good," he said. "Now keep your balance! Come back at me. Fight me off."

I tried a jab at his head, and he blocked it. I then tried to swipe a leg under him, and he blocked that too.

"See? This is why I need my powers to come back. Then I wouldn't need to know this stuff."

"Come on, chin up. Aim for my rib cage," Sebastian explained, walking me through a couple of good offensive moves.

We worked on that for a little while, falling into step with one another. Fighting felt like a dance; we could move in time together and feed off each other's energy. After a little while, I could read his movements, blocking what he was about to try before he even tried it. I also got some punches in, including one that I combined with a kick to the side of his leg, finally knocking him down.

"Yes! You're getting the hang of this," he said, pushing back up. "Do you notice how much easier it is when you are paying attention to body language?"

"Yeah, that helps. I think I'm starting to understand how this is supposed to work. We can learn with each fight: The more we fight S, the more we will know what to expect."

"And don't forget what Theo said about keeping your eyes up and locked with your opponent."

I looked up into his eyes. My heart fluttered. *Ok maybe I did have some sort of feelings.* We practiced a bit more before eventually deciding to call it quits. While we put our shoes back on, I decided to ask him about his powers since we hadn't discussed it much before.

"So, you can take anything and make it a weapon?"

"Yep. Anything can become a weapon, and somehow I know exactly how to use it. For example, you can toss me a banana, and I can kill a man with it. If I really want to."

"There's no way that's possible." I stopped tying my shoes and stared at him. He reached into his bag and pulled out a banana.

"You can't kill someone with a banana," I said.

"Yes, you definitely can. I don't think my powers are so much about physical strength and skill. It's about math. It's instinctively knowing, without thinking about it before the moment comes, the angles, speed, power, et cetera. My power is being able to know all of that. So for the banana …"

He swung the banana at my neck, and I flinched. He stopped it inches from my throat.

"See, I've never actually used a banana as a weapon. I've never done any research on the matter. However, I know the exact place I need to hit someone, the angle I have to come in at, and the speed and force I need to use in order to kill someone."

"Ok," I said, understanding a little more. "What about a ping-pong ball?"

"I can't know for certain unless I have one in my hand, but I would assume you'd have to come downwards at the throat at a 72-degree angle. Funny enough, it's gonna be the throat again. Throats are a pretty solid target if you want to kill someone."

"Ok, ok. What about if you had a handful of shaving cream," I asked as we walked to the van.

"Is this going to be a new thing for you?" he laughed. "Are you going to start listing random objects to test me?"

I laughed too. "Oh definitely. And now I understand why you're working as a researcher for a math professor. You're a nerd!"

"I am not. I enjoy math and I happen to be incredibly and unusually good at it. Especially geometry and physics."

"Angle boy," I teased, "helping write a nerdy book."

He laughed and bumped into me. I bumped back. Regardless of what this was and what feelings I did or didn't have, it felt good to laugh with someone.

CHAPTER FOURTEEN

For the next month or so, training continued as normal, and so did the calls for help. We entered Victory about once or twice a week, stopping things like bank robberies and auto theft. As my friends said before: your friendly neighborhood Spiderman kind of stuff.

I either stayed by the van and watched or helped Jasmine with civilian evacuation. While not as persuasive as Jasmine, I found that it's not too hard to get people to run away from dangerous situations. I got people moving quickly, and Jasmine kept them calm: a system that worked well.

Jasmine was anything but enthusiastic about my help. In fact, she often tried to take control and box me out of helping entirely. On at least one occasion, I reluctantly retreated to the van, annoyed at the thought of being so unwanted.

I wanted to be of use and because of one person, I often couldn't be. I came here for a reason, one I didn't quite understand. And I was staying for a reason. I knew that I had something to give, and I wanted Jasmine to stop getting in the way.

The missing reasons for being in Victory remained ever present in my mind. Each time we went into the city, I couldn't help but wonder what brought me here in the first place. Something pretty significant had drawn me out here, away from home.

Home.

Where was my family? I could remember everything up until about two months before my college graduation, so I knew where my family was and should still be, but were they still there? What did they think of me moving out here? Did they worry about me?

On the first Saturday in July, I was standing by the parked van dressed in black. One question about my family stuck in my mind: Why was I not motivated to go back to see them and ask them what happened to me?

Probably because they didn't know. I don't think anyone really knew my motives. Not even me. At least from my most recent memories, there was no evidence of dissatisfaction or a desire for change. And not only that. What would happen if talking to them revealed something I didn't want to know? What if I hadn't left by choice, maybe been abducted, or stolen away? Before seeing anyone close to me, especially my family, it was important that I first figure out what happened to me. It was better for me to bring them answers than the other way around.

I quickly snapped out of these thoughts when I saw a black figure moving towards the Victory post office where my friends were inside stopping a solo gunman intent on robbing the register while the actual police were distracted by another major issue across town. I pulled up my sweatshirt hood and followed behind at a safe distance.

I spotted Sebastian, coming out of the post office, talking on the phone. He didn't see the approaching shadow. The figure moved his right arm away from his body, and I suddenly saw it: the long, tall staff. S was back.

The man tapped it on the ground twice as he walked and a fireball appeared, hovering over the top. S was heading straight for a clueless Sebastian. I picked up the pace and kept following.

Come on, Sebastian! Turn around!

I wanted to warn him, but I knew S would see me. My brisk walk turned to a jog, which turned to a run. If I couldn't get to Sebastian quickly, it would be too late. He needed to know who was coming for him, so I ran and I focused my mind on my hands. Distracting thoughts populated my mind, but none were strong enough to produce the flame I so deeply desired.

Sebastian, you complete idiot, you're going to get burned alive, and it's all your fault.

The anger was coming on stronger and stronger, and my body began to warm. But it wasn't strong enough to produce anything real. The intrusive thoughts kept coming, one piling on top of the next.

Sebastian was about to be burned alive, and if he was, it would be my fault. It would be all my fault because I couldn't concentrate. If only I had my memory and knew how I got these powers, I would have more control and I could save him.

Time seemed to slow as I ran. I felt hot and angry, really and truly angry. I wanted to save my friend, and the only thing stopping me from being able to do so was myself. But thinking this made my gut twinge. Self-guilt didn't feel right. Something in my core felt that it wasn't my fault. Something I couldn't put my finger on told me that *someone* did this to me.

In this moment, I finally realized I didn't just have amnesia. Someone intentionally took my memory from me. They wanted me to forget. I didn't have evidence; only a gut feeling. But that feeling was so deep, I knew it had to be true. I may not have my memory, but I had the same body, and that body knew the truth.

I despise whoever did this to me, whoever made me lose my memory, whoever stripped me of everything I knew. It was their fault. And now I have to save my friend because I wouldn't dare let whoever did this take anything else from me.

My hands burned. I didn't even bother looking down as I ran. I knew.

Stopping about ten yards from the man, I yelled a stupid phrase, one I had seen in the movies. In a moment of nerves, it came out. The words were already spoken when it was too late to change my mind. "Hey fire guy! Pick on someone your own size."

He now turned to face me, and I held up my hands, each with a softball-sized flame above them. A stunned Sebastian also turned to look at me, and backpedaled to the post office door, yelling inside for everyone to come quickly.

The man with the staff smirked. He sized me up and down with a sense of recognition. I planted my feet firmly and waited for him to attack. Instead, he spoke. "Welcome back, Miss Williams. I must say that I was quite surprised to see you a few weeks ago. And with those superkids too. Now that really surprised me. And here you are again! And once again, in their company."

I kept my anger steady, but his words instilled fear into the situation. If I got too scared, I knew the flames would go out. And the chance of getting them back …

"How do you know who I am?" I asked, trying my best to keep my voice firm. "How do you know my name?"

S completely ignored my question and continued speaking, approaching me slowly as he spoke. I began to inch backwards.

"It's no surprise they wanted to recruit you seeing how powerful you are. Or were." He smirked. "Let's see if you've still got it, shall we?"

He dramatically wound back his staff and threw a fireball at me. I dodged his flame and fell to the ground, turning my orbs into whisps of smoke. He didn't throw another while I was down. In fact, he paused while I took a deep breath and pushed up. In this particular moment, he wasn't trying to kill me. This was a test.

Centering myself again, I miraculously reignited the flames. With great satisfaction, I hurled them both, one after the other. S used his staff to deflect them, sending them back at me. And then my body took over. Some sort of muscle memory seized control, and I began to move in ways I didn't know were possible.

I don't know how I did it, but I waved my arms and combined the two balls into one, which I blasted back at him. He stumbled and stared up at me. He was astonished.

"I must admit, I did not expect you to have such control after your little … accident. That boy must be training you, I presume? He's quite talented, but not nearly as much as you have the potential to be. Oh look! Here he comes now," S said, turning to fight off Sebastian.

One-on-one became two-on-one, with our opponent primarily fighting off Sebastian, while also using his staff to counter my weak flame balls. With a low level of fear still diluting the pure anger I needed to feel, all I could produce were the same small, flammable orbs. However, I knew that there must be more in me somewhere. I mean, I combined two balls into one! What else was possible with these powers?

Penny came running from the bank, and Sebastian yelled to me, "Bianca! Flame!" He gestured quickly over his shoulder at Penny, who I realized was carrying a broom. He didn't need to say anything else. I knew exactly what he wanted.

Penny tossed me the broom and I used my hand to ignite the bristles. I now held a massive fireball on a stick.

"Sebastian, catch," I yelled. He stepped back from the man and caught the broom. It wouldn't stay aflame for long. The fire crept down the handle. Sebastian swung high, aiming for S's head. S countered with his forearm on the dry handle and used the bottom of his staff to hit Sebastian between the legs. Sebastian fell, tightly clutching the broom with both hands. The fire continued to burn down the handle, and when it reached his hands, he cried out in pain and threw the entire thing.

Time slowed down. Sebastian burned himself. On my flame. My mind flashed back to the burning carpet and reminded me once again that my powers didn't just exist; they were dangerous in a way that some of my friends' powers were not. In moments like this, I truly understood how Penny felt when she accidentally hurt the girl in her dance class.

Another sound quickly jerked me out of my thoughts and back into the surrounding battle: Penny was screaming. Horrified at the man towering over her friend, she charged in.

I followed suit, picking up on her emotion, I threw flame after flame. But I no longer had full control: Fear began to shake me. I tried to focus on not hitting Penny, but it became more and more difficult.

I stopped suddenly, unwilling to risk hurting them both. I pulled back and stood, prepared for hand-to-hand combat. Sebastian finally regained his balance; his hands were curled into fists and shaking slightly. I knew he felt pain, but he wasn't giving up the fight. S now faced three of us.

He must not have liked the odds very much because he stopped and stepped back, holding up his hands to halt us.

"Come and get us, you coward," Sebastian barked.

S ignored him. Swirling the staff overhead, he surrounded himself with a wall of fire. Over the noise of the burning, crackling, and whooshing, I heard a single clap and knew that he had disappeared within his flaming force field.

We all were breathing heavily. As his flames disappeared, we said nothing. We stared at the charred circle on the ground, surrounding where he once stood.

"He knows me. S knows me. I don't know why or how. But he knows me," I said and stared at the circle. Sebastian reached over and placed his balled hand on my shoulder. I jumped a little and turned my attention to him.

"It's ok," he said. "We'll figure out what he's after and take him down."

I glanced at his hand, red and enflamed.

"My gosh, your hand. I'm so sorry. I didn't mean to." I teared up a bit. It felt horrible knowing I had caused this.

"Oh, it's just a small burn. It'll be good as new tomorrow. Besides, it was my mistake," Sebastian said. "I didn't let go of the broom when I fell, and I should have. It's not like you hit me with a fireball or something."

But I could have.

"We at least need to rinse your hand! And probably ice it."

"You're right. We should go. I don't think he's coming back. Our job here is done for the day," Penny said. "Come on, Theo and Jasmine are finishing up with the police and will meet us at the van."

The other two walked ahead, and I waited behind for a moment, staring at the char. I had done it. I had fought off a bad guy with my powers. And I had controlled them fairly well. With more training and practice, I could be fighting side by side with Sebastian, and S would never stand a chance against us.

Why, then, was I not thrilled? Why did I feel so off balance? Because I hurt Sebastian. Because my powers needed to be properly controlled. Because I had the potential to be dangerous if I *wanted* to be.

Suddenly, from behind a car, I heard a *crack*. My head snapped up towards the noise. S was back again. I glanced behind me to see that Sebastian and Penny were too far away. Before I could say a word, S spoke: "You don't know how powerful you are." He then clapped once and only a circle of char remained where he once stood.

As I caught up with my friends, I decided not to tell them about S coming back. Understanding who this man was and how he knew me was my mission and my mission alone. I couldn't risk them getting hurt again. My past remained a mystery, and the last thing I wanted was for them to get tangled up in my mess.

But despite my decision, I couldn't quite get the echo of his words out of my head:

You don't know how powerful you are.

CHAPTER FIFTEEN

I spent the evening of our bank mission alone, mostly passing my time outside in the backyard. A lot clouded my mind, both good and bad. For starters, I had finally gotten my powers to cooperate. I could bring them out at will, most of the time, but it took a lot of effort and there were a lot of negative effects. It was physically, mentally, and emotionally taxing trying to propel that kind of energy out of myself.

Second, since negative emotions fueled my powers, I now felt massively depressed. The amount of anger it took to initiate anything horrified me. And pushing it away after the storm had proved to be difficult. It lingered. To be frank, I didn't want my powers to be associated with anger. In short, anger is a bad emotion that hurts people.

Hurts people. Sebastian. It was my fault that inside the house, Jasmine tended to Sebastian's burns. And it was also my fault that I wasn't the one inside helping him.

I needed time to cool off and let the anger fade, which took a bit longer than anticipated. In the midst of battle, I had to let it consume me, and therefore, it wasn't easy to erase the emotion when the job ended. I didn't like that reality. I didn't like that I felt awful leaving the scene, while everyone else reacted in real time with real feelings. I felt devoid of every emotion.

How could I feel like a real hero when my powers made me feel like a villain? When they hurt people. When they couldn't be fully controlled without burning away the good and the positive in me.

Was it even possible to fix that, to use my powers without their taking over my entire being? Or was I doomed to become an angrier person as a result of my efforts? My stomach hurt thinking about it. Considering the possible consequences of my powers suddenly brought back anger.

I made a fireball and tossed it from one hand to the other. Then I caught it, split it in two, and threw them up in the air, one after the other.

I thought about S and what he said to me before he disappeared. I now understood what he meant. Playing with fire wasn't the game I thought it was. I wasn't taking all of this seriously enough. I had the power and the potential to help so many people and to bring justice to the world. But I also had the power to burn it to the ground.

I heard my friends chatting and laughing together through the back door. Their laughter stung. I couldn't feel that same kind of happiness. I couldn't even muster a smile. The anger had suffocated me. I broke down sobbing but was unable to drown out the sound of joy coming from inside the house.

"What are you watching?"

When I had finally pulled myself together enough to stop crying,

I came inside to find Sebastian watching a movie on the couch. It appeared that everyone else had gone to bed.

"The Avengers," he said, casually. "Do you want to join me? I made popcorn."

I laughed at him for watching such an ironic movie and reluctantly joined him on the couch. He offered me the popcorn bag, and I looked down at his bandaged hands. I felt it best not to say anything about them.

"Isn't this a bit loud for Theo?" I gestured toward his closed door.

"Oh no; he can sleep through anything. His snoring drowns out any noise; it's amazing. You should know. You had to hear it for weeks on end."

We watched Iron Man and Captain America take turns beating a giant alien while Thor and Loki engaged in hammer-to-staff combat. To have a villain with a staff seemed exceptionally ironic.

I glanced over at Sebastian, observing him as he studied the screen. He wasn't just watching the movie; this was an examination. While it was a work of fiction, he watched it as if it were a historical documentary and he sought to learn something from each punch.

"Is this what you think we look like?" I asked.

"I think this is what we *should* look like, yeah! Not skill-wise, per se, but in terms of coordination. I think we struggle a bit when we fight as a group. We tend to work one at a time, and the others stand back and watch. I think we would be more powerful if we could coordinate our attacks and come at the enemy from all angles at once."

Sebastian grabbed the remote and muted the movie.

"So in this scene, see how their actions are fluid? They all attack at once but work around each other. Natasha and Clint are especially good at it. Here, I can go back to this other scene," he said, but I stopped him. This was getting to be too much for me. How could he talk about tomorrow's strategy as if today never happened?

"No, it's ok. I believe you. And I get what you mean," I said, taking the remote and pausing the movie. He looked startled.

"Sebastian, I feel like a liability."

He looked even more startled.

"What do you mean?"

"I don't like that I hurt you. Even though it was unintentional, you still got hurt. And what if Penny weren't there to stop S from finishing you off? How can I be sure that I'm not the reason one of you gets hurt or killed? I don't want to be that person."

Sebastian sat quietly for a moment, but then without speaking, offered me his bandaged hand. I hesitated, but took it, and he scooched closer to me, just enough that our legs touched.

"I guess that's why we're a team," he assured me.

I didn't feel much like a member of a team. A teammate wouldn't let another teammate burn both his hands.

"I know what you're thinking, Bianca, but we are a team. And you're part of it."

I smiled a little, "Like the Avengers?"

"Just like the Avengers," he laughed. "The Avengers get beat up all the time when they're fighting these villains. I don't know if you noticed in the last scene, but Thor, for example, gets slammed around like crazy when he's fighting individually. And look here."

He un-paused the movie. "See here. Cap is on the ground, bleeding. He is giving everything he can, but he knows he can't do it alone. He needs his team. Oh, and then look who comes to save him."

The Hulk jumped down from the sky and pummeled the alien.

"The guy with uncontrollable anger," Sebastian said. I could hear the smug smile in his voice. We stared at each other. Oh, the way he looked at me—like he could see past my flaws and my fears and stare straight at my soul.

"We need to be a team," Sebastian said. "All of us fit into the puzzle somehow. Even you. We need to figure out how to make that happen in the smoothest way possible. We need everyone to feel comfortable with the part that they're playing and the skills that they have. Because we can't win alone. Hell, we've never been able to beat this guy. Maybe now, with you, we stand a chance."

He squeezed my hand, and I thanked him and attempted to pull away. He didn't let go. He continued looking into my eyes. I became increasingly aware of my heartbeat. I didn't expect this, especially not tonight.

"You really are an important part of this team," he said softly.

"I don't want to hurt anyone. Especially you," I whispered.

"You won't. I promise. I know you won't hurt me," he said and leaned in closer, whispering, "You've got too much good inside of you. And I trust you."

I held my breath. My heart pounded.

"Prove it," I whispered.

And then he kissed me.

CHAPTER SIXTEEN

Over the next few days, we continued to train individually, focusing on strengthening our bodies. More importantly, however, we began training as a team, strategizing how to best combine our strengths. We were aware that we acted powerfully as both individuals and as pairs, but we wouldn't defeat our mysterious, staff-wielding villain unless all five of us worked together. As movie-like as it sounded, we needed to be in sync. Not just on the same page but acting in unison as one being. Essentially, we needed to be one superhero with the powers of five.

This, however, proved difficult, since only three of us had powers useful for combat. There was a reason that Jasmine and Theo never found themselves in the thick of the fight unless Theo was practicing only hand-to-hand. Their powers seemed to lend themselves towards preventing destruction and clearing out civilians.

However, as Sebastian pointed out one afternoon, this was not ideal. We needed to find a way to get the two of them into the combat zone. Sebastian and Penny couldn't take down S as a duo, and we still didn't quite have the power as a trio. While we didn't want to admit it, we knew he had far too many powers to keep up with. He seemed to have some new trick with every encounter. It would require all five of us to take him down.

"We need to figure out how Theo's float flying and Jasmine's Voice can be used to fight," Sebastian said. He leaned back on the couch and put his hands behind his head. For such a serious topic of conversation, he lounged as though he were discussing the big game with the boys.

"Pretty sure that's not possible," Jasmine replied. Always a downer. She lay on her stomach on the floor, tracing circles on the carpet. Theo kicked back in the new armchair we purchased a few weeks earlier when we realized that we didn't have enough furniture for five people. Penny paced around the room in front of the TV.

Seeing as everyone else appeared to take this meeting casually, I settled on the couch next to Sebastian, leaving a decent amount of space between us. We hadn't talked to each other about what happened a few nights prior, and we certainly hadn't talked to anyone else about it. The last thing I wanted was everyone getting involved, especially since I wasn't even sure what was happening between the two of us.

It felt like it came out of nowhere, that kiss. I hadn't been able to get it out of my head. The moment he took my hand, the way his eyes locked with mine. The soft caress of his lips …

But no matter how many times I replayed the scene in my head, I still wasn't positive whether he meant something by it or if it came from the heat of the moment. I certainly didn't want to ask him, since more than likely, he would then ask how I felt. And at this point, I didn't know. In the moment, I knew one thing. But now, after some time, I felt confused.

"Float flying mixed with some good punches could be possible, right? If it's windy enough," I said, trying my best not to sound stupid. But it wasn't working—I was starting to sound really stupid. "Like what if you could jump and get blown *at* him and then sock him once you get there."

Yeah, really stupid. No one even bothered to reply.

"You could maybe try floating around him to keep him distracted?" Penny tried, but no one seemed interested in that idea either. At least it wasn't only me.

"I'm sorry, Theo, but your powers kind of suck," Jasmine scoffed, rolling onto her back, "Not that mine are any better, but still."

"If I'm being honest, I genuinely don't know how we're going to get either of us on the front line in a useful way," Theo said. "Unless we secretly have some skill that we don't know about."

That got me thinking, and not in a stupid way this time.

"Theo," I said, "your power isn't really 'floating.' It's weightless-ness, right?"

"Yeah, I guess you could call it that," he replied. "I never found much I could do with it other than float around like an idiot. Fun for jumping off buildings but not much good for anything else."

I stood and began pacing around the room. As everyone watched me, I felt an immense amount of pressure to *not* say something dumb.

"Have you ever held onto something while floating?"

He looked confused.

"Why would that matter?"

"No *really*," I continued, still trying to work out the vision in my head, "if you're holding something, does its weight affect your fall? Or do you affect its weight?"

Theo thought for a moment.

"I guess I haven't tried to hold anything since I'm usually trying to keep my hands free and ready to fight. But I assume it would add weight and prevent me from getting anywhere. Or it would drag me down."

My heart stopped and then it fluttered. I continued to press, "But you don't know that for sure, right?"

"No, I guess I don't." He didn't seem to be picking up on what I was suggesting.

"So what you're saying is that you may not even know the extent of your powers," I replied, getting a bit giddy, like I had solved the greatest mystery of our time. Maybe I had … maybe. We still had to see if I was right.

Sebastian cursed to himself, understanding where I was going with this thought. He suddenly stood up from the couch.

"This could be a Mjolnir scenario," he said.

"Yes!" I yelled. "Oh my gosh, *yes*. That's exactly what I'm saying." Absolutely thrilled that I had finally provided the group with a sensible idea, I rejoiced. Even more thrilling was being on the same page with Sebastian. Theodore Martin, however, was not.

"What the hell are you talking about?" he asked, looking at Sebastian as though he spoke Chinese.

"Mjolnir is Thor's hammer," Sebastian said. "When Thor picks it up and swings it around, it's practically weightless, but as soon as it hits someone, they get smacked with the full weight of the heaviest hammer in the universe."

"Sooo …" Theo replied, gesturing for Sebastian to continue his argument.

I cut in, "So what we're thinking is that your powers might be similar."

"But I don't have super strength." He didn't get it. And clearly neither did Penny and Jasmine.

"You don't need super strength," Sebastian patiently replied, "We think you may affect the weight of objects when you hit the wind rather than the other way around."

"Exactly. And if this is correct, then we need to get you a heavy-handed weapon and bam, you pack a Penny-like punch," I said. Everyone was starting to catch on. We may have actually figured out a solution.

"So how do we test this?" Jasmine asked. It was nice to see her participating for once, the only time since I arrived. If even Jasmine was chipping in, we had to be onto something.

Theo ended up consenting to our crazy idea and climbed onto the roof. Through the window, Sebastian handed him his backpack, which was full of heavy books.

"Here goes nothing," Theo said, dramatically taking a step off the roof. As I suspected, he floated to the ground with no problem whatsoever. The rejoicing continued.

"That's incredible! Your powers handled the extra weight with no issues," Penny said, bouncing with glee.

"But can it handle a person?" We turned to look at Jasmine who had a question. "Look, I don't mean to be a downer, but what if a living thing doesn't work the same way? I just mean that a person is bulkier and heavier than a bag of books. I worry you think this is foolproof and will jump off the roof of a skyscraper with a civilian in your arms. What if that goes wrong?"

Jasmine had a good point, even I had to admit it.

"Ok, well how do we test that?" Penny asked, knowing the answer but not wanting to accept it.

"I'll jump off the roof with one of you, obviously," Theo laughed.

"You laugh, but you're probably right," I replied. Everyone stared at me.

"It's like Jasmine said, Sebastian's backpack doesn't have the same weight, motion, and bulk of a person. We also need to know if a living being makes a difference in how the powers work. If Theo can carry people safely to the ground, it will be beneficial for both civilian rescue and for combat."

Surprisingly, no one fought me on this. Penny and Sebastian nodded, and Theo quipped that it made sense. Jasmine stood stone-faced with her arms crossed.

"Can't he do it first with a smaller animal to test the theory? What about that cat?" she asked.

"Nah, if I'm going to jump off the roof with a living thing, I might as well go big. Keeps things more interesting," Theo said and smirked.

It was crazy, for sure, but we needed to know if this could work. I didn't know why, but I was enthusiastic. And since this idea was the brainchild of my insanity, Theo decided that I would be the one to jump off of the roof with him. Jasmine was excited about that detail. Sebastian reluctantly agreed, trusting my judgment. It was yet to be seen if I'd even be vindicated.

As I pulled myself up and out the window, I started to regret my idea. Our roof wasn't that high, but it felt like it once I got up there. Theo grabbed my hand and hoisted me up. Once I had my feet under me, I crouched and tried my best not to look at the ground.

"You don't have to do this, Bianca."

"No, I think this is a good idea," I said, trying to focus on my balance. I took a few deep breaths.

"Ok," I slowly stood up. "I'm ready."

"I think you should get on my back. Does that make sense? I don't know how to hold you so you won't get hurt if this doesn't work."

If this doesn't work.

"It'll work, but in the slimmest chance that it doesn't, I don't know if there's a good or bad way to do this. Since it's just the two of us now, I feel like I can admit with full transparency that this is incredibly stupid."

He laughed, "Yeah, it's really dumb. But I have faith. You seem to know what you're talking about."

I winced, certain that I did *not* know what I was talking about. He recognized my reaction and added,

"And I trust you."

"Well I don't know why because my track record *isn't* fantastic."

"It doesn't matter. Sebastian trusts you, so I do too," Theo said.

My stomach flipped. If I fell off this roof and died right after Sebastian and I finally kissed … maybe this was an abysmal idea after all.

"Theo," I said, taking a deep breath, "It's your lucky day. You never asked me to prove my trust in you, but I'm about to. So, you're welcome."

I climbed on his back and held on around his neck like a child being carried by his father. My legs squeezed tightly around his waist.

"What are you, like ninety pounds?" he laughed. "My gosh what if I have to save a fat person? I'm totally screwed."

"While I love the compliment, please shut up and jump off the roof already." I wanted to get this over with. I closed my eyes as tightly as possible and said a quick prayer.

This felt dumb. Beyond dumb. Why did I continually put myself in horrendous situations? With my current track record, it didn't surprise me that I ended up in Victory without my memory. Maybe it really was my fault.

Theo asked, "Ready?" and I silently nodded. I felt him take a few steps backward, get a running start, and jump.

I screamed. Down below, Penny also screamed. Jasmine cursed in shock. But Sebastian cheered. We floated gently to the ground.

Time seemed to slow as we drifted through the air. It wasn't a slow, straight descent. Rather, we floated along with the breeze, my hair lifting up around my face like the leaves in the trees as they rustled in the wind.

I could fly.

"*Yeah!*" Theo yelled and pumped his fist. My screams turned to laughter as we landed safely on the ground.

I dropped off of Theo's back and hugged him tightly. We were thrilled to be alive and excited about what this meant. Penny was jumping up and down; Sebastian and Jasmine hugged, and we all celebrated the minor victory. This detail helped us toward completing the puzzle. If we kept thinking, we could find a way for all five of us to incorporate our powers in one fighting force. That's what we wanted.

"So now," Theo said, "I guess I need to focus more on lifting. I always thought I had the worst power, just floating around like a dingbat. But this could be like super strength in a roundabout way. And that's pretty cool. As you said, if I can hold something before hitting the air, I can use it as a weapon."

"Yeah, if you're not picking up and throwing cars by the end of the week, I'm going to be super disappointed in you," Jasmine said and smiled.

I turned to her. "Ok, so now we need to get you in this mix. How can we use your powers on the ground? Does anyone have any ideas?"

Jasmine quickly crossed her arms and stopped smiling.

"I'm going to stick to evacuation duty," she said.

"But surely you want to get in the fight," I added. "And we can use all the help we can get."

Surprisingly, Sebastian backed her up.

"No, I think Jasmine's right. Evacuation duty is a good idea. I don't think she's up for combat-type situations. While it would be nice to have extra hands, she's great at evacuation. And you must admit, it's a necessary role."

"But," I questioned, "what if there's no one to evacuate? What are you going to do? Stay in the van and watch?"

"We will see when we get there. Ok?" Jasmine turned and walked into the house. I stood there stunned, but no one else looked surprised.

"Good work today, everyone," Sebastian said as he followed her. Apparently, that meant we were done for the day.

And we were just getting somewhere too…

CHAPTER SEVENTEEN

We continued getting minor calls from Victory for a few weeks. We used those opportunities to perfect our four-man fighting force.

I continually found Jasmine's absences bothersome. She talked big but was clearly too scared to engage in combat. Either that or she lacked confidence in her skills and neglected to try. While her quest to save all civilians was occasionally noble, there weren't always civilians in danger. At those times, she dawdled on the side, and it grew increasingly infuriating.

We often needed an extra pair of hands since in several cases we faced more than one opponent. A pair of shooters, a group of bank robbers, three guys wielding machetes who tried to hold up a Wendy's: We could have used her, even if her powers never manifested in a physical way.

The most recent incident of this came when we got a call about a robber in a bank after hours. While this initially seemed to be a classic call for us, that wasn't the case. Over the last few months, I had learned what kinds of calls we received as opposed to the ones the police received. There were two fighting forces in Victory, and we got specific missions.

The police handled most crimes, and we handled anything unique, anything with too many civilians, or anything related to S. In those cases, our powers were better suited to stopping criminals than relying on a few officers.

However, most of the time, the police handled standard situations. And they did a great job of it, too. We were there as support more than anything except when they expected that S may be involved. In that case, we were always called. Sometimes, they were wrong, and S wasn't there, but we would help anyway. Regardless of why the call came to us, we showed up when needed and fought the troublemakers.

Since we technically lived outside the city limits, it was hard to get there as quickly as the local police. This further demonstrated the need for them to handle anything small and quick. But when S was involved, it didn't matter where we were; we were called in.

This particular bank robber call seemed like something outside of our lane, but the police insisted this one was definitely ours. They noticed in a drive-by that someone they hadn't seen before had been sticking close to the bank since mid-afternoon, examining all the doors and windows. They expected a premeditated attack. Additionally, police discovered charred circles on the ground near the bank's back entrance and immediately called us.

By the time we arrived, the robber was already in the back door, working on the first vault. Jasmine, as expected, refused to come inside. Sebastian and Theo, the gentlemen they were, went in first. Penny and I crept silently behind. When we could see the robber, we realized it wasn't S.

This man looked younger and well-built. S was incredibly tall and bone thin. He looked a lot like your classic Dr. Strange or Jafar sorcerer-type. This guy was bulkier, but he looked strong. Definitely not S. The char circles must have been unrelated. Guess this call shouldn't have been ours after all. Our suspect fiddled with the lock system, and Sebastian initiated communication.

"Excuse me sir, but this office closed at five o'clock."

The man whipped his head around. Dark circles surrounded his bloodshot eyes. He looked rough and breathed heavily, like a madman. He slowly turned his full body towards us. I quickly realized that he was bigger than Theo—not great news. But with four of us, we could definitely take him. At least I hoped so.

After a look into the man's eyes, I didn't feel the need to continue the conversation that Sebastian had started. I quickly conjured a fireball and threw it at his hand, which still rested on the locking mechanism. He cursed and pulled back, massaging his palm. His eyes flashed with anger.

"Step away from the vault," Sebastian said as he approached. The man didn't move.

"Make me."

It was a standoff, and the one person who *could* make him step away wasn't present. For the love of all things good …

I suddenly heard what sounded like the air conditioner kicking on. Out of the corner of my eye, I saw Theo crouch. The sound definitely came from the air conditioner, and Theo knew it. He jumped up into the softly blowing air and shot directly at the man, foot first.

This should have knocked the robber over, or at least made him stumble, but he stood unmoved. Instead, it was Theo who fell. The man picked him up, gripped the back of his sweatshirt and lifted him in the air with one hand. He simply tossed him across the room. Theo slammed into a wall and fell to the floor with a thud.

That shouldn't have been possible. Theo was a big guy; a man of any size should have been moved, at least slightly, by the impact. But this guy stood completely unfazed. I couldn't help but react.

"What the he—"

Penny and I suddenly fell to the ground; our legs had been kicked out from under us. The man hadn't moved. I glanced around, panicked, but didn't see anyone. Hearing a soft noise coming from the corner of the room, I turned to see. Still, I saw no one.

But there was something, or someone in the room with us.

We pushed ourselves to our feet, but the same force knocked us down again. This time, it distinctly felt like a person had swept their leg and knocked my feet out from under me. I looked around wildly. Theo tried to stand but was knocked down as well. As he lay there, a girl suddenly appeared, dressed in blue, standing over him. She was tall and thin with long, brown hair. She stretched her arms a little for effect, as if this was no big deal for her, and laughed at Theo.

"Try and stay on your feet, big guy!" she laughed. "You look like an idiot, lying there all helpless on the ground."

I blinked and she disappeared. Theo recoiled, crying out in pain. A drop of blood appeared on his lip, and he cried out again.

"She's kicking me in the face," he yelled. He recoiled again and swung his fists in the air, trying to prevent her from kicking again. She suddenly appeared again, this time, next to the man at the vault door.

"Hey Zeke, let's get the stuff and get out of here. These kids aren't worth our energy." The man turned and started working on the door again. Penny charged in and roundhouse kicked him in the gut, but he didn't budge. He was a wall.

Sebastian pulled the fire extinguisher off the wall and approached the woman. I followed suit, fireballs in hand. Before we could do anything, Theo yelled out in pain again.

"She keeps kicking me!"

But it didn't appear that she had moved; she stood in the same spot, smiling. Sebastian blasted her with the extinguisher. White foam flowed from the extinguisher, covering the floor. Theo kept yelling and tried to block more attacks. His face was bloodied. I noticed foam tracks leading from the woman to him and back.

"Invisibility," I said softly. That must be it. I raised my voice and continued, "Is that your schtick? That's pretty lame and definitely overdone in the movies these days."

"Super speed, actually," she said, winking. "So much more effective."

"Still pretty freaking lame," Sebastian said, taking the first swing with the extinguisher. She dodged and disappeared again.

I remembered Jasmine outside, clearly seeing through the window what we were dealing with. Why on earth did she not come in and help us? I made eye contact with her through the glass and screamed at her to get in here, but she didn't budge; she just turned her back and looked out to the horizon.

Jasmine! What are you doing?

Sebastian, still wielding the fire extinguisher, continued battling Miss Superspeed while I shifted my attention to helping Penny take down Mr. Rockwall. I threw more flames his way, and he yelped in pain. It worked. A few more hits and he'd have to give up. They'd have to retreat. I kept firing, advising Penny to stay out of the way.

While the man focused on stopping my fireballs, Penny kicked him behind his knees, and he fell with a deafening crash. It became clear that he could only be rock solid and unmovable if he concentrated on doing so. Penny found his weakness—the key was to distract him.

Luckily, we quickly experienced one. Tired of blindly swinging the extinguisher around, Sebastian released the rest of the foam all over the floor. Miss Superspeed slipped and fell on it. Sebastian proceeded

to hit her over the head with the empty canister, knocking her unconscious.

One down, one to go.

Sebastian grabbed her under the arms and dragged her out the front
door to the sidewalk. Jasmine started searching her pockets for ID, or
anything that might help us later.

Penny continued her hand-to-hand with the man. She had grown
tired from the fight; I could tell. Her hits appeared visibly weaker than
when they started, and her kicks weren't anything special. Mid-punch,
he grabbed her wrist, and pulled her up in the air. She dangled there,
whimpering. In one swift motion, he threw her across the room where
she landed next to Theo. He screamed and grabbed her, pulling her to
his chest, talking to her softly. He maneuvered his body between her
and the man, attempting to create a protective barrier.

Before I could see if she was ok, the man grabbed me by the collar
and jerked me up to his eye level. Unable to breathe I clutched my
throat as the fabric tightened around my neck; when I gasped and
wriggled, he laughed in my face. I was in a panic. I tried to make
myself angry, make myself hot. If I could burn him, maybe he would
drop me.

But I couldn't. The fear was too strong.

Where was Sebastian?

I was losing consciousness, and no one was coming to rescue me.
My two friends lay on the ground. They were no help. Alone, terror
overcame me.

Suddenly, the man looked up over my shoulder and froze. His eyes
were locked on whatever or whoever stood behind me. "Drop her," a
voice said. The man's grip on my throat immediately relaxed, and I
fell on my stomach, gasping for air. I glanced up to see the man in a
trance, staring forward. His eyes were locked with Jasmine's.

"Now sleep," she said, and at that moment, Sebastian hit him in the head with an oversized cash register, sending him tumbling to the floor. Barely able to hold the register's weight anymore, Sebastian dropped it to the ground with a thud.

It was over. We had won.

The police arrived shortly afterward. They took our two unconscious suspects out in handcuffs and put them in the back of the cruiser. Jasmine tended to Theo and Penny's wounds while Sebastian and I talked to the officers about what had transpired.

"We knew there was something suspicious and assumed it was the 'usual suspect,'" one of the officers explained. "We had no idea there were more people out there like … him. Or you all. At least not here in Victory."

"We didn't know either," Sebastian said. "We've never seen anyone before. I don't understand where these two came from."

"And their special … talents," the second officer began and pulled out a notebook. "Were their 'powers' like yours, or could they have been learned skills?"

"They were powers, at least for the female. I know that for certain. She moved faster than the human eye could detect," I said. "And the male was a wall, and I mean a *wall*. If he concentrated, nothing could make him budge, not even Penny's kicks. We're under the impression that he has super strength. He picked Theo up and tossed him like a wad of paper."

I gestured to my friend who was lying on the ground and bleeding from several wounds. Penny lay next to him, and they whispered softly to each other. Jasmine was nowhere to be seen. I looked around, and finally spotted her through the window as she rounded the corner of the building.

"Could you excuse me for a moment?" I asked the officers and Sebastian. Angry as ever, I shoved through the door and rounded the corner, following Jasmine.

"Hey!" I yelled.

She stopped, turned around, and looked at me. I kept approaching.

"What do you want?" she asked, crossing her arms in front of her chest.

"What on earth was all that back there?" I walked straight towards her, infuriated.

"What? In the bank?"

"Yes, in the bank!" I stopped about eight feet short of where she stood. "What were you thinking? How did you think staying outside was the right choice? There were no civilians! You just stood there!"

"Oh, calm down. I came inside," she shot back, stepping towards me.

"Yeah, only at the last possible second. You could have come in sooner. You know, when you saw them take down your friends? Maybe if you had actually cared, Penny and Theo wouldn't be hurt! Did you think of that? Did it even cross your mind to care about other people for a second?"

"I saved your life, Bianca. Stop acting so pathetic."

"We shouldn't have gotten to the point where you had to do that! If you came in with us and at least tried to help, maybe I wouldn't have needed saving!"

As I approached her again, my hands started to burn. I could feel little flames licking my fingertips. I twisted my wrists, forming small orbs.

Jasmine's face changed. She looked scared and backed away slowly. I had never seen her like this. Her eyes remained locked on my hands. Terrified, she searched my eyes and pleaded with me. "Please stay away from me. Stay back."

I could feel my arms lowering and my feet trying to make me stop. She was using her Voice. That angered me even more.

I escaped her spell, screamed and threw an orb at her. She ducked under it and fell to the ground. "Please, Bianca," she cried as I stood over her. "*Stop*. I didn't mean to leave you in there alone." She wasn't using her Voice this time. She was terrified that I would hurt her. I extinguished my hands but continued to stand over her.

"Either you're a part of this team or you're not. You've hated me since day one. Well guess what? I'm here now whether you like it or not, and I'm not playing games. I want to take down S and whoever these other villains are. I'm not so sure that you feel the same way."

"What do you mean? Are you saying I don't want them defeated?"

"You don't seem to! You never want to engage them. At first, I thought you were scared, but now I'm starting to think you might have other motives."

"You're calling me a villain!" Jasmine looked both shocked and furious. She pushed herself to her feet and looked me in the eyes.

"If I'm a villain," she continued after a pause, "what does that make you?"

"Me?" I questioned her. "Are you joking? Seriously, are you joking? My intentions have been completely pure."

She started laughing.

"You know nothing, Bianca Williams."

Before I could push back, Sebastian and one of the officers rounded the corner and ran up to us.

"I don't want to interrupt what looks like a fascinating and intellectually stimulating conversation, but we have a problem," Sebastian said.

I glared at Jasmine one last time before we followed Sebastian back to the police cruiser. Theo and the other officer were talking. Theo's arm was wrapped around Penny, who supported herself on her left leg and leaned on Theo for balance. It hurt to see her in so much pain. Her expression was sullen as she stared at her feet.

"What's the issue?" I asked. Without looking up, Penny pointed to the ground in front of her.

A large, char circle was burned into the cement.

The police cruiser sat empty, its rear door handle blasted off.

"What does it mean?" I asked, almost at a whisper. Sebastian sighed,

"It means our new friends have been bailed out by their boss."

CHAPTER EIGHTEEN

I held fire in my hands.

Completely at ease, I walked down an alley, not at all stirred by the darkness or the quiet. I had no fear. I had fire.

A noise rang out around the corner. I jumped a little in surprise, and the flames in my hands flickered. I shifted my concentration back to the quiet and calm, and the flame stabilized again. I didn't need to be scared. I wasn't the one being hunted.

"Reveal yourself," I yelled. "Come out."

A shadowy figure stepped out from the darkness, and I smiled. Before I realized what I was doing, I attacked. I threw balls of fire from my hands and charged the figure who came at me with a crowbar. I kept moving forward, releasing flames. A fireball brushed the figure's arm, and they yelled in pain. I didn't stop. I couldn't show weakness. I kept approaching, fireball in hand. I planned to finish my mission.

The figure lay on the ground. Clutching her burned arm, she whimpered and squirmed in pain. The flame clearly did more than simply brush her arm. It burned deeply.

Standing over her, I looked into her eyes and found only terror. As she pleaded, my hand hesitated slightly, but I fought off the urge to hold back. I was angry at myself for considering mercy and threw a flame next to her head. She screamed and covered her face.

"Please! Stop! Please," she sobbed. She was done for. She and I both knew that, but she pleaded with me anyway. This was a different voice: one with no confidence, one scared of death.

"Please. Please, I beg you, please."

I only laughed and made another flame.

I woke up shaking.

My goodness. What was that?

I sat up in bed and looked to see Jasmine fast asleep. Did I dream about killing her? I felt mad, but I didn't want her dead, did I?

I was getting into my own head, focusing too much on our fight and calling each other villains. I wasn't a villain; these were bad dreams. Besides, Jasmine lay across the room, alive and fine. This was all in *my* head. Still, I struggled to fall back asleep, dreading that I would wake up to find the dream had come true.

CHAPTER NINETEEN

To no one's surprise, the next day felt incredibly tense. In ordinary circumstances, it wouldn't have been, since it was a Saturday, the most relaxing day of the week for all of us. To add to the irony, the weather had been gorgeous. The signs of fall surrounded us and beckoned us outside. We should have been enjoying the fresh air and one another's company, but instead we spent the afternoon inside, surrounding the table. Angry.

Sebastian thought it would be good for us to talk things out since our last mission revealed such shocking information. And also, because Jasmine and I still hadn't made up after our fight. That was the part I wasn't so excited about.

Jasmine clearly resented me, and to be quite honest, I was angry. At myself. It scared me to think about how aggressive I could be. It felt so out of character, especially the part where I prepared to finish her off.

I didn't hate her. She simply irritated me and intentionally caused me constant self-doubt. I didn't hate her. But at the same time, why did "dream me" want her dead?

I knew for certain that I didn't want to sit at the table and fight with her, especially not in front of our friends. To that end, I tried my best to keep the conversation focused on the events in the bank, purposefully avoiding any discussion of Jasmine or our fight afterwards.

"They were definitely working with S, right?" I asked. "The char circles prove that."

"I think they do," Sebastian said. "How else could they have disappeared like that? I'm certain that S was involved. Maybe he was the mastermind behind it."

"How did we not know that he had allies?" I inquired. "This is information we should have known."

"I mean, he's had allies in the past," Theo said, leaning back in his chair. "They've usually been in a sidekick-type role. But we took care of them."

This was news to me. I thought S worked alone. That's what they made me think, at least. I wish I had known this information sooner.

Practically speaking, however, it didn't surprise me that more supers existed in Victory, even if they were villains. If five heroes ended up in one place, a couple of villains showing up shouldn't surprise us, especially if they had such a powerful man luring them in. I suppressed the doubts in the back of my head and decided not to press my friends on why they hadn't told me about S's past sidekicks.

"That makes sense," I replied, "if he's used other supers like us, but been defeated. It would logically follow that he wanted to take matters into his own hands since his previous plans clearly had failed."

"Exactly," Sebastian confirmed. "So what's interesting is that he started using other supers again. It's been a long time since he had accomplices. I thought he gave up on that after the first few tries. So why now? What caused him to start again?"

"Maybe he's scared," Penny added. "I mean, we've added another member to the team. It's five on one now."

Four on one, but I didn't plan to say that out loud. Instead, I silently looked over at Jasmine. She kept her eyes locked on the table and seemed to be uninterested in the conversation.

"I think he's scared of what Bianca brings to the team," Sebastian said. He glanced up at me, made eye contact, and quickly glanced away. Butterflies multiplied in my stomach, and I held back a smile.

"He's not scared of me. I think he's merely intrigued," I said. "He knows I'm powerful, but he's not scared. He and I have the same power, and he has more skills on top of that. He's essentially me but better."

The energy in the room shifted. I knew I had crossed the line into the realm of saying too much.

"How do you know that? He didn't start sending in his goons until you showed up at full force. How do you know what he's thinking?" Theo asked.

It flattered me that my friends believed I was the cause of worry for a super villain, but they were wrong. I still hadn't told them about my last encounter with S when he appeared but didn't attack me.

You don't know how powerful you are.

I knew I should have told them at the time, but I didn't want them to be upset or worried about me. We were a team, and I needed to trust them. I needed them to know everything, and even if it upset them, the truth must be told eventually.

"I know how he's thinking because he told me." They stared at me, confused, and slightly concerned.

"What do you mean?" Penny asked. "He told you?"

This was it; the moment it would all come to light. I braced myself for the consequences.

"Remember that day when he almost attacked Sebastian outside of the post office? After he disappeared, we started to make our way back. My head couldn't stop spinning after everything that had happened, so I hung back a little bit. Trying to be alone, you know? And he reappeared. Just for a moment."

I took a deep breath. Tears came to my eyes, and I felt like a traitor for not telling them sooner.

"He looked at me and said, 'you don't know how powerful you are.' And then he disappeared again," I said and choked up.

Everyone was silent. I couldn't read their expressions, whether they were mad, concerned, or merely confused. I couldn't even look at Sebastian. I didn't want anyone to be mad at me, especially him. He told me we were a team; I didn't want to betray his trust.

"I am so sorry," I said, and then I began to cry. Tears poured down my face. I buried my face in my hands. "I wanted to tell you, but I felt a tremendous amount of guilt for accidentally burning Sebastian. I didn't want anyone to be more angry at me than they already were. But I promise; you know everything now. He said that one thing and then disappeared again. I'm sorry."

I couldn't stop crying. The emotions of that day flooded back to me. The fear started building again. I felt like I was running away from something. The pain instantly returned—the pain of hurting Sebastian; the pain of seeing Penny and Theo lying on the ground, injured; the pain of my nightmares. I didn't want to hurt anyone, not even now, sitting at this table looking at my friends' shocked faces and Penny's bruises, Theo's black eye and bloody lip—I broke down.

Unlike those moments of anger where my body pulsed with the heat of rage, I felt cold, sad. My body seemed to float in a void. They deserved to be mad at me. And I deserved their anger. My body shook and shivered. Penny reached over and grabbed my hands, rubbing and patting them gently.

"It's ok," she whispered.

"Bianca," Sebastian said, "we aren't mad at you. You were concerned about other things. A five-second encounter with S isn't going to make us hate you. You had a lot going on. I understand why you didn't tell us. It was an overwhelming day."

"Besides, S messes with people. He intentionally got in your head, which would've driven anyone crazy. You didn't do anything wrong," Theo added.

I sniffed as my nose started to run. I felt pathetic. Penny let go of my hands, got up, and grabbed a tissue for me.

"We aren't mad, Bianca. Thank you for telling us," Sebastian said. This time, he took my hand and squeezed it. I squeezed back softly, still aware of his injured palm.

"Speak for yourself," Jasmine scoffed. Through all this emotion, I had forgotten that she sat at the table with us.

"Excuse me?" I asked, dropping Sebastian's hand. "What?"

"You heard me," she said. "You think this little pity party is going to cover your mistakes? You're such a cute little actress."

This shocked me so much that the tears stopped flowing.

"What did you just say?" I whispered.

"Jasmine, stop," Sebastian intervened. "This has gone too far. I'm sick of you attacking her."

Jasmine laughed in an unsettling way.

"Of course you're defending her! I've seen you two. So you can stop pretending and sneaking around. We all see the way you look at each other. And besides, I saw your little make out the other night. By the look of it, it certainly wasn't your first."

My cheeks became hot, and I looked at Sebastian with my heart racing. His expression was hard to read; he looked straight at the table, not at Jasmine.

"Wait they did wha—" Penny started, but Jasmine cut her off.

"And on your point about me 'attacking' Bianca," Jasmine raised her voice. "That's the biggest freaking joke I've ever heard. Are you *really* going to pretend you don't know her, Sebastian? Are you going to let yourself forget what she's done? I am *sick* of acting, sick of pretending to be friends."

I opened my mouth to object, but she held her hand up to stop me. My jaw immediately snapped shut. I couldn't tell if it was from shock or if her Voice was more powerful than I had realized.

"I tried so hard at first," she continued, "but I can't be expected to buddy up to someone like her as if nothing happened! I'm not playing your games anymore, Sebastian! If you want to keep playing them, fine, but I'm not going to participate. And I'm not going to continue lying."

"Jasmine, stop it. Please. You're not helping anything," Penny begged. This conflict clearly upset her, almost as much as it was up-setting me.

"Oh, I'm the one not helping? How is it helping someone to lie to them for months on end and take advantage of their amnesia? I'm sorry, but you guys wanting to make allies and turn the tide was a stupid idea. It was stupid then, and it's stupid now."

"It's worked, Jasmine," Theo said. "The tides have turned, and Bianca is a valuable member of this team."

"Yeah, but what's going to happen when she remembers?" Jasmine snapped. "Have you thought about that?"

Everyone was silent. I couldn't take it any longer.

"What the hell are you going on about?" I asked, a little louder than I had intended.

Jasmine scanned her eyes around the table, looking at each of her friends. They were silent and avoided looking directly at her. She laughed. It wasn't a malicious laugh, but rather the kind that comes out in a moment of relief, a moment when one finally gives up after a long fight, or a moment when a decision has been made.

"Sorry to ruin the game everyone," she said. Then, looking directly at me, she pulled up her shirt sleeve to reveal a big, dark scar. A burn scar.

"You're the villain, Bianca," she said. "Congrats! Now you know something."

Then she pulled her sleeve down and left the room.

CHAPTER TWENTY

MAY 25, 2017

The elevator took forever. I checked my watch and once again examined the business card in my hand. *Helping Hearts: Victory*, Suite 225. I needed to ask for Alexandra at the front desk.

The suite was one of many in a large, standard looking office building. Unlike a company with their own building, Helping Hearts appeared to be renting a floor of office space. The company was clearly quite small. When the elevator finally came, I made it up to Suite 225, and I hesitated.

Was it really a good idea to go into a place I'd never been, filled with people I didn't know and request a job? I wasn't sure how this sort of thing worked. I had just graduated from college, after all, so what I knew for sure was that you needed a resume and to make a good impression at an interview. Maybe showing up unannounced wasn't the way to go about this.

In all honesty, I didn't know exactly what this group did. Alexandra had described the work as "philanthropic," but that could mean a variety of things. Besides, the place was named *Helping Hearts: Victory*.

The name didn't add useful information, and I couldn't find mention of them online.

However weird the situation, I was running low on prospects and needed a job as soon as humanly possible. I had been in Victory for a week, and I'd had no luck with my job hunt. I figured that using a connection couldn't hurt, even if I had only met the connection once. In a diner. In the middle of nowhere. But people use one-time connections to get jobs all the time, right? Isn't that the whole point of networking? And besides, maybe the job wouldn't even be a good fit. And I could quit if I wanted to. There was no harm in asking.

I opened the door, forgetting to knock. This startled the receptionist and she jumped. My first *faux paus*. Great. Regardless, she smiled at me kindly.

"Hi there, can I help you?"

"Hi," I said. "I'm here to see Alexandra Oliver."

"Is she expecting you?" the girl asked, flipping through a day planner.

"Well no, but she knows who I am."

Somehow.

The woman picked up the phone and dialed.

"Alexandra? Hi, I have a young woman here to see you." She paused and nodded to herself.

"That's right, yep," she continued. Then she looked me up and down, describing me into the phone.

"About your height, blue eyes, strawberry hair, looks a bit lost." There was a pause. She nodded, thanked Alexandra, and hung up.

"She will be right out. Please, take a seat." She gestured toward a small couch and coffee table. I made my way over and sat down.

The front office felt very empty. Other than the reception desk and this little lounge setup, the only other thing in the room was a filing cabinet. No art on the walls or any type of company logo could be seen. Besides the one we came in, there was only one other door.

Alexandra had mentioned that they recently moved out to Victory; essentially they were a startup. I couldn't fault them for not having a website or not covering their walls in waiting room art. But still, it felt a bit odd not to have a logo.

As I waited, I started to get nervous. An excited *type* of nervous, but still nervous. I closed my eyes and said a little prayer. This was going to be good. I could feel it.

The door opened, and the woman I recognized as Alexandra appeared. She exclaimed, "Bianca! Oh my goodness! So happy to see you here! Come in, come in!" She ushered me through the door and into a small hallway with three office doors. She took me into her office and told me to sit down. Boxes covered the floor.

"Sorry, I'm still slowly unpacking everything. It's been a bit of a process. Just ignore the boxes and make yourself comfortable." She sat down at her desk and asked if I wanted coffee or tea.

"No, thank you," I said. "I appreciate your taking the time to meet with me, especially without an appointment."

"Of course! I am so happy to see you," she said and took a sip of her coffee. "What brings you here today?"

Oh no, it was exactly as I feared. I had to directly ask for a job. I didn't know what I expected. I guess I had foolishly hoped that she would call me into her office and hand me a job. I wasn't prepared for this.

"I wanted to take you up on the offer you extended when we met. About a job or an internship?" I swallowed hard and suddenly wished that I had asked for a bottle of water.

"I looked for an application online, but you don't seem to have a website."

She laughed.

"We take all of our applications in person. You see, we are always looking for very specific types of people, ones who will take the necessary risks. We look for people like you. People who don't sit back and wait for their life to change. We need people who will seize what they want."

I breathed a sigh of relief. This really was my lucky day.

"So is there paperwork or anything you need me to fill out?"

Alexandra ignored my question and continued, "Our mission at Helping Hearts is to make the world a better and safer place. That's not an easy goal! It takes guts, risk. We need our team members to understand that risk and be entirely dedicated to our mission. Do you understand?"

"I think so? Maybe?"

"So our application is more of a meeting. An interview, if you will. Especially for our apprenticeship program."

"Apprenticeship program? Is that like an internship, or is it a full-time job," I asked, pulling out a notepad to jot this down.

"It's full time but similar to a fellowship. You would be studying under our founder and CEO, Dr. Fadel. It's a type of mentorship pro—" She stopped and stood up, looking out the open door behind me.

"Actually, Dr. Fadel just walked by! Follow me. I will introduce you!" I followed her out the door.

"Dr. Fadel," she called to an incredibly tall man who was walking away from us down the hallway. He turned and smiled at Alexandra.

"Miss Oliver, hello. Who is this?"

He stood tall and slender with the mustache of a sorcerer or a magician, and his skin was noticeably tan. He spoke with a light accent, perhaps of some Middle Eastern country.

"Nice to meet you, sir. My name is Bianca Williams. I just moved out here. Miss Oliver gave me her card and informed me that you were looking to take on apprentices. I came here to submit an application."

I tried my best not to look nervous, but Dr. Fadel was rather intimidating.

"Wonderful, come into my office and we can begin the interview!"

My heart rate picked up. I hadn't expected an interview with the founder this soon.

"Are you sure? Right now? I bet you have a million other things going on," I said.

"Nonsense," he replied. "This is the most important thing right now."

I followed him into the office at the far end of the hall and took a seat facing his desk. Alexandra stood behind me, checking emails on her phone.

Dr. Fadel's office was much bigger, and much tidier, than Alexandra's. Books covered every wall. In the corner sat a red armchair and a tall reading lamp. Still no art, nor any sign that this was a business and not a college professor's office.

"What brought you here, Miss Williams?"

I started to explain how I bumped into Alexandra on my way to Victory and how I struggled to find a job, but he cut me off.

"No, what brought you *here*? To Victory?"

I thought about the night I saw the superheroes on the news. How it made me feel watching them bring justice to people who deserved it. "Victory seems like a special place," I began, "with special people."

Dr. Fadel never looked away from my face. He examined my every move, taking mental notes rather than physical ones. I tried to examine him in return, to read him, but it was impossible. His eyes said nothing.

"What are you hoping to do with your life?" he asked. "What do you want to do more than anything?" The interview suddenly grew intense. The questions were not particularly easy, especially for a fellowship interview.

"Helping people. I want to help people," I said, nervous that my answer wasn't good enough. There wasn't anything else to say. I came here because I wanted to help people like the Victory superheroes did. It sounded dumb, but it was the truth.

"Well you're in luck," he laughed. "We are called Helping Hearts for a reason." He leaned back in his chair and put his arms behind his head.

"Do you know what we do here, Miss Williams? We help people, just like you said. A lot of bad things happen in places like Victory. It's our job to make sure that those things are stopped and that people can be free to live their lives in peace. Do you follow?"

"So you're defending Victory from bad things and people?"

He put his arms back on the desk and looked at me quizzically. "Your choice of the word 'defend' interests me." He picked up a pencil and started twirling it between his fingers.

Without looking at me, he asked, "Do you know of the Victory supers, Miss Williams?"

My heart began racing again. Besides the one news program I saw, I'd never heard their name said out loud. What I saw on television wasn't a dream. It was real.

"Yes," I said, quietly.

"Aha," he replied. "I understand now. You want to … help people like they do? Yes?" I swallowed and nodded. He put down his pencil and stared at me.

"Well that's precisely what we do. We help make Victory what it *should* be. We help bring it to its fullest potential. Does that interest you?"

"Yes," I said, "it does. I want to help people and make Victory better."

"Well it sounds like you're in the right place. But one last question before we finish the interview. This one is very important, so I need you to be honest with me."

I nodded. He looked me in the eyes.

"Do you have any special skills, Miss Williams?"

"Special skills?" I repeated. "I'm incredibly organized and have some experience using Excel—"

"*Special* skills. Do you have any *special* skills?"

My heart pounded in my chest. I had never told anyone about what I could do. I had always felt so alone, too scared to share what I'd accidentally discovered about myself one night after a high school dance. I didn't really want to show them, but a part of me knew this was my one chance to do something to change the world.

I closed my eyes and concentrated. Dr. Fadel said nothing.

A few seconds later, I raised my hand above the desk, the fire licking my fingertips. I opened my eyes to see Dr. Fadel smiling.

"Alexandra," he said, "draw up the paperwork." Offering his hand to me, he smiled. "When can you start, Miss Williams?"

CHAPTER TWENTY-ONE

I couldn't breathe. The burn scar was real. My dreams hadn't actually been dreams. They were memories. I had hurt Jasmine, *really* hurt Jasmine. And if I had hurt her, who else might I have attacked?

Me ... the villain.

I gasped for air between sobs. No one said anything.

"You all ... you ..." I couldn't get out what I wanted to say. How dare they pretend to know nothing of my past? How dare they try to make me into a fighting machine?

"Why ... how ..." I couldn't stop crying. I didn't want to be at the table anymore. I needed to get out of the room. Maybe even out of the house. I couldn't do it anymore.

I pushed back from the table and tried to stand, but my legs wobbled; blood rushed to my head; and I sank to the floor. I couldn't breathe. The room spun around me. Theo quickly got up. I thought he was going to leave the room, but instead, he knelt next to me and pulled me into his arms. I melted into him, sobbing as he whispered that it would all be ok.

Penny and Sebastian didn't move from the table. Neither spoke. After a few minutes of silence and soaking Theo's shirt with my tears, I tried speaking again.

"I don't understand any of this," I said. "I don't get why you would bring me here after I hurt one of you. And I also don't get why you kept denying that you knew me. You've used me."

"We didn't use you, Bianca," Penny hastily replied. This was the first time I'd heard her anger towards any of us. "You didn't have your memory, and we knew you needed help. We couldn't just leave you there and risk S finding you."

"How did you know that I didn't have my memory? I was *unconscious*, Penny. There's no way you would have known that when you took me to the van."

Then it hit me. "You had Jasmine wipe my memory. You had her persuade me to forget."

My blood boiled; the heat trickled from my core into my upper body, down my arms, and into my hands. I glanced down at them, trying to suppress the fire. Sebastian must have seen my glance and began speaking quickly.

"Bianca, I think you and I should go for a walk. This isn't Penny or Theo's problem," he said, getting up and offering me his hand. I didn't accept it. It was almost laughable that he wanted to grab my hand knowing full well the transformation about to take place.

I couldn't hold them back any longer. Flames danced around my fingertips. I rotated my wrists, keeping them alive. If it wasn't Penny or Theo's problem …

"Sebastian, it was you. You told Jasmine to do it."

"Please," he said, "can we go and talk about this privately? This isn't fair to Penny or Theo."

I certainly didn't want to go off in private with Judas.

"No, this is happening here and now." I held my hand at his eye level. The flames kept growing, sparking a little with each angry breath I took.

"See what you're doing to me, Sebastian? See what you've all done to me? You tell me that I'm the villain, and I become more and more the villain."

I thought about our talks over the last few months, just the two of us. I remembered our walks, all the times that he'd held my hand, our first kiss. I had told him my fears and my insecurities. That all felt so far in the past now.

"I can explain. I had my reasons," Sebastian said; his eyes glistened, wet with tears that hadn't yet fallen.

I wanted to feel sympathy, but pain overshadowed it.

"You know," I said, overwhelmed by the intense emotions that came from such bittersweet memories of our time together, "I don't want to talk to you. I don't want to do this."

It was ironic that I had begged for answers since the day I met these people, and now that I had finally been given the truth, I didn't want to hear it. Somehow, I missed the naïve little world I lived in yesterday, one I was previously desperate to leave behind.

"Please," he begged, "I owe it to you to explain everything. But you have to let me tell you."

"I don't want to listen to your excuses!"

Tears poured down my cheeks as I screamed. My body seemed to melt from the heat of my anger, and flames pulsed in my palms.

"You've been lying to me for months! You took *my memory* from me, Sebastian! Do you know how insane that is? Do you know how humiliating it is to be me at this moment? And yet you can't understand why I don't want to talk to you right now?"

"Please."

He looked at me endearingly. His face expressed exhaustion and sadness; all of this was so clearly draining him. He didn't want to fight. And deep down, despite my anger, I knew I didn't want to fight with him either. I took a deep breath and extinguished my hands. Silently, I stood and went to the front door, pulling my shoes on and grabbing my coat.

Sebastian moved to follow me, but I put my hand up and told him that I wanted to be alone. He silently retreated to the table. I went outside, sat down on the porch, and cried until I saw the lights go out. I slept on the couch that night.

I spent the next several days outside, away from everyone. In all honesty, I would have left if I'd had somewhere to go. But despite knowing a little more about my past, I still didn't have my memory. Therefore, I didn't know *where* to go.

I briefly considered going back home, or at least to the place I thought was my home before I left to join forces with a supervillain. But somehow, that didn't feel right. Maybe it was the idea of returning to my parents, having done terrible things since they had last seen me. Or maybe a hidden memory existed, one I didn't remember but still pulled at my gut, warning me against hopping on the next Greyhound out of town. Regardless of reasoning, I chose not to go home. And if not home, to the only place I could remember. Where else? So I remained on the back porch.

It wasn't necessary for me to be outside all the time, but I usually stayed there by choice. While the others went out for the day, I went inside to use the bathroom and make myself something to eat.

I left the good food for them, eating things like ramen and crackers instead. Standing in the kitchen, looking around the empty house, I recalled how I used to feel in this place. How quickly that had been ripped from me... Almost every trip inside ended in tears, so outside remained preferable.

It wasn't all that bad being alone. There were perks. For instance, I got to sit outside for hours on end, petting the stray cat. Thankfully, the others didn't try to find or bother me. I had all the space I wanted. All the space I needed. All the space I deserved.

I continued sleeping on the couch at night, which was comfier than most couches, but it was incredibly unpleasant. I had gotten so used to the bed upstairs that returning to the couch felt like penance for all of the horrible things I had done in my villainous past.

The group went out on a mission to Victory, but I insisted on staying behind. Funny that for so long I begged to go, but now I begged to stay. I knew that I wasn't mentally or physically stable enough to go. I didn't want to risk hurting anyone. Besides, I wasn't a hero.

I had resigned myself to the knowledge that I may never be able to go out on another call. Clearly, I had been partial to the other side at one point. What was the likelihood that I could turn back in that direction? My powers were fueled by anger and hatred; it was only a matter of time before I let that go too far. My brief run as a hero was coming to a close.

I tried to mentally retrace my steps, to fill in the blanks of the last two and a half years. I had graduated college two and a half years earlier, or at least I had planned to. Shortly afterwards, I must have come straight out to Victory. If the dreams I had been having, the ones where I hunted Jasmine, were real, then I had been a villain. And Jasmine told me that herself, showing me the scar to prove it. These hadn't been dreams. They were memories. Wiped memories.

I finally understood why Jasmine avoided conflict. She didn't want to get hurt again. I guess I couldn't blame her, since—if the "dream memory" was correct—I definitely harassed her, tormented her, *burned* her. It explained her distaste for my presence. In fact, distaste was generous. She deserved to despise me.

I was lucky—she tried to be kind to me at first, welcoming me into the house as if nothing had happened between us. And then it all changed when I started trying to bring back the flames. The flames that hurt her. It all made sense.

She must have known that it was only a matter of time before I figured it all out. She must have worried for months, concerned that I would revert to my previous ways. I felt bad for her. I spent months being upset with her, all because I couldn't understand why on earth she didn't want me around. I wouldn't either if I were in her shoes.

So Sebastian had her wipe my memories. All of them, starting back two weeks before graduation. He didn't want me to remember what I had done and who I was working for. He wanted me to think I had come to Victory to fight the good fight. But had I? How could I be sure that my motives were pure if I couldn't remember them?

The back door suddenly slid open, and the cat on my lap darted off into the bushes.

"I see that you made a friend," Sebastian said, shutting the door behind him and sitting down next to me. I hadn't seen him in days. A little stubble lined his unshaven face. His eyes were dark and drained of emotion. He hadn't been sleeping much; that was obvious. And yet here he was, the olive branch already extended towards me. Taking care, I hesitantly, cautiously took it. I wasn't interested in diving deep with him, but I could at least give him a chance. I had spent days alone. I needed a brief interaction, whether I liked it or not.

"He's really friendly," I said, stroking the cat's fur. "He'll come back if you sit long enough." I stared down at my bare feet and rocked a little, unable to concentrate nor look at Sebastian.

"Could have used you out there. We got our man. Well, our woman. It was a woman who tried breaking into a pet store to free all of the animals. Honestly hilarious, in my opinion. The police had noticed char circles around, so they called us in to be safe. False alarm on that front."

I sat silently. They didn't need me. They could fight their own battles.

"We should go for a walk," Sebastian said, standing up. My head snapped up.

"Why?"

"You have been in this backyard for days. You could use a change of scenery."

I didn't want to go off with him, but he made a good point. Still, walking was what we did before. When we were friends. When we thought about being more than friends. I didn't want to go.

But he looked at me with those pathetic eyes. Pathetic, but I couldn't ignore them. Unfortunately, despite my desire to say no, my gut told me *yes*. Those eyes won out.

"Fine, let me grab my shoes."

CHAPTER TWENTY-TWO

Sebastian met me outside the front door, and we ambled down the street with no particular destination in mind. The sun started to set over the houses and surrounding hills, filling the sky with different shades of red and gold. At any other time, in any other moment, this would have been a truly romantic walk, hand-in-hand. Instead, Sebastian and I walked with a few feet of space between us. A cloud of negative emotions hung in that empty space.

I couldn't stand the discomfort. I didn't want to talk to him, but I did want closure on this situation. He gifted me the olive branch, so I could at least cooperate with his plan to hash things out.

"Sebastian," I said, speaking first, "You betrayed me." A perfect way to open the conversation. A few beats of silence passed; now the tension hung in the air unbearably thick.

"I know," he finally replied, surprising me. I didn't expect him to agree with me. I continued, letting it all spill out at once. Every thought, emotion, and fear came tumbling out. No use in holding back now.

"I honestly feel like a fool. I thought you actually cared about me.

And I mean *really, truly* cared about me. But now I know that I've just been a fixer-upper project for you," I said. I wanted to be angry. I was angry. But I also sounded like a wounded bird, and I hated it.

"Was I just a game to you?" The words caught in my throat, bringing tears to my eyes.

I could sense him turning to look at me, but I continued facing forward, holding my ground. I couldn't dare risk looking into his eyes. When he spoke, he sounded exasperated, as though he had been bottling up a plethora of emotions all day. And now, he finally had a moment of release.

"Bianca, I don't know where to begin. But if it's alright with you, I want to start by apologizing. I'm sorry that you feel like this. I'm sorry that I never told you the whole truth, or even part of the truth. I'm sorry I lied. I'm sorry I … had Jasmine strip you of your memory. I'm sorry that I thought it was even a good idea. I'm sorry I've made you feel like I don't care because I really do. That part was true."

This time, I glanced over at him. He stared at the ground as he walked; he looked as if he were about to throw up. My heart ached through my anger. His apologies were kind, but they still didn't reach the heart of the problem.

"You knew that I was scared of my powers," I said. "You knew that I was frustrated by how dangerous I felt. You knew I didn't want to be the villain but also that I actually had been, so why lie and tell me that I could never become one? That I'm too good for that life, when clearly I'm not because I've lived it before?"

He looked over at me with doubt.

"Do you think you would have been confident enough to fight S and do the right thing if you had known that you used to do the wrong thing? If you knew you used to work for him? Really, do you think you would have?"

This caught me off-guard. I hadn't considered what I would have done if I had known these facts.

"I don't know. Maybe?"

"I don't think you would have," he said, matter-of-factly. "I think you needed a blank slate to discover what you were capable of. And look! You used that fresh start to do good. So really, I didn't lie when I said I knew that you were truly capable of good; that your powers could be meant for good. Even though I saw you before, I refused to let that be the entire story. I'm not saying what I did was perfect, but I wanted to give you the chance to change your narrative. So I'm sorry for wiping your memory, but I did it because I saw your potential. And at the time, it felt like the right decision."

I didn't speak.

"You weren't an experiment," he continued before I could respond. "I wanted you … we wanted you to have a chance to be back in your actual mindset. To begin anew. We thought you deserved that opportunity."

I didn't know what to say or even what to think. My head had been spinning for days, and I wanted it to end. "I don't think I can be this person, this hero anymore," I said, kicking a pebble down the road. "I think I need to figure out where my family is. And then go home to them. Put my powers in the past. Good, bad, or otherwise, I don't think I can do this anymore."

I knew it wasn't true, the part about finding my family. But the other part was. I felt exhausted, and I didn't want to do it anymore.

We walked in silence until we reached a grassy patch that led off to a trail. Without speaking, we wandered over and sat in the grass, still leaving an adequate amount of space between us. The tension lingered.

I didn't know how he would react. I told him I wanted to leave, and if he let me, he wouldn't just lose a member of his team. He would lose a woman he cared about. Unless he really didn't care like I thought he did. Like he said he did. By confessing my desire to leave, I would know for certain how he felt. But regardless of his answer, I would have to go. I wasn't up for this challenge, no matter how much I cared about him, or Penny, or Theo. Losing them caused me more pain than anything.

After a minute or two of sitting, Sebastian finally broke the silence.

"I don't hate the supers we fought in the bank," he said. "I feel sad for them."

I looked at him, puzzled. Was he ignoring the fact that I expressed the desire to leave forever? Maybe this was the answer I needed. But he didn't seem finished talking.

"After you all went to bed last night, I did a search on the big guy, Zeke. Found him on Facebook. His name is Zeke Nicholson, and he's a twenty-seven-year-old from Alabama. Moved to Victory about eleven months ago looking for a job."

"Yeah, what about him?" I asked. Part of me didn't care, but another part was curious.

"I requested a background check on him, and the crazy thing—the guy is clean. Not only is he clean, but he seems like an incredible man. All over his Facebook page were pictures of him building homes with Habitat for Humanity and doing mission work overseas. There are also several pictures of him with his little sister. She's seven and clearly adores him."

He pulled out his phone and showed me a picture of a screenshot: Zeke with his sister in his arms, both smiling. "Notice the date," Sebastian added while I examined the photo. December of last year. A little over eleven months ago.

"Oh my gosh," I said, covering my mouth with my hand. I gave the phone back.

"Until I saw this photo, I assumed that he was your typical bad guy, and he came out here last year to join forces with S. But knowing this," he said, holding up his phone, "makes me believe that there's more to the story."

He looked at me, and this time, I looked back.

"Also," he said, keeping his eyes locked on mine, "it confirms my theory."

"What theory?" I asked softly.

He scooched close to me, like he used to do. I didn't back away.

"You're not a villain. You're not evil. You and Zeke and that girl—you've all been pawns." He reached out and took my hand. I started to pull it away but stopped.

What he was saying might not have even been true, but for some inexplicable reason, relief flooded my body. I allowed doubt to challenge this notion.

"I don't understand how that's possible. I clearly came to Victory by choice and worked with S. I did that, whether I like to admit it or not." But Sebastian didn't back down.

"When you look at that photo, do you believe that Zeke willingly came to Victory to team up with S? Be honest," Sebastian said, looking right into my eyes.

"No," I replied, honestly. "I don't think he did."

"Well I don't think *you* did either," he said, squeezing my hand.

I thought about what Sebastian said. What did Zeke and I have in common? We both were living seemingly nice lives and then ended up in Victory, helping a super villain. That's all I knew in both our cases. So maybe Sebastian was right. Maybe we ended up with S by mistake.

"So you think he lured us here? Under some sort of spell?"

"I think you were under a spell for sure, or at least brainwashed into thinking what you were doing was good," Sebastian said. He let go of my hand and pulled out his phone again.

It would make sense. Take Zeke for example. He had a history of community service. He clearly enjoyed helping people. It may not have been hard for S to convince him to do something if that something was disguised as helping others.

"Ok, so how did Zeke and I get in contact with him?"

"It sounds like you're starting to believe me."

"Don't get too excited," I replied. "I'm just trying to see the full picture you're painting. How did we get in contact with S?"

"I think I also happen to have the answer to that question," Sebastian said and handed me his phone. It was on Zeke's LinkedIn page. "Zeke is currently listed as working for an organization called Helping Hearts: Victory," Sebastian said. "If you click the link to their company page, it doesn't have a logo or a description. But it does have other employees."

I clicked the "employees" link.

"None of these people look like S," I said, scrolling slowly through the names and headshots. There weren't many employees, so I took my time, examining each one thoroughly.

"Yes, because a villain like that would be stupid to put his name and picture on the Internet. Keep scrolling; that's not what I want you to see."

I stopped scrolling when I saw the girl. "It's the girl from the bank," I said. "Zeke's partner in crime. Her name is Margaret Andrews. She looks so sweet and innocent. Not at all like I remember her looking that night."

"I saw that too," Sebastian said. "But keep scrolling. You're almost there."

Then I saw it: my face. That was my name. It was my profile. I had been working at Helping Hearts since May 25, 2017. This was S's organization. "You were right," I whispered.

I immediately started to cry. This was the first time I truly knew what happened after I graduated college. I came to Victory, somehow ended up at this Helping Hearts place, and then snapped out of whatever spell S had me under. And now, sitting on a grassy patch in the dark, I was with Sebastian, the man who both rid me of my memory and saved me from it. The man I wanted to burn to a crisp but also hold on to forever. It didn't matter what he had done to me. He wasn't the enemy. S was.

Sebastian pulled me up against his chest and held me tight. Any last trace of anger turned into a cold wave of sadness. I shook as I cried.

"I'm so sorry, Bianca," he said.

May of 2017. Two years. I had been there for two of the last two and a half years.

"I can't believe that I worked for him for over two years," I sobbed. Chills ran through my body and I shivered. "What kind of monster—"

"Hey, hey don't think of it like that," Sebastian said, stroking my hair. "Really you should just be happy that you've snapped out of it. And you know you haven't always been like that. You definitely aren't now."

"Yeah," I sniffed. "I guess so."

I continued to breathe into him, the rise and fall of our chests falling into sync. I felt calmer, warmer, and the fog in my head began to clear.

"So," he said, breaking the silence, "you aren't mad at me?"

"I'm still a little mad. Mostly that you didn't tell me sooner. And that you clearly knocked me out and then wiped my memory. That's going to be very hard to get past."

"Yeah, I'm not going to deny that I did those things. But I really am sorry, and I want us both to move forward. You aren't defined by those two years. You're defined by what you're doing now. And what you're doing now is good."

"I just want to be good," I said. "I never want to hurt anyone again."

"You are good, even if that's hard to believe right now. And I'm going to do everything in my power to help you truly understand that."

I squeezed him tighter. "Thank you," I whispered.

"You're welcome," he replied, "And don't worry; you don't have to talk to anyone else yet if you don't want to. You can sleep in my bed tonight, and I will take the couch. I want you to have a bit of space to breathe since things were left a little rocky with the others."

"I appreciate that," I said. We sat in silence again for a minute or so. "Sebastian?"

"Yes?"

"Do you think we can find an address for Helping Hearts?"

"I thought you didn't want to do the hero thing anymore? Thought you were going home." I could hear the smirk in his voice, but I maintained my composure.

"Well I changed my mind. For now." He smiled at me. I fought the urge to smile back, even though I wanted to.

"What? It's not like you can take down S without me. And I personally think that he needs to be taken down. I may be a villain, but I'm not a psychopath."

He laughed, and this time I smiled. My eyes cut back to the grass under my feet. "For real though," I continued. "Do you think we can find an address? I have a good feeling about what we could find there."

"I'm already on it."

I looked up and met his eyes again. They still looked tired, but I could see the life in them again. He didn't need to say anything. I knew for sure in that moment. He cared for me. "I'm still mad," I said, smiling. "But you can make it up to me, if you want."

He grabbed my waist and pulled me close to him. "I plan to make up for it. No matter how long it takes," he said, kissing me softly.

And I didn't fight it. I was still mad at the situation, at Sebastian, and at myself. However, I knew the only way to get over the past was to move forward with hope that I could be who Sebastian wanted me to be: a hero.

I knew that tomorrow would be difficult, facing the others and finding the location of Helping Hearts. I also knew it wouldn't get easier after tomorrow. Knowing about the last two years dumped a lot of fear and doubt into my system. Things would only get harder from here. But for now, I was in Sebastian's embrace, knowing someone trusted me. Which felt pretty good since I really didn't trust myself.

CHAPTER TWENTY-THREE

OCTOBER 11, 2011

I was getting antsier by the minute. Two hours into the dance and the DJ still hadn't played anything slow. That was the entire purpose of my even being at the dance. I desperately needed a slow song, and now.

Kimberly had heard from Amy Miller who had heard from Justin Levenson that Matthew Ryerson might be asking me to dance tonight. I'd liked Matthew since the seventh grade, so if the rumor was true, then this would be the best night of my life.

My parents let me go over to Kimberly's to get ready. I spent more than an hour getting dressed, making sure every detail of my outfit was perfect. Kimberly's mom had eyeliner and said we could try it on, just for the night. I never felt so beautiful.

"Do you think Matthew will like this dress?" I asked Kimberly as she held my head against the wall with one hand, trying to apply the eyeliner.

"Oh duh! You look perfect. He would be so dumb not to fall in love with you and that dress."

Kimberly finished putting my makeup on and told me to look in the mirror. I looked good. And I mean *good*. I looked at least a year older, which was perfect because Matthew was a junior, and I was short compared to most of my class. After all, I had to make sure that he danced with a woman and not a little girl.

I looked down at my dress and sighed. I didn't love it for one simple reason: It had little sewn-on tulle sleeves. My mother insisted that my shoulders must be covered, or I would "attract the wrong type of boy." I pulled at the sleeves, trying to widen the neckline a little. Maybe show a little collarbone. Matthew wouldn't want a stuffy girl, right?

I looked at Kimberly. Compared to me, she looked stunning. Unlike my dress, hers had no straps—it didn't even touch her knees. She also wore heels, which amazed me, since I didn't know how to walk in them. While I looked maybe a year older in my new makeup, Kimberly could definitely pass as a senior in hers. She always came across as confident and beautiful. All the boys worshiped at her feet.

Six different guys asked her to the dance, and she turned them all down in order to go with me: a true friend.

When we got to the dance that night, she stuck right by my side the whole time. As I started to get antsy, she reminded me to uncross my arms and try to "look tall and available." I stood as tall as I possibly could in flats. I also tried to stick my chest out a bit, pretending I had one.

Suddenly, the music faded and changed to a slow song. This was my moment. "Oh my gosh," I said, looking around in a panic. "This is it. It's happening. Where is Matt? How do I look?"

Kimberly tucked some hair behind my ears and did a once-over. "You look so good, Bee. He's got to be here any second."

I spotted him across the room. He, too, stood on the side with a friend, watching the dancers. Why wasn't he coming over to ask me to dance?

"Kimmy, he's over there. He's not even moving!" I pulled on my friend's arm and pointed him out. I tried not to be obvious about it, but the panic set in. I wanted him to come dance with me, and we were losing time.

Kimberly looked around and began taking her heels off.

"What are you doing?" I asked.

"Switch shoes with me. Put these on," she said, holding me for balance as I slid my feet into heels for the first time. I wobbled just standing.

"You look so hot, Bee. Absolutely smoking," she said. "Come on." Grabbing my arm, she dragged me across the room, all the way to Matthew. My heart pounded in my chest.

"Hey, my friend, Bianca would love to dance with you," she said to him, letting go of my arm. "Are you down?"

Matthew, confused by Kimberly's assertiveness, nodded, took my arm, and walked me to the dance floor. I wobbled the entire way, nervously trying not to fall down. I tried to concentrate on acting tall and sticking my chest out.

This was happening. It was finally happening. After four years, I finally got to slow dance with *the* Matthew Ryerson. We didn't talk at all. He just held my waist and swayed from side to side. My arms hung around his neck, and my eyes stared down at my feet, still horrified that I might fall over.

This was the best moment of my life. I would never forget this. I, Bee Williams, was the luckiest girl in the whole school. As the song finished, he pulled away and smiled at me.

He smiled at me!

"Hey, Bianca, right?"

Oh my gosh! He said my name out loud.

"Yeah," I said, "Bianca Williams. My friends call me Bee." I tucked my hair behind my ear and smiled up at him like I learned how to do from Disney Channel movies.

"Thanks for the dance, Bee."

"No problem at all," I said, nervously. "It was super fun. You're a great dancer."

"Thanks," he said, looking around. "Hey what's your friend's name? The hot one over there?"

I hesitated.

"That's Kimberly," I said, awkwardly glancing over at her. She waved and gave me a thumbs up.

"Kimberly," he said. "That's a great name. Do you think you could give me her number? Or her email? I would love to go out with her sometime."

My heart plummeted. "Oh, yeah," I said, biting my lip to fight back sudden tears. "Sure."

My heart was now on the floor, maybe even beneath the floor. This was no longer the best moment of my life. I looked around, starting to panic.

"I'll try and get that for you," I said. "But right now I have to go, sorry." I quickly took off across the gym and out the back door, losing one of Kimberly's heels along the way. As I ran, I completely forgot about acting tall.

Standing alone in the parking lot, I tried to catch my breath. Since I didn't have a cell phone, my mind raced, trying to figure out how to call my dad and ask him to come pick me up. I didn't just feel sad; I was furious. Angrier than I had ever been.

How could this happen? I liked him for four years, and then he decided that he wanted to ask my best friend out instead? I started feeling really hot, probably because of the stupid sleeves.

I was seeing red, furious at Matthew, at Amy and Justin and all the people who thought that he might have liked me back. I was even furious at Kimberly for some reason.

Why did she have to look so perfect and mature, and I had to look so ugly and young? Why wouldn't my parents let me wear a dress without sleeves or a little makeup? Why didn't I know how to walk in heels?

I was about to burst. I took a deep breath and screamed into the night. And that's when flames shot out of both of my hands. The anger stopped, and the panic began.

How did I do that?

I looked around wildly, making sure that no one saw anything. I stood alone, but only for a moment longer. Kimberly ran out the door, yelling to me. "Bee! Oh my gosh, I've been looking everywhere for you! Come on. I called my mom to come pick us up. This dance is boring, and I've got a new movie for us to watch at home. It's got Zac Efron, so I know you won't say no." She winked at me. "I hear he even takes his shirt off in this one."

I wasn't mad at her anymore. My mind drifted elsewhere. I could barely acknowledge the words she said to me. As she talked, she handed me my flats. I brushed the asphalt off the bottom of my feet, and slid into my shoes. Relief took over; what a joy to finally be in shoes that I could walk in. We waited for a bit, and eventually Kimberly's mother came to pick us up.

All night, I tried to concentrate on my friend and Zac Efron. I tried to push the flames out of my head, but they wouldn't leave me alone. Those flames would haunt me for the next seven years. In those years, they would reappear four times, all at moments of intense anger. Eventually, they would spark the need for answers and a road trip out east.

CHAPTER TWENTY-FOUR

S ebastian and I spent the next few days sitting at the table, looking for an address. Occasionally, Penny or Theo joined us.
Sebastian clearly had talked to them about our conversation,
as there seemed to be some sort of unspoken agreement that
we would all move forward and not discuss the events of the other
evening. Luckily, Theo and Penny didn't seem bitter at all. The four
of us had moved on and could return to life as before. I even started
sleeping in my own bed again.

Jasmine, however, continued to avoid me. Worse than that, she
began to avoid everyone else too. Annoying as it was, I still didn't
feel like sending out an olive branch. We didn't have time for drama.
Instead, the rest of us dedicated our time and energy to searching the
Internet for answers.

"There is nothing, absolutely nothing on this stupid Helping Hearts
place," Theo said one morning, pouring himself a bowl of cereal.

"And we are positive it exists, right?" Penny asked, taking the box
from him, reading the label, and pouring some for herself.

"Positive. It comes up on Bianca's LinkedIn, even if the main page is blank," Sebastian replied. "I don't think it's a coincidence. There are too many people linked to it."

"True. And also, while I can't remember it, there is this part of me deep down that knows it exists," I added. "I know it sounds crazy; part of my brain remembers being there. But I can't recall when or why."

"I plan to make some calls today. I want to see if any other businesses in Victory have heard of it or know where it might be," Sebastian said.

Just as he stopped speaking, his phone started ringing. He picked up, listening and nodding. A beat later, he pointed to the door and mouthed, "Get your shoes on."

"Yes, yes, we will be right there. Yes sir, we're hurrying," he said into the phone before hanging up.

"No time to change, guys. This one is extra urgent. Just get running shoes on. We've got to go," Sebastian said to us.

He and Theo quickly pulled on their shoes. Penny said her shoes were upstairs, and I could really use a hair tie, so the two of us sprinted up to the bedroom. We found Jasmine on her bed, reading. "Come on, Jasmine, we have to go," Penny said, pulling a sweatshirt over her head.

"Tell Seb I'm not coming. I don't feel well." We didn't challenge her, and neither did Sebastian when we told him. He was outside by the van.

"We can figure it out in the car. We've gotta go. Now," he said. There seemed to be an added urgency to this call. More than usual.

"Where are we going this time?" I asked, getting into the backseat of the van. Sebastian looked more worried than I had ever seen him before a mission.

"Beckworth Elementary School."

"I feel like this is one of those times when we could really use Jasmine on evac," I said as Sebastian sped towards Beckworth Elementary. He hit 50 in a 25. I gripped my seatbelt, hoping we would make it to Beckworth Elementary alive.

The school year had just started for these kids. Whatever was going on there, having us show up to defend the school and protect the kids wasn't a great way to kick it off.

"Was it S this time?" Theo asked. "Or one of his guys?"

"One of his minions again. A different one this time," Sebastian answered. "I don't think we've seen him before. Sounds like he's a teleporter, just like S."

"Oh well that's not good," Penny chipped in, pulling her hair up into a ponytail.

"Yeah but at least he appears to be working alone. So we've just gotta get in there and stop him. Quickly," Sebastian said, taking a sharp right turn. My body smacked into the window.

"I don't like the fact that we're about to fight a break-in at an elementary school," Theo said. "Kids are in there!" I didn't like the sound of that either. Fire and children did not play well together. Maybe it would be best if I stuck to evac, replacing Jasmine for the day. I expressed this to the others.

"Exactly," Sebastian said. "We need to get in and stop him as quickly as possible with as few of our 'more dangerous' powers as possible. That means no fire from Bianca and no dangerous weapon wielding from me. I'm thinking we go hand-to-hand only, if that's even possible. I'll lead up front with Penny. Theo and Bianca—you two follow up in the rear and be ready to run. We need you two clearing out rooms and making sure everyone is safe. We also may need you to help us out if our new friend decides to play the disappearing game."

Evacuation sounded like a good plan for me. Having just learned that I had been a minion of S, I wasn't sure that I would be in the right headspace to perform properly. Best to be as far away from the fight as possible.

Sebastian turned one last corner onto Beckworth Drive and sped up the road to the school. When we pulled into the front circle, the assistant principal was standing outside, already waiting for us. The police had arrived slightly before us and were setting up a barrier in the parking lot.

"He's inside," the assistant principal yelled, trying her best to stay calm in such a terrifying situation. "He went towards our upper wing, the fourth and fifth graders."

Sebastian and Penny nodded and ran inside.

"Ok, ma'am, we want to start evacuating your lower wing, the first through third graders," Theo said. "Can we go in and start doing that?"

"They're all under lockdown in their classrooms; they should be safe," the assistant principal replied.

"No, they'll be much safer out here," I explained. "This guy can teleport, and he might enter any of those classrooms. We don't want that. I think getting the kids outside into the parking lot would allow us to best protect them and make sure they're all accounted for."

The assistant principal teared up but held strong. She wanted to be a strong model for the kids. And she was. She represented a rock for them when they needed it most. Still, I could hear the distress in her voice.

"Why would someone come here? Why would he hurt children?"

I didn't know what to say. Only a truly evil person could do such a thing. Luckily, Theo spoke for us both. He put his hand on her shoulder.

"Don't worry, ma'am; we won't let him hurt any children."

"Come on, Theo," I said, and we took off running towards the school. As we ran towards the building, the assistant principal called after us.

"Please help us! Please save the children! He's got a gun!"

CHAPTER TWENTY-FIVE

W e started in the computer lab, the room closest to the front doors. Without hesitation, Theo smashed the door down, and the children inside screamed.

"It's ok," Theo said, calmly. "We're here to get you to safety!"

"Are you superheroes?" a little boy asked. "Like the movies?" He cried and clutched a backpack in front of him.

"Yep," Theo said, grabbing the boy's hand. "And we're going to get you out of here."

We told the teacher to follow Theo and for the kids to follow her. The teacher nodded calmly and told the children to follow. Between us, the police, and the staff, we had a great team and a solid plan. We planned to quickly get each class out the front door under the escort of either Theo or myself. Theo would take the first classroom, and then I would begin emptying the next. We would leave the students in the parking lot with the police.

We weren't sure that was the right thing to do, but we didn't have much time to think about it. The goal was to empty the school as quickly as possible, so the officers could keep an eye on everyone at once. They would keep the kids safe, and we would take down our suspect.

I ran to the next door. *Mrs. Donahue's First Grade.* Little handprint cutouts covered the door. My heart rate picked up. These were real, live children we were working with. I got angry thinking about whatever villain would dare come to a school and attack children. My hand melted the door handle and lock. I kicked open the door.

To no one's surprise, the children screamed when Theo broke down the first door. However, this time, they didn't stop screaming.

"No, it's ok!" Theo said.

I tried doing as Theo did, assuring them that I would help them escape. They kept screaming and crying. With their little hands outstretched in front of them, they cowered against the far wall. Even the teacher froze, overcome with terror.

For a moment, I looked behind me, imagining the gunman stood behind my back and the children were screaming at him. But no one was behind me. They weren't screaming about a gunman. They were screaming in fear at *me*.

"My name is Bianca," I said, approaching and crouching down to their level. "I'm going to help you get out!"

They screamed louder and continued to cower. "You're the evil lady with the fire," a little girl cried, "from the TV." My heart sank as I pled with them.

"Please. Please just come with me. I promise you, I'm a good guy! I can get you out of here. To somewhere safe."

"Stay away from us," they continued to yell. "Don't kill us, please!"

Just then, Theo ran into the room. "Bianca, what's going on?"

"They won't come with me; you've gotta take them. I don't think I can do evac—no one will listen to me. I'm going to find Sebastian and

Pen, maybe swap out with one of them."

Looking around at the crying children reaching for him, Theo nod-ded and took Mrs. Donahue and her students outside. They followed him obediently.

Attempting to brush off the crushing blow, I took off in the other direction, searching for Sebastian or Penny.

I found them in an empty fifth grade classroom.

"Where is he?" I asked. I was out of breath. For all the training I had been doing, cardio was not part of my usual routine. I was feeling it now.

"We don't know," Penny said, wiping the sweat from her forehead. "We've seen him multiple times, but each time we've cornered him, he's snapped his fingers and disappeared."

"Why aren't you with Theo?" Sebastian asked.

"Change of plans. Kids knew me as the evil fire girl from the TV, so I'm now helping you."

"That works for us; we need the help. Theo can handle evac," Penny replied.

"The good news is that this guy hasn't been alone in a room with kids yet," Sebastian whispered as we followed him down the hall, searching for the perpetrator.

"The school did a great job of locking down quickly," he continued, "The teachers handled this phenomenally, getting so many classes outside on their own. Plus we've been able to get some of the upper classes out a backdoor."

We kept searching. Every classroom was empty. "I think we got everyone out," Penny said. We suddenly heard a crashing noise down the hall and ran towards the sound. I saw movement behind a door that was ajar.

"In there," I said, and we ran in. As I had expected, we found our man. He was tall and lanky. His mischievous grin sent a chill down my spine.

Without hesitation, Sebastian charged in and began fighting hand-to-hand. The man disappeared and reappeared around Sebastian, punching him from different directions. Sebastian swung his arms, and the man found this hilarious, laughing and mocking him the entire time. Even when Penny joined in, he still seemed unreachable.

That's when I noticed the stunned children pressed silently against the wall. We had to get them out.

While the man was distracted and fighting the other two, I gestured to the teacher to round up the kids and follow me. The children looked terrified like the children in the other classroom. However, to my advantage, they seemed more scared of what transpired across the room, and they decided to listen.

They began to escape via the doorway when suddenly the man stopped fighting Sebastian and Penny. He fired his pistol above the doorway as a warning shot. The children screamed and froze on the spot; a few dropped to the ground, covering their heads.

Sebastian jumped on the man's back, attempting to wrestle the gun from him. Someone was about to get hurt. No matter how dangerous my powers were, I needed to do something.

Without thinking about the consequences, I whipped around and blasted a flame on the hands of both men who immediately cried out in pain. While I felt bad for what I did to Sebastian, I achieved the results I had hoped for: The man dropped the gun.

Penny kicked it across the floor to me. I picked it up; dropped the magazine into my hand, and shoved it in my pocket. I racked the gun, and the bullet in the chamber fell to the floor. The clink was definite; the man was now unarmed.

I noticed a few kids still standing in the doorway. "Go!" I yelled at them. "Go out to the front parking lot!" I sucked in my breath and immediately knew that I had made a mistake.

The man was smiling again. "Parking lot, eh?" He snapped his fingers and disappeared.

"No!" I screamed. The three of us ran as fast as we could out the door and down the hallway. We met up with Theo running back inside to find us, but he whipped around and ran with us.

"Parking lot!" Penny screamed. "Now!"

When we got outside, we found both the principal and the assistant principal trying to calm the dozens of screaming children.

I was panicked. "Where is the intruder?" I asked. "Is he here?" The principal shook his head. "He was just here, but he's gone now. I think he left the grounds."

"Wait!" Penny commanded and added, "What makes you think that?"

"Because he clearly got what he came for," the principal replied.

"Which is what?" I asked. The pit in my stomach was ready for my heart to drop into it once again.

The assistant principal looked at me with tears in her eyes. "Two children are missing. He took them."

CHAPTER TWENTY-SIX

The principal notified the parents about what had transpired, and the school day ended early. Everyone needed
the extended weekend to sort things out. While Theo and
Sebastian helped walk students to their cars and chatted
with the principal and teachers, Penny and I sat together on the curb.

I pulled the gunman's magazine from my pocket and examined it.
This magazine could hold ten rounds, but it had only eight bullets.
Plus the one I had dropped from the chamber. That meant the only
shot fired was the one we witnessed. Thank goodness.

"I don't think he intended to use it unless he had to," Penny said,
handing me the empty gun. "What I mean to say is that I don't think
he planned to hurt anyone."

I emptied the rest of the bullets from the magazine and popped it
back into the casing.

"I'm still confused. Did he come to Beckworth just to steal kids?" I
asked. "Why? All this stuff usually happens in Victory. This is outside
of their usual territory. And the crime … so unexpected."

"Again," Penny replied, "I think he came here for a good reason."

"He did," the principal jumped in as he walked up to us with Sebastian, Theo, and the assistant principal. The principal gestured for us to follow him back inside, so we made our way to his office in silence.

"Take a seat," he said from behind his desk. The assistant principal stood next to him, and the four of us took chairs facing his desk.

"This man didn't take two *random* children," the principal said and started flipping through what appeared to be a directory, "He took siblings: a fifth-grade girl and her second-grade brother." He turned the directory towards us to showed us a small, blonde girl.

"This is Molly Meadows, a very bright girl with incredible talent." He flipped a few pages and showed us an even smaller child, a boy who looked like Molly.

"And this is James Meadows, a quiet boy, very dedicated to his sister. A little mischievous."

I fought to hold back my tears. These two innocent children were now in the hands of a villain. While my heart had ached for his new minions, Zeke and the others, they were adults. The young and innocent children were helpless victims of this dreadful tragedy. My stomach churned thinking about their little faces, scared and longing for rescue.

"Do their parents know?" Theo asked. Our minds went to the same place. This was a tragedy for the Meadows family, the school, and the Beckworth community.

"Yes," the assistant principal replied. "I called them a few minutes ago." Her eyes dropped to the table, and little tears formed in the corners. I could only imagine the conversation. What would it be like to be told your two children were abducted from their school by a supervillain? How lonely and empty their house would feel tonight. My heart plummeted.

The principal continued. "But I assured them that we would get their children back. Well, not we. *You*."

"Sir," Penny replied, "we don't know where they went! I hate to say it, but we can't promise that we will find them quickly."

Penny was right. We could try as hard as we wanted, but we didn't know where S was, so we didn't know where the kids were.

"We know that this is a big thing to ask of you, but you're Victory's defenders," the principal said, folding his hands on top of the closed directory. "If these villains could so easily abduct two children, think of how many more people are at risk. The police will do everything they can, but these are actual villains. You're our best shot."

Before any of us could speak, Sebastian stood and reached towards the principal. "We will do everything in our power to bring them home," he said, shaking the principal's hand.

While everything in me wanted to smile and agree with what Sebastian had signed us up for with that handshake, reality rang in my ears. This task was huge. How on earth were we supposed to find those kids? How much time did we have?

Upon further reflection, however, it struck me that we had planned to find S anyway. This would force us to speed up the process. A lot rode on our shoulders.

"I have one question," Theo stated. "You said that Molly has 'incredible talent.' What did you mean by that?"

The principal and assistant principal shifted uncomfortably. "I think you know what I mean," the principal said. His voice was low, almost a whisper. "She has *skills*. Not unlike all of yours."

We glanced around considering the disturbing statement.

"She can electrocute people. Shock them. It's quite horrifying, honestly," the assistant principal chipped in.

"It's no surprise that he came here for her," the principal added. "And he must have assumed that James would also have these skills.

So he took them both. We never saw signs from James, to be frank. But it was probably worth it for him, and by him I mean the man, to know for sure."

"This is all making a lot of sense, sir," Sebastian replied and stood to leave. "I'm starting to piece together what's going on here. We will do our best to stop them and bring the children back."

We stood to leave.

"Thank you so much for your help—all of you," the principal said. "We have faith that you will bring the Meadows children home and protect our city from these villains."

We waved goodbye and got in the van.

"He's collecting supers," Sebastian said, pulling onto the main road. "We were right. But now that he's collected two kids—ones far too young to fight for him—I'm starting to think his collection is for more than an army."

"What do you mean?" I asked.

"I think he wants his army for sure, but that's not the whole story. Think about all the people he has under his control. Or at least the ones that we know about."

"Ok, so we got this new guy, the teleporter," Theo listed. "and the speedy girl and the strong guy."

"Yes and he had Bianca," Sebastian added. I grimaced.

"Don't remind me."

"Sorry, but that's important in my theory," he continued. "What powers has S proven to have so far? When he's fought us?"

"Teleportation, fireballs, and a bit of super strength," Penny said.

Her eyes widened, and Theo's mouth opened a little in realization.

"Are you saying—"

"Yes," Sebastian said, completing the thought we had at the same moment. "I think he's sucking the powers from his minions and making them his own."

"So," I said, "you think he's making an army to send on side tasks while he also drains them of their powers."

"Yes, that's exactly what I think," Sebastian said.

"So he also has superspeed, we assume," Theo added. "And it sounds like he's about to add electrocution."

"Yeah, that's not good," Penny said. "He's getting more powerful with each person he collects."

"And he keeps the powers of those he's previously collected," I said. "He still has my powers, even though I'm no longer there."

"That also means even if we conquer his friends, he still will be the master of many powers," Penny said. She sighed and dropped her face into her hands.

"Eh, I'll still beat 'em up anyway," Theo said, rolling up his sleeves and doing slow motion punches in the air. "I'd much rather fight one stupid looking wizard than an army. We should get the little jerks out of the way, so we can show that mustache who really runs this city."

"Yeah let's hope we find the kids before we have to fight *them*," Sebastian laughed, morbidly. "I don't feel like punching a fifth grader anytime soon."

"So what I'm hearing is that we're about to pull an all-nighter trying to find the location of Helping Hearts," I said, in all seriousness. I expected them to take it as a joke, but Sebastian had other plans.

"Oh you better believe it," he replied, turning into the driveway. "Better nap now, it's going to be a long night."

CHAPTER TWENTY-SEVEN

I've never been so scared in my entire life.

I knew that running was my only option. Whether I stayed put or ran, danger would find me. I figured that I might as well keep running since staying put made me a sitting duck. And nothing is worse than being a sitting duck in times like these …

However, my body couldn't do it much longer. My legs shook uncontrollably, and my heart pounded so hard it made my head hurt. I didn't have a lot left to give, but I had to keep trying. I had to keep running.

I tried to make flames as I ran, but that proved impossible. The fear had taken control. All my defenses were gone.

I could only run.

As I heard someone getting closer and closer behind me, I blocked out the pain and kept sprinting.

I was running for my life.

Getting absolutely nowhere in our search, we decided to call it quits a little after midnight. Penny fell asleep on the floor and Theo, in his kindness, carried her up to bed. I decided to follow suit and called it a night.

But I couldn't sleep. I lay there for hours, tossing and turning. My mind kept wandering back to those two kids. Terrifying thoughts populated my worried mind, all about where they could possibly be and what could be happening to them. I couldn't stop myself from thinking the worst.

Finally I gave up, I rolled out of bed and pulled on a sweatshirt. The clock by Penny's bed read 3:13. I crept down the stairs where I noticed the living room light on. I intentionally made a little noise as I reached the kitchen, shuffling my feet a bit in an attempt to avoid scaring whoever was in the living room.

Despite my best effort, an alarmed Sebastian poked his head up over the couch. "Bianca, why are you still awake?"

I opened one of the kitchen cabinets and pulled out a glass. "I'd ask you the same question, but I'm guessing we have the same answer." I filled the glass with water and made my way over to the couch to join Sebastian. He had his laptop and about fifty tabs open. "Are you having any luck so far?" I asked.

"No, not really." Sebastian yawned. "I'm exhausted, but I can't sleep until I figure this out."

"I understand," I replied. I really did understand. This fear ate away at me.

"I can't stop thinking about what S may have done to them. I want to find Helping Hearts, but I'm also scared that when we find it …"

"They'll be dead," I said. It was morbid but true.

"Yeah."

We sat silently for a second. Sebastian looked down, tracing a square on his plaid pajama pants with his finger. He yawned, causing me to yawn too. He then spoke, snapping my attention back. "The hope I'm holding onto is that he didn't abduct just any two kids. These are kids like us. They're special. More importantly, they're useful. Why would S get rid of something or someone useful?"

"Yeah, but we don't know about James. S is running on the assumption that he has powers, since Molly does. But I don't know if there's a correlation between families and powers. We all seem to be one-off freaks."

"But it's too soon for S to know that. He'll likely keep both of them around in the off chance he does have powers," Sebastian said.

"Do you really think he will use them to fight though?" I asked.

"I don't know, but I do know that his main objective is collecting powers. So he will at least need them for the time it takes to collect Molly's power. Who knows how long that will take, but if we can find his headquarters, we can find the kids and rescue them before he decides he's done with them."

"I hope you're right," I said, scooching down the couch and leaning my head on his shoulder. He put his arm around me and pulled me close against him.

"We have to keep looking," he said. "We know they're around here somewhere. It's called Helping Hearts, Victory for a reason. We'll have an address by sunrise."

We spent the next hour or so in this position. Sebastian typed with his left hand and held me with his right arm. I watched as he searched databases and maps, trying to find any hint of S's headquarters.

I felt incredibly and surprisingly relaxed. I knew in my heart that Sebastian wouldn't stop until he found the location. He was as loving as he was determined. There wasn't much I could do without a laptop or a phone of my own, so I continued to watch him.

Shortly I was asleep. At around six, I was jolted wide awake. Upon opening my eyes, I found Theo sitting on the floor, leaning up against the TV stand and smirking at me.

"Looks like you had a comfy night," he said with a smile.

I pushed myself up into a seated position. Sebastian's arm remained around me. I could feel an indent on the left side of my face from lying on his shoulder. Theo's smile grew wider.

"Oh shut up," I said, and threw a couch pillow at him. He laughed. Sebastian had passed out. His laptop lay on the floor. So much for us having an address by sunrise.

"Any luck so far?" Theo whispered, getting up off the floor. I gently unwound Sebastian's arm from around my back, pushed off the couch, and followed Theo to the kitchen. Sebastian didn't budge. He clearly needed the rest, so I decided not to wake him.

"No, not really. At least not while I was awake. Maybe Sebastian found something after I fell asleep and then decided to sleep a bit himself in order to recharge before our mission. But I doubt it. I assume he would have woken us all."

"And are we still sure this place exists?"

"Yeah, I think so." I refilled my water glass. Theo got a box of cereal from the cupboard and poured a bowl for each of us. I continued, "As we've established, all of our suspects—like Zeke, the speedy girl, and myself—we are all shown on LinkedIn as currently working at Helping Hearts. Last night, we also found the teleporter listed as working there. But when you click the company name, there's no address or website. So it exists, as far as I'm aware. However, I'm not so sure the building is labeled. I think they must be renting out a house or apartment or something. If that's the case, though, I don't think we will ever find it."

As we sat at the table and eating our breakfast, I could tell that the wheels in Theo's brain turned, as he tapped his foot and gazed into the distance. "Hmm," he said, "have we tried looking at office spaces? Like shared office buildings? A lot of those rent out single suites and don't necessarily advertise."

Now that was an idea.

"No, we haven't. Can I use your laptop? I can start a search on that."

Theo laughed. "We need to get you your own laptop," he said, "Not that I mind you using mine, but I think getting you a laptop, or at least a phone, would do you some good."

"Yeah, that's probably a good idea," I said, realizing I would likely never get my old phone or laptop back. Who knew where they were now.

"We never brought it up because we didn't want you doing a Google search and seeing your face on the news," Theo replied. "Sorry about that, by the way. I know it's a touchy subject, and we all still feel terrible about it."

"No, it's fine," I said. "I'm getting over it, honestly. You did it for my own good. I agree though, it would be smart to get something like that. I'll have to resist the urge to find those news stories."

"Good plan," he replied. He went off to his room and came back with his computer.

"Ok, I'm going to search for office space to rent. We can get a list and then investigate each."

"That's smart," I said, pulling my chair around to sit next to him and watch.

He pulled up the Internet and searched for, *Victory Office Spaces, Office Space Rentals, Victory,* and *Office Suites for Rent Near Me.* We found only five rentable office buildings in Victory. One of them didn't allow for long-term renters, so we ruled that out. Another had just opened two weeks ago, so we ruled that out as well.

"Ok, so it's one of these three," he said. "Probably. Hopefully."

"Hopefully," I repeated, looking at the list, praying it was one of these three and that in a matter of hours we could have the Meadows kids back with their parents.

"I'm banking on this office theory," Theo said. "You could be right that it's in a house, but I think that's pretty unlikely. If you're going to trick people into thinking you're a legitimate operation and want them to join you, an office is way more believable."

"Agreed. So we should check these out this morning."

"Definitely."

We heard a groan, and turned to look at the couch to see a startled and groggy Sebastian.

"Good morning, sunshine," Theo said, smirking. "While you were slacking by taking a nap, we were working. Get some fresh clothes on. We have an address."

CHAPTER TWENTY-EIGHT

B y about 8:30, we were ready to go. However, Sebastian got a call shortly after waking up, requiring us to "divide and conquer" for the morning. "Penny and I can probably handle this one ourselves," Sebastian said as he tied his sneakers.

"Besides," Penny chipped in, "you and Theo are the ones who got the addresses, so you two should go deal with that."

Theo nodded.

I took in the scene around me. While Penny and Sebastian wore their classic all-black uniforms, Theo wore khakis, a button-up, and a tie. Theo and I were going as a "young couple trying to rent an office space for their family business startup," a direct contrast to the black athletic wear of our friends. Consequently, I had borrowed a dress and cardigan from Penny and stole a pair of Jasmine's dressy sandals. She hadn't gotten up yet and probably wouldn't come down regardless.

We decided that Penny and Sebastian would get the van for the day since their matter was much more pressing. "Besides," Theo said, adjusting his tie in the mirror after our friends left, "it would be much more 'cityish' of us to take a bus or a taxi. It would follow our characters' motives.'"

"Our characters?'"

"Oh yeah," Theo replied. "Today we aren't ourselves. No no, Bianca Williams and Theodore Martin are far too poor to rent office space. They also are far too busy kicking butt to start a business."

"So who are we? I want you to give us a backstory," I laughed.

"Our names are Benedict and Amelia Clearwater, and we recently moved from Houston."

"Oh gosh, you're not going to make me do an accent are you?"

"Sure, if you think Amelia would do it," Theo replied in a ridiculous and very inaccurate southern accent.

"She wouldn't," I said, definitively, "and Benedict wouldn't either."

"Oh you're no fun," Theo said, switching back to his normal voice. "So we moved from Houston to get married and open our small business."

"What do we sell?"

"Our time," he said as I followed him out of his bedroom and to the front door. "We are tech consultants. That's how we have the money to rent the place. Our urban apartment is far too small for us both to be on client calls all day, so we need to rent a space. Plus we're thinking of expanding and hiring another consultant, so we definitely need a bigger space."

"I can go along with that. It's actually pretty believable … without the accent." We walked to campus and caught a bus to Victory.

As we got close to the city, Theo quizzed me about our made-up lives. It was ironic, really. I spent the majority of my life as one character, small town Bianca Williams. Then I spent some time playing a different character—this unknown villain by the same name. Now, I was in my third role: Bianca Williams, Victory Super.

I wondered if this role would last the rest of my life, or if there would be another character to play. Would I always and forever be this new version of myself? Or after defeating S, would I retreat to my home and do a revival of my original role?

I asked Theo these questions, and he pondered them for a moment before answering. "I don't think we can ever go back to old versions of ourselves. It's like they say: 'You've seen too much and, therefore you know too much. 'Gotta keep plugging along, moving forward. Besides, even if you go back to the place you were before, you won't be that same person. You know things now; you have new scars on your body. And you know and love new people."

"If you're trying to ease into a conversation about Sebastian and me, you're not going to get it," I said and laughed.

"No, dummy, I meant the rest of us," Theo said and gently hit my arm. "We all care about you, and we know that you have to feel the same way since, of course, we are far too loveable. However, if the word 'love' brings Sebastian to mind, that's good to know."

"Oh, uh, not at all," I said, feeling my face turning red. "I know you're dying for me to come out and say something like that."

"Yeah," he said, "Hmm. I'm clearly the one who wants you to get that off of your chest. Makes perfect sense."

"What do you think I need to get off my chest?"

Theo gave me a mischievous smile.

"Was Jasmine telling the truth? Have you kissed yet?"

"Theo!" My face throbbed with heat.

"Oh, so you have!" He looked incredibly satisfied.

"I never said that," I retorted.

"You didn't have to. I can read it on your face. It's ok. I won't ask for details. You at least deserve *some* privacy."

"Yes, fine," I said. "We've kissed a few times. It's not a big deal."

We both sat in silence for a moment. Theo smiled and closed his eyes. He put his hand behind his head and leaned back in the bus seat.

"What?" I questioned.

"And you're happy?"

Puzzled, I replied, "Yes, I am."

He opened his eyes and looked at me, keeping that same stupid grin. "Good," he said. "I want you to be happy. And I want Seb to be happy, honestly. He was starting to get really depressed before you showed up. I think you've been good for him. Good for all of us, really."

"Oh yeah?" I asked.

"Oh yeah," he replied. "We've really needed you. Not just in the field but in the house. You've given a lot to us. So thank you."

I smiled. I spent so much time thinking about how much they had done for me. I never bothered to consider that maybe I had done something for them too.

"You're welcome," I said, starting to get a little emotional. Theo snapped me out of it by reaching over and patting my shoulder.

"You don't have time to get all teary-eyed," he said. "We're here."

He pushed the Stop button, and we hopped off the bus at our first location.

Our first stop turned out to be a bust. Unless S and his colleagues disguised their business as a veterinary clinic or a small law firm, this wasn't our building. By the time we reached the second stop, nerves had taken over. What would we do if none of these places were it? Or worse, what would we do if we stumbled in on S? I wasn't totally sure that Theo and I could handle him, or any of his friends, without Penny and Sebastian. This probably wasn't the brightest plan we'd ever had.

"We aren't going in," Theo assured me when I started panicking. "We need to investigate. See if any door stands out—ask the right questions, see if the building owner knows anything."

"Got it," I replied as we approached the building. I still felt nervous, but I knew I had to trust Theo. We were in it together. This building was a little smaller than the first. I doubted there were more than three suites in the whole complex.

"Get in; get the information we need; get out," Theo said. Compared to the last building, he spoke more cautiously before heading into this one. He believed this to be it. Once inside, we met a woman named Caroline. We explained to her that we were looking to tour the building and wanted to see if they had available office space we could check out.

"We just got married and moved from Houston," I told Caroline, repeating the story that Theo and I crafted on the bus.

"Congratulations," Caroline replied. "Such wonderful news!"

"And we're launching our new consulting business," Theo added, right on cue.

"Yes," I said. "Our small apartment is a bit too tight for us to be working simultaneously. We get a lot of client calls! You know how it is."

"I completely understand," she replied, falling deeper into our web. "Living spaces around here are far too small. I've been living in about 500 square feet for the last year, and it's been miserable! You are in luck, though. We have one unit available."

She grabbed some keys and beckoned us to follow her up the stairs. Theo and I followed and kept an eye out for anything unusual.

At the top of the stairs, I noticed a door with a darkened window and no signage. As we passed it, she gestured further down the hall towards a different suite.

"Excuse me, Caroline," I said. She stopped and turned around.

"What's up, dear?"

"Is there a business in the suite back there? You said you only had one unit available, so I'm assuming that all the other units are being used; is that correct?"

"Yes, ma'am, that's correct. We have three other rented suites in the building."

"What kind of businesses?" Theo asked. "We want to get a feel for the building and the other occupants."

"Of course," Caroline replied. "At the end of the hall, that door down there, that's a law office. And upstairs in our large suite is an optometrist."

"And that door we just passed?" I asked, my heart racing. "What do they do?"

"I'm not sure exactly. They're very private people. Some sort of philanthropy work if I remember correctly. Helping something?"

Bingo.

Caroline continued down the hall and unlocked the available suite. Theo and I glanced at each other.

This was it.

Caroline proceeded to show us the empty unit, giving us pricing and amenity information. The layout of the suite, she explained, matched the others in the building. Inside was a small entry area and then through a door there was a short hallway and three offices.

Listening was pure torture. On the other side of a wall sat S's hide-out, and yet I had to stand and listen to a woman try to sell us a suite for a fake business. As time slowly ticked by, I began to lose my nerve.

"Excuse me, but is there a bathroom nearby?" I asked. "I don't mean to be rude, but I'm sure that my husband has a lot of questions that he can ask while I am gone."

"Certainly, there's a bathroom at the end of the hall," she said, pointing towards the door.

"Thank you," I said and slipped outside.

My heart rate picked up momentum. What would I find behind that door? Theo had specifically advised that we shouldn't go in, but the dark window meant that it was empty. Right? Which meant that I wouldn't get caught. Right? Well, so long as Theo could keep Caroline occupied. We had done a great job convincing her of our story.

Look out Jasmine. Your powers are becoming irrelevant, I thought.

Thinking about Jasmine kicked my fear back into anger. I could use that. My hands filled with heat, and I sparked a flame in my left hand. Cranking up the emotion, I began to melt away the door lock.

I knew I just played my calling card, but at this point, it didn't matter. I didn't have much time, so fire it would have to be. I pulled my sleeve down over my hand to protect it from being burned, and slowly turned the knob. The door opened.

It was dark inside, and I didn't want to turn on the lights, which would have drawn attention to me. Instead, I sparked another flame and carried it into the center of the tiny room.

I could barely see, but it didn't really matter. I didn't need a light to tell me that the room sat entirely empty. There wasn't a desk, a bookshelf, or anything that I had expected to find. Through the darkness, I detected the shape of a door on the far side of the room. I went over and opened it slowly.

Inside I found a short hallway with three doors, like the other suite. There was still no signage or furniture to be seen. I tried each door, and the first two led to small, empty rooms; however, the third opened to a mess: Papers and empty cardboard boxes were strewn all over the floor. Paper cups and other trash had been dumped on the floor. I didn't know what had happened here, but I also didn't have time to think about it.

"Ok, ok," I whispered to myself. "Clues. Gotta be clues."

I gave up on trying to be sneaky and opted for speed. I flicked on the light switch and dropped to my hands and knees, digging through the piles for something that might be of use. Most of it was worthless trash, but then a scrap of paper caught my eye.

It was a parking receipt. I shoved it in my pocket, deciding that I had been gone too long. It didn't look like there was much else to find anyway. Whoever had been here was long gone, and they didn't leave much behind.

Turning off the light and closing the doors behind me, I crept out of the suite and into the shared hallway. I could still hear Theo and Caroline talking in the other room. Relieved, I walked back in.

"Hey, are you ok?" Caroline asked, definitely crossing my privacy boundary. "You were gone for quite a while."

Seeing this as an opportunity to get out, I replied, "I'm not feeling fantastic. I think we need to take a raincheck and come back another day. If that's alright with you, Benny."

Theo suddenly remembered the name of his alter ego and joined in. "Of course, sweetie. We need to get you home so you can rest. Thank you so much for the wonderful tour, Caroline. We will be in touch."

Caroline walked us back to the front door and told us to give her a call to reschedule. We thanked her, and she went back inside. I immediately turned to Theo.

"You won't believe it," I said, as we began walking back towards the bus stop. "It's completely deserted. They've fled."

"No way." Theo's eyes widened. "What the heck? Why would they pick up and leave?"

Relieved that he didn't seem to notice that I had gone in to get the information, I continued, "And they appeared to do it quickly, too. The rooms were all empty. Like, completely empty. No signs, no furniture, no indication of anyone recently being there. However, one of the offices was trashed. Really disgusting stuff."

"Anything useful? Any idea where they went?" I pulled the receipt out of my pocket.

"This was the only potentially useful thing I could find. I didn't take time to look at it closely since I really wanted to get out of there. Could just be trash, but I figured it was the closest thing to a clue I could find."

Theo and I examined this parking pass for a hotel in Victory, maybe not useful after all.

"Wait a second," Theo said, looking closer. "isn't that the hotel we fought S in?" He was right. "Yeah, I think it is. And look," I said, pointing to the date. "The pass was from about a week after our run-in. Why would S be going back and forth between the hotel and this office?"

Theo suddenly looked enlightened and lifted his hand to his mouth.

"I think I know what he went to the hotel for," Theo said and pulled out his phone and started texting Seb. "He went in for a room key. That's where they've been hiding out. They switched locations to keep us off their trail. And they never told the building owner that they were leaving. That way, no one would know they were on the move."

"That space was far too small for the little army he's creating. I think you're right. I think he's fled."

"Why steal a key though?" Theo pondered aloud. "Why couldn't he just check in?"

"If it's a long-term thing, that would cost a lot of money. Stealing the key and hoping no one tries to check into that particular room saves a lot."

"But wouldn't a hotel room be smaller than the suite he had in the other building? I don't see the point. Maybe he got multiple rooms?"

"Or the penthouse on the top floor," I said, piecing it all together. "Which would explain why he went all the way up there and you had to go up on the roof."

I kept looking at the receipt. Something else about it seemed off.

"Theo, look at this registered plate." I handed him the receipt.

"What about it?"

"Look at the state," I pressed.

"This is from Indiana. Do you think this is a clue? Is he from Indiana?"

"No," I replied, taking the receipt back. "But I am."

Theo stared at me as he discovered the final destination of this train of thought. I looked at him, annoyed beyond belief.

"I think that jerk stole my car."

CHAPTER TWENTY-NINE

AUGUST 18, 2017

I actually enjoyed the testing.

When Dr. Fadel originally told me that he wanted to examine the extent of my skills, which would involve a variety of tests, I wasn't so sure. I pictured myself lying on a surgical table, attached to a hundred wires and beeping machines. I pictured being electrocuted every time I missed a target or some other sort of Pavlovian torture. Luckily, that wasn't exactly the case. Occasionally there were wires and beeping machines. However, Dr. Fadel worked with kindness and patience, talking through each test beforehand. And I never felt any sort of pain.

Most of the tests were fairly simple, primarily questionnaires, asking a variety of questions like, "When did you first discover your skills?" and "What exactly is the direct trigger of your skills?"

Dr. Fadel stressed that we should be using the word "skills," rather than "powers." Skills had a more positive connotation, he explained. We were helping people, after all.

In addition to the written questionnaires, he also had me test my skills in simulated scenarios. He kept one of the offices empty except for a computer stand in the corner. The room had thickly padded green walls where the doctor would project images and record which ones triggered a reaction. He always encouraged me to follow my emotions and to release them if I felt the urge to.

Occasionally, he'd have me drive him and other colleagues out to a rural farm, where I would complete target practice and other physical training exercises. I always found it interesting that he had me drive. In fact, I wasn't even sure he owned a car. But I never minded; the drive wasn't too bad, and the trips were great for practicing my skills. Besides, it felt nice to get away, out to the country. The fresh air reminded me of where I grew up.

The tests acted as fun challenges, and I improved with every testing round at the farm. I began to control my skills, and I knew it was only a matter of time before Dr. Fadel would let me out on the streets to fight the bad guys.

I wasn't the only recent hire. A week or so after I got to Helping Hearts, a new recruit showed up: a tall, beautiful girl named Margaret, whose skill was moving at super speed. But the doctor didn't like calling it that; he wanted us to refer to it simply as "speed."

"We don't like the word 'super,'" he explained to Margaret and me one day. "People assume a lot of things when they hear 'powers' or 'super.' Their minds go to a preconceived notion. We don't want them to have expectations or make snap judgments about us. We want them to see us and know that we are here to change the city for the good."

His logic seemed to make sense, and because we were in no position to question it anyway, we obeyed.

The other new hire was a thinner guy named Eric. He could teleport. Dr. Fadel didn't have a better name for teleporters, so we continued to use that term. "That's incredible," I told him one day at the farm as he practiced disappearing and reappearing around me in a circle.

"I've been doing it for a long time, so I'd like to think I've gotten quite good at it," he said, disappearing again. I heard rustling behind me and turned around to see him leaning on the fence, eating an apple.

"How'd you get that?" I was amazed.

"Bopped inside real quick," he replied and shrugged. I couldn't believe his mastery.

"So you said you've had these skills for a long time?" I asked, climbing the fence to sit on top of the rail.

"Yes, since I was about six years old," he said, joining me on the fence. He took another bite of his apple.

"What brought you out here?" I asked.

"Same reason as you, I bet. I saw some people like me plastered all over national television. I knew of some near where I grew up, actually. Decided I wanted to be a part of that. Thought I could use these skills for something good. And I figured out that Dr. Fadel could actually train me, so I came out here to learn from the best."

I nodded. We all had so much in common; we all wanted to change the world and help people. I considered the doctor a hero for bringing us together and allowing us to fulfill our purposes.

"When did you figure out you had fire skills?" Eric asked me.

"Two years ago I got angry at my dad, stormed up to my room, and boom. There it was," I lied.

"The fire?"

I nodded.

I didn't know if I wanted to tell him the truth. I mean, I trusted him, but that story was private. I wasn't ready to share it, not even with Dr. Fadel. I stuck with my same false story every time, and no one questioned it. Maybe someday I would tell Eric. Or Margaret, or Alexandra, or the doctor. Or someone. I wasn't there yet.

"Are you ready to get out there and fight?" I asked him. "Do you feel prepared?"

He thought for a moment and then sighed. "I think I've been ready for a long time. I want this so badly, and I know that I can make a difference. I'm ready. What about you?"

"I think I'm getting there. The doctor wants to make sure that I'm perfectly confident before I begin the fight."

"Well, when he thinks you're ready, you'll know."

"How?"

"He calls you in for what he calls the 'final test.' Mine's tomorrow. He told me this morning."

Overjoyed, I threw my body forward and hugged him, almost falling off the fence. He gripped my shoulders, steadying me and laughed.

"That's amazing! Congratulations!" I said, bursting with excitement for my friend.

"Pass that test, and I'll be out there doing what I've always dreamed of. I think that tomorrow might be the best day of my life."

Eric looked so happy. It was obvious that he wanted to change the world—wanted to help people. He came all the way from Utah to be a part of this. I was sure that starting tomorrow, he would finally be fulfilling his destiny.

I smiled at him. I hoped that I would be that confident and excited when it was finally my turn to take the final test. "Do you know what it is?" I asked. "The test, I mean?"

"Not a clue, but I'm positive I'll pass. And I'm sure that yours is coming soon. And you'll totally pass. Then we can get out on the street and fight crime together."

Eric's prediction came true. The next day, he passed the test. He was also right in his prediction that mine wasn't far behind. One evening a few weeks later, Alexandra found me taking a walk around the outside of the building.

"Bianca, so happy to see you! I have amazing news."

I knew what she was going to say before she opened her mouth. Mixed with excitement and nerves, I smiled as she spoke.

"Tomorrow morning, Dr. Fadel would like to see you in his office for the final test."

CHAPTER THIRTY

L ater that afternoon, Theo and I sat in a coffee shop down the street from the hotel. As soon as we realized that S might actually be in the place where I first encountered him, we called Sebastian, and requested that he grab Penny and Jasmine and meet us as quickly as possible. They'd be there any minute and they were bringing a change of clothes for both of us.

About thirty minutes after we called Sebastian, the three of them walked into the coffee shop with two backpacks, which they tossed to Theo and me. I was surprised to see Jasmine, but also felt relieved knowing that we had someone other than myself on evacuation. After the incident at the elementary school, I never again wanted that role.

Penny followed me into the bathroom, bolted the door, and sat on the counter. She prodded me with questions while I went into the stall to quickly change.

"Are you sure he's in this hotel?"

"No, I don't know for sure, but there was a parking ticket for the hotel in the abandoned office. So either he's there or he *was* there. If it's the latter, we can ask around and investigate some more."

I thought for a moment while I pulled my dress over my head and switched into a black, long-sleeved shirt.

"But I honestly think they might be there. I have this deep gut feeling," I said, shoving the dress into the backpack. "I mean, S making the hotel a hideout really lines up with our little incident a while back."

"Yeah," Penny said as I came out of the stall. "It makes sense that he would stake out a place that allows him to get off the map entirely."

We joined the others outside and began walking towards the hotel. "Do we have a plan?" Jasmine asked, sensibly. She looked nervous—not surprising considering she hadn't been on a mission in weeks. That last mission didn't exactly end well for her or for our relationship as a team.

"We always have a plan," Sebastian laughed. It wasn't an assuring laugh, especially since what he said wasn't really true. And even when we did have a plan, one of us (usually me) often strayed from it.

"For real, Sebastian," I added. "What's the plan?"

"I think we need to go into the hotel, straight up to the top floor. We start investigating from the top down, since Theo's convinced he took the penthouse style suites on the top floor."

"I mean, just suggesting it doesn't mean that I'm convinced per se, but sure, we can start there," Theo said, rolling up his sleeves. I knew we were both thinking the same thing: Encounters on the ground were safer. And not only that; encounters that were not on the ground suddenly became Theo's problem. None of us wanted the float-to-the-ground-after-jumping-off-a-high-rise-building experience. Regardless, it was the most likely spot, so the risk became unavoidable.

"Might as well start somewhere," I replied, nodding.

"Now keep your heads down and walk straight to the elevators," Theo said as he opened the door and held if for all of us.

One word described the state of the lobby: construction. Since part of the hotel had caught on fire the last time we visited, much of the place required renovation. Luckily, nothing had been too fire-damaged besides one floor of guest rooms. But since I *also* set off sprinklers that day, the lobby and floors with working sprinklers (luckily not all of them) also needed water damage renovation. That being said, much of the hotel remained under construction. However, since the hotel wanted to minimize profit loss, they continued to operate with the remaining rooms available for booking.

Not too far into the lobby, Jasmine stopped cold.

"What's up, Jas?" Penny asked.

"I have an idea," she said. "Give me a second." It wasn't like Jasmine to come up with plans, especially not after an official plan was declared by Sebastian. Everyone stared at her.

"Trust me. I know what I'm doing," she said, strolling up to the front desk. Leaning on it, she looked straight into the concierge's eyes. Penny laughed and twirled her hair.

"We don't have time for this," Sebastian said, glancing at his watch.

After a minute, Jasmine thanked the concierge and made her way back to us, waving a few sheets of paper in one hand and a stack of room keys in the other.

"You're welcome," she said, handing Sebastian the key cards. The printed pages contained a list of every hotel room and its vacancy status.

"Dang," Theo said, flipping through them. "This has got to be illegal."

"Yeah well so is everything S does on a daily basis," Sebastian replied, pulling the pages from Theo's hands and scanning them up and down, looking for evidence of our culprit's whereabouts.

"I got room keys too, just in case," Jasmine added. "However, I only asked for the top two floors since I figured we didn't want to carry too many. I can always come back down and ask for more."

"How did you get all these?" I asked. She looked at me as if I were stupid.

Oh, duh, her powers, I thought.

"Come on," Sebastian said, gesturing to the elevator.

"Maybe I should stay down here in case we need to evacuate," Jasmine quickly replied as she lingered anxiously wringing her hands.

"No, I think you should come," I replied. I wanted all hands on deck, to be safe. She looked at me skeptically.

"I promise I'm not going to hurt you." I sighed. "Just come on; we should all stick together. I don't like the feeling in the pit of my stomach."

She was hesitant but followed us into the elevator. Sebastian hit 12 and the elevator lurched to life. At least *something* hadn't been destroyed by our last encounter here.

"This spreadsheet indicates that one of the two penthouses is validly booked under the name Clifton," he said. "There's no name listed under the other, which probably means no one reserved the room."

"But there's no room key in the stack for either suite. So someone has the key to the un-booked room," Penny said. She looked through the room keys as the elevator rose towards the twelfth floor.

I think we all knew what that meant.

"Look alive, people," Theo said with a sarcastic, over-enthused grin. "This could get crazy."

The doors opened to the twelfth floor, and we stepped out, unsure of what we'd find.

As we slowly and silently inched down the twelfth floor's main hallway, it felt like an action movie. With the full team assembled, walking as one cohesive unit, I visualized us as the Avengers. For the first time, I could see it clearly in slow motion: Penny and Theo stretching and warming up their arms; Jasmine throwing her hair over her shoulder; Sebastian pulling out a crowbar, and me making a flame in each hand.

This is what it felt like to be super.

Reality, however, quickly snapped me out of it.

"This is the door," Sebastian said, crouching to look under the crack. We all stood on either side of the door in case someone decided to look out the peephole. We couldn't take any risks.

"I'm not seeing movement under there," Sebastian whispered. "To be honest, it looks dark. I don't think anyone is home."

"So what do you want to do?" Jasmine whispered back. "Do you want to go in or leave it alone?" By the sound of her voice, I was pretty sure she preferred the latter option.

"I guess I didn't think that far ahead," Sebastian replied.

I saw this as further proof that we didn't always have a plan.

Sebastian tapped his foot and Penny started rocking back and forth, visibly balancing creative thinking with pure nerves.

"Well what were we going to do if people *were* in there?" Jasmine asked, crossing her arms. Her whispering voice was gone.

"My plan was to try to listen in through the door. And if we could prove it was S, I would have had Theo break the door down. Then we would have had him cornered."

We stared back at him in disapproval.

"That's the worst plan I've ever heard," Theo said. "We don't need proof if he's in there. We go in; we get him."

"And if it's not him staying there? If it's random people, what do we do then?" Jasmine questioned.

She clearly didn't want to burst into the room. S was afraid of what she'd find there. But Theo wasn't hesitating. He was a man of action, after all.

"I don't know; you could convince them that everything is fine and that they should go back to whatever they were doing," Theo replied.

"I'm not a band aid to cover your mistakes," Jasmine snapped.

"Guys, stop it!" Penny whispered sharply looking back and forth between her two friends. "Are we going in or not?"

"Well no one seems to be home anyway," I said and started pacing. "So it doesn't matter whether or not Jasmine will have to use her Voice. But one thing I know for sure is that I don't intend to be sitting here in the hallway when he gets back."

"No," Sebastian agreed. "We might have to come back some other time. I want to get him when he least expects it. I assume he doesn't travel without his creepy staff, but he probably doesn't keep it constantly on him when he's in there. If we are correct and his powers are connected to that staff, I want to get him when he's unarmed. I also don't want him to be able to run. We can try again tomorrow."

Jasmine looked pretty angry at this point. I took a step back and let her unleash her fury.

"Is everyone going to ignore my concerns? What if this isn't his place? And no, I'm not worried about us bursting in on other people. I'm worried about wasting our time. If we wait and we are wrong, we'll be wasting time scoping out the wrong location while he sits comfortably somewhere else in the city. It's idiotic to simply wait without proof."

Jasmine was right. I didn't want to waste time. Not when he had the Meadows kids. I wouldn't be able to live with myself if something happened to either one of them just because we took too long.

"You're right," I said. "We need evidence that this is the place. And the parking ticket isn't unquestionable proof."

"I'd say we should go in," Jasmine shrugged. "But the room key wasn't at the front de—"

We all jumped at the loud clang. Penny had roundhouse kicked the door handle, opening the door a bit.

"What?" she asked, innocently. "I got tired of waiting for you all to make a decision."

Everyone stared at the slightly open door in silence.

"After you, sir," she gestured to Sebastian. He slowly pushed open the door, and we crept inside.

I wasn't sure how we'd get away with that damage. If S really was staying here, he was definitely about to know that we were here looking for him.

Fortunately, when we looked around the big penthouse living and dining rooms, it became clear that we might not need to worry about S finding out. Unfortunately, like the office, this place also looked abandoned.

It had clearly been lived in recently, as there were dishes on the counter, chairs not tucked in, and a few newspapers scattered throughout the penthouse. However, there were no personal artifacts anywhere.

Walking around, Sebastian whispered that our last hope would be the bedrooms. There appeared to be three, which seemed excessive for a hotel. I had to say, it was quite a nice setup. I wished we had more time to explore since it was unlikely I would ever see a hotel room that nice again.

We split up and decided to enter the bedrooms all at once. Penny and Theo went in the first bedroom; Sebastian went in the second; and Jasmine and I went in the third. When we opened the door to our room, we noticed the unmade bed and towels on the bathroom floor. Not a soul could be found.

"I wonder how long ago they left?" Jasmine pondered, flicking on the lamp. I went further into the bathroom to investigate.

And that's when I noticed the water.

"Jasmine, the shower is still wet. I think they *just* left."

"Oh my," she said as she looked in. "So either they take everything they own with them each time they go out on the town, or they decided to abandon ship within the last few hours. And in that case, they aren't coming back."

The answer came to us quickly, as Sebastian yelled that he found the room keys on the dresser in the second bedroom.

They were gone. Again. We hit another dead end.

"You guys!" Penny called from the first bedroom. Her voice shook with fear. "Come here *now*. Hurry!"

When we ran around the corner, we found her standing in front of the bathroom door. She burst into tears, causing Theo to quickly pull her into his arms to calm her down. Sebastian moved past them, stood in the doorway, and cursed. I looked over Penny's shoulder to see what they were staring at.

"Oh my gosh," I gasped.

There on the floor was an unconscious, young woman, splayed out with her hair across her face. Her arms were bruised, her tights torn, and her white shirt tinged red from recently dried blood. The tiles around her were bloody too. In her hand, she held a complimentary hotel notepad with one word written on it.

Traitor

CHAPTER THIRTY-ONE

AUGUST 19, 2017

Alexandra walked me down the hall to Dr. Fadel's office. My hands shook uncontrollably. I had to pull myself together if I wanted to pass the final test. Taking a few deep breaths, I followed her inside the office.

"Miss Williams, welcome! Are you ready for your test?"

Dr. Fadel stood and pushed his glasses on top of his head. He smiled at me, like a proud father. I didn't want to let him down.

"I am, sir. I've been looking forward to it for a long time."

"Excellent," he said, coming around the desk and gesturing us out the door. "Miss Oliver, if you'll leave us. Miss Williams, if you'll follow me."

Alexandra wished me luck and retreated to her desk. I followed the doctor down the hallway and into the training room.

On the far end of the room was the table usually covered with machines, screens, and wires. However, today wires ran down the leg of the table and wound their way to a platform in the middle of the room. On the platform, locked into the ground, stood a large staff. It looked like a wizard's staff, with a large glass-like ball at top. Delicate wiring encircled the ball, twisting like vines and attaching it to the base.

"Come over here, Miss Williams," Dr. Fadel said, as he pulled out more wires and attached them to a computer. He picked up a wire, attached it to a wristband, reached for my arm, and placed a band on my wrist.

"Other wrist, please," he said. I extended my other arm, and he attached a second band.

"Do you feel mobile enough?" he asked. "Can you move your arms freely without the wires getting in the way?"

I moved my arms in wide circles and changed my stance and arm position a few times. "Yes, I'm good."

He then handed me a heart monitor that was attached to yet another wire and asked me to place it under my shirt and over my heart. While I did that, he fiddled around with a few settings on the screens.

He led me to the other side of the room, commanding me to stay in this section, away from the staff and his computers. He then went back to the table and sat down.

"Miss Williams," he said, loudly, lowering his glasses and looking at the screen in front of him. "The final test is very simple. All you will be required to do is bring your skills to their peak—that is, I need you to channel them as fully as possible and hold it there. Can you do that for me?"

I looked at my hands. I knew they contained power, but how much did he want? How much was enough? I didn't want to fail.

"Yes."

"Very good. In a moment, I am going to turn on the machines. You will feel a buzzing in the wristbands. It will not cause pain, but it will be noticeable. As soon as you feel that, you may begin. Remember to hold it as long as possible. I want to understand the full extent of your powers."

Powers.

I nodded and prepared for the test.

He flicked a switch, and I jumped in surprise. The wristbands tingled. I closed my eyes and held my hands out in front of me, palms up.

I thought of the horrible gang of young people, the ones with skills like mine. The ones that the doctor had told us tales about. I pictured them breaking into buildings, attacking innocent citizens. I pictured a crumbling building with the group of young people blocking the exit, not allowing a soul to escape, claiming that they were getting out as many people as they could. I pictured them on my TV screen at home, fighting those bank robbers. They pretended to act for the common good, pretended to be heroes. It was all a publicity stunt. They stopped the robbers, and when no one was looking, they took the money for themselves. I remembered the stories that Dr. Fadel had told me about them, about all the evil they had done.

My hands grew warmer and warmer. I started to feel the little flames, licking my fingers. I twisted my wrists to keep them alive. Keeping my eyes closed, I continued to concentrate.

No one knew the truth about the "Victory Supers." Everyone saw them as heroes, but they merely used their skills to help themselves. We were the real heroes. We were the ones who would take them down. And with my help, they could finally be eliminated.

I could feel the flames grow larger. I brought my hands together and pulled, stretched, and molded the flames. I opened my eyes to see a flaming ball hovering above my palms.

They would come for us. But we would come for them first.

I hurled the flames, one after another, at a blank, fireproofed wall. I screamed and blasted ball after ball, flame after flame. Like a fire hose of lava, I sprayed the wall with fire, screaming in fury the entire time.

After about a minute, I felt as though I had hit a wall myself. Taking a deep breath, I extinguished my rage and the flames in my hands. I sank to my knees. I had given him all I had. I had never felt so tired, so drained.

I panted. Looking up I saw that the staff in the center of the room glowed; a pulsing red light shone in every direction. I looked over to Dr. Fadel. He was smiling.

Without speaking, he strode to the staff, pulled it out of the platform, and tapped it on the ground twice. A little flame ball, just like mine, hovered over the top. He smiled again.

At that moment I knew I had passed the final test.

CHAPTER THIRTY-TWO

"Is she dead?" My voice shook, and my body began to feel weak. Stumbling back a bit, I grabbed the doorway for support.

"Theo, take Bianca and Penny to the living room. Jasmine, help me set her up." Sebastian dropped to his knees and brushed the woman's hair from her face. Jasmine joined him.

The room around me echoed in silence—well not silence, because I knew for a fact that Sebastian kept talking. But for me, only a dull ringing remained. Time appeared to slow down. It was like watching a car crash; I didn't want to see this, but I couldn't stop staring.

I didn't even know her, but somehow I felt connected. My mind told me that I didn't know her, but the blood pulsing through my body told me I *did* know her. Had this woman and I shared history? Was she like me, taken under the spell of S, and like me, awakened?

Traitor.

S knew she had turned and he …

Suddenly, Theo's hand grabbed mine and pulled me from my thoughts and out of the room.

"Bianca, it's ok. Come on. Let's get you some water."

I squeezed his hand, grounding myself in the unfortunate situation of reality. He led me to the couch and sat me next to Penny. He insisted we sit for a moment while he ran off to get glasses of water for us. Penny continued to cry. I continued to sit, dazed. I felt cold and sad.

"He killed her. He *killed* her," Penny repeated over and over. She pulled her knees up to her chest and hugged them, rocking a little.

Penny's fear snapped me out of my daze.

"We don't know that," I said, scooching closer to her and grabbing one of her hands.

Theo came back from the kitchen just in time, handed me a glass of water, and set Penny's glass on the coffee table. "I don't think she's dead, Pen," he said. "I think she's just unconscious. Jasmine and Seb are going to wake her up, and then we'll get her somewhere safe. It'll all be ok."

"Ok," she said softly. She was crying and continuing to stare into the distance. I let go of her hand, pushed myself off the couch, and gestured for Theo to take my spot.

"You've got her. I'm going to join the others."

"Are you sure?" Theo asked. "You don't have to."

"I just needed a second to breathe. I'm fine now."

That wasn't exactly true, but Penny needed Theo, not me. And honestly, I had to suck it up and face what lay in the other room. As I made my way into the bedroom, I heard muffled talking—Jasmine speaking softly in her Voice. Then, I heard another woman's reply.

She was alive.

I slowly pushed the bathroom door open, so as not to startle them. The woman sat propped up against the cabinets under the sink. Jasmine sat close by, holding her hand and stroking her hair. Sebastian knelt on her other side and checked her arms for injuries. They all looked up when I entered. The woman's eyes sparkled with recognition.

"Bianca," she whispered. "Bianca, you're alive."

Taken aback, I got down on the floor with them.

"Yes," I replied. "I'm alive and so are you. Thank goodness you're ok."

Sebastian kept checking her limbs, asking if things hurt, or if she could move them.

"What's your name and how did you get here?" I asked. "If you feel up to speaking."

"I'm up for it," she said, weakly. "Your friend calmed me down quite a bit, so I feel much better now."

Jasmine smirked a little. Honestly, she didn't know how valuable her powers were. If we weren't in such an urgent situation, I would tell her.

"My name is Alexandra Oliver," the woman said. That name echoed in my mind.

"Alexandra," I said, letting it naturally roll off my tongue. "It's a pleasure to meet you. My name is Bianca, and you've already met Sebastian and Jasmine."

"Bianca, I know you don't remember me, but we worked together." The hair on my arms stood up, and I could feel my heart rate pick up again.

"I worried that was the case," I replied.

"We worked together for quite some time, but then he discovered your secret, and he got angry," the girl said, "He tried to find you, but thank goodness you escaped."

Her eyes widened again. "*They* found you."

A tidal wave of questions flooded my mind. I wanted to ask her about what happened to me; what I discovered; what she meant by him "trying to find" me. But I wasn't the priority; she was.

"What happened to you? Why did he leave you like this?"

She coughed a little and readjusted herself against the cabinet.

"Shortly after you left, I grew suspicious and started observing Dr. Fadel more closely."

"Dr. Fadel? Who's that?" Jasmine asked.

"S," I replied. "I think we've been referring to him as S. Is he the man with the staff?"

"Yes," Alexandra replied. She continued her story, "I knew you must have had a reason to leave, and he was clearly livid. I trusted you; I trusted your judgment. I grew more suspicious when he suddenly decided to move us to this hotel. I didn't like his fear of being tracked, his desire to be off the grid.

"And then he kidnapped the Meadows children. Then and there, I decided that it was time for me to leave. I told him it was my calling to go elsewhere, to take a normal job like teaching or writing. He didn't like that one bit. Before I knew it, he locked me in this bathroom with the kids. We sat in here for days before he grabbed the kids, hit me several times with his staff, and apparently knocked me out. And now I'm here."

"The Meadows children," Sebastian exclaimed. "They're alive!"

"Yes," she said. "I think so. They're scared, but they're proving their worth. He won't get rid of them until he's captured the full extent of their powers. They aren't quite there yet, so they still have time."

"*We* still have time," I replied. "We are going to save them, Alexandra. But first, we're gonna get you out of here."

Sebastian and I helped her to her feet.

"Are you ok?" he asked her. "Do you feel stable?"

"I do," she said, taking some steps towards the door. We held her around the waist and put her arms across our shoulders, helping her out the door as Jasmine led the way.

"Ok gang," Sebastian yelled to the others as we approached. "Let's get Alexandra home."

Seeing us emerge and seeing Alexandra alive, Penny gasped and hugged Theo again. Theo gave a huge sigh of relief. We all felt that.

I wasn't a runner.

Even with all the training, I barely considered myself athletic. But the fear … the fear kept me running for my life.

I felt them closing in behind me. In a matter of seconds, I'd be trapped. I had to keep running. I panted and coughed; my heart was in my throat. I didn't want to run anymore, but I had to keep moving.

"Bianca!" I heard someone call in the distance. It was a man's voice. My stomach twinged. I had to get away from him. Immediately.

I took another turn and suddenly halted, coming face to face with an open street. I didn't want to be exposed, but I couldn't stop moving. I eyed a side street across the way. Taking a deep breath, I sprinted directly towards it.

Almost there … almost there …

Suddenly, an explosion to my left threw me off my feet, and I turned to see a car on fire.

Keep moving …

I tried crawling, hoping to get enough momentum to bring myself to my feet, but it proved useless. The pain seized my body. I wasn't going to make it.

I inched towards a side street on my hands and knees, trying to block out the sound of screaming and the smell of smoke. I focused on finding a place to hide.

Out of the corner of my eye, a shadow flew overhead. Behind me, I heard screaming, shouting, the clashing of metal on metal, and a throaty laugh.

Terrified, I crawled for my life, but my arms were giving out. I lost focus … unbearable pain … dropped to my stomach … losing consciousness … trying to get air.

Come on, Bee. Whatever you do, don't lose cons—

CHAPTER THIRTY-THREE

W e decided to give Alexandra as much time as she needed to peacefully recover before peppering her with questions. I wanted answers more than anything, but I knew that she needed rest, so I set my desires aside for the time being.

When we got home, Sebastian and Theo carried her to Sebastian's bed, and after that, we didn't bother her. Penny went in once to give her some water and crackers. Other than that, we sat around the house and waited. I finally understood what the others must have felt when I was the one passed out on Sebastian's bed. The wait was excruciating.

"How do you feel about everything she's told you so far?" Sebastian asked me. The two of us sat out on the back porch together. The sun had set a while earlier, so the only light came through the glass door and the tiny kitchen window.

Fireflies floated along in front of us, little lights flickering here and there. Some swooped down and skated on the ground, and others hovered in the stars.

"It was a lot. Emotionally, I mean," I said as I traced shapes in the dirt with my finger.

"I understand," he replied. "You wanted information, something to tell you what actually happened to you. However, once you heard the truth, it was devastating. Not only that, but it still didn't give you the full picture you were hoping for, and it didn't reset your memory."

"Yeah," I said. As much as Sebastian tried to console me, it was hard for him to truly understand. It was hard for anyone to understand. The silence lingered.

"Are you still bothered about the kids?" he asked me, changing the subject to a possibly more depressing one.

"The Meadows kids? Of course I am," I said, shocked that he would even ask. I may have been a villain once, but I had a heart.

"No, no. I mean the kids that were … scared of you. The ones that remembered you from the TV."

My stomach churned and my heart raced. That wasn't much better.

"Yes," I said, truthfully. "It's been on my mind, even with everything else going on. It's really difficult, knowing that whoever I was before … that she did horrible things. Things that scare me to think about now."

"You can't control what you did in the past; that's behind you. Thinking about it won't make it better."

"Yeah, but from here on out, every time I go out in the field and see civilians scared of me, terrified of me, my heart shatters. I don't know if it will ever get easier. That kind of thing stings, Sebastian."

Trying my hardest not to cry, I sighed and hugged my knees to my chest. The cool breeze pricked my skin, and I shivered. Why did it bother me so much? What others thought about me? About who I used to be? I was a different person now, but something painful remained in my past. And even if I wanted to, I could never outrun that—that old Bianca would always be a part of me.

I turned to look at Sebastian, about to ask what he thought, whether I was crazy or overthinking. However, I turned to find him watching me, seemingly concerned. I stopped, speechless.

"What?" I asked, confused.

He thought for a second, sighed, and replied, "Have I ever told you why I came here? Why I left home?" He looked at me with sincerity in his eyes.

He'd never talked about life before Victory.

"No," I said, "you haven't."

He laughed a little. "Probably dumb that I asked, since I don't think I've told anyone that story." He faced out into the night and leaned back, resting on his elbows and forearms.

"Well the tale I'm about to tell is not a happy one," he said. "But I think you need to hear it. We both have something about the past that we can't outrun."

He sighed and continued, "I grew up in a small town called Durango. I had two great parents and a little brother. We were a tight-knit family.

"A few years ago, things were starting to get a little crazy in Durango. People … like us started emerging … not all of them good. Actually, the first ones were very bad, which then led more supers to rise up and fight them. The battle lasted a few years, causing a lot of destruction. In Victory, we have destruction; don't get me wrong. But in Durango … we had … death. And not an insubstantial amount of it."

Sebastian paused. My stomach churned. I didn't like his silence. I reached out and placed my hand on his.

"I felt called to do something about it. I wanted to be a part of the fight. So one day, I went to the gym, trying to train myself so that I could go out and fight alongside the heroes. At this point, I had already discovered that my math and fighting skills were little better than average. I thought maybe they could lead to something. Anyway, I was coming home from the gym that evening, and I pulled into the neighborhood. Or what was left of it."

"What do you mean?" I asked. My voice was shaking. I knew what he meant, but my brain, or maybe my heart, didn't want to accept it.

"My neighborhood had been wiped out. There wasn't anything to return to. I panicked. So did everyone else. People ran around through the rubble: police, firefighters, medics. I had no idea if my family was alive. Everyone kept screaming about a fight. Heroes versus … them. This fight burned the neighborhood to the ground and left many dead."

"And your family?"

"Good or bad, I wanted the truth. I asked everyone I could. I ran to the remains of my home, tearing through the ashes and the rubble; nothing remained to be seen. Hours later, I finally got the answer, and it wasn't the one I wanted to hear."

"Oh my, Sebastian, I'm so sorry," I said as tears started to stream down my face. "I had no idea."

"They all perished in the fires, including my little brother. I was alone."

"I'm so sorry," I said, crying and squeezing his hand.

"The worst part is that the heroes lost the battle. They were all killed. Every last one of them. The villains wiped them out."

"And then what happened to Durango?" I asked, wiping my face.

"Durango was left alone. The villains had succeeded in what they intended to accomplish—they wiped out the threats. Then they moved on to the next city."

My heart raced to put together the pieces of this sorry tale. They moved on to the next city …

"Wait," I replied. "You can't mean Victory?"

"The same villains we fight today are the ones that killed my family. The ones that destroyed everything I love. And I couldn't help but think that it was partially my fault because I didn't have the ability to stop them. I knew that I needed to find people who could truly defeat them, once and for all."

Suddenly, I understood.

"Sebastian," I asked, "you … couldn't defeat them because …"

"Because I don't have powers."

Silence.

Sebastian leaned forward on his knees again, running his hands through his hair. He stared at the ground between his feet, almost in a daze.

"When I began working out, boxing, wrestling, I thought I had something special. Especially combined with my skills in mathematics. The thing is, I didn't realize at the time that I didn't actually have powers. I thought I was one of them. I needed to grow into my gifts. I tried to force something that was never going to happen."

"But you can calculate the angles, the velocity of every object to be used as a weapon? I don't understand."

"That's not a power, Bianca. That's the art of prediction. I take my best guess and roll with it, calculating speeds based on weight and size and angles based on shape. It's nothing special, it's just math. Fancy math, but still, just math."

"When did you realize it wasn't …"

"That it wasn't anything? Well I guess I realized that the day my family died. But I was so determined to avenge them that instead of backing down, I continued to embrace this self-created gift. I continued to train and to get strong. I guess I had the mindset that while I couldn't be a superhero, I could maybe still be a hero. I could still be a great man. I could still be a great son and brother, even if they would never see it themselves."

"You are those things, Sebastian. Just by wanting to fight for them, you've honored them as a great son and a great brother. You're a fantastic man, and you know what else? A great leader," I added. He looked up at me. His eyes shone so bright, even in the dark.

"I can't be a leader," he said matter-of-factly. "A leader is meant to *lead* his men into battle and fight alongside them and for them. I can try my hardest, but I don't have powers like all of you do. I can't fulfill the role to the fullest. I am not the best suited to lead you all. I'm not even sure I'm suited to fight on the front lines anymore. Fadel is far too strong. The leader should be someone with actual powers, strong, amazing powers. Someone like you."

I sat in silence, glancing up again at the fireflies above my head. Quietly, I reached up and grabbed one, letting it crawl around my hand. Sebastian watched the tiny creature, observing how I turned my hand to make a constant path for it.

"You know," I said, "I could say the same thing. That I'm not meant to be a leader. That I don't have the qualities or proper skills to lead us into battle. However, in my case, it's true. I don't have those skills.

"Just because I have powers, no matter how strong, I don't have the power of courage, the power of ambition, the power of justice. Not like you. To be a leader, to be a great man, you need courage and confidence. You need to know right from wrong and be fully ready to sacrifice yourself for what is good and true. And you need to be able to inspire confidence in those who will fight by your side.

"I wasn't born to be a leader. For many, many reasons. But I was born to fight for the good, alongside someone strong and courageous," I said.

He looked over at me, somewhat skeptically.

"I truly believe that," I continued, "I have these gifts to use for good, but I am not meant to lead us. That's not my story."

I turned the little firefly over into my palm and closed my fingers gently around it. With my other hand I grabbed Sebastian's. I unfurled my fingers and let the firefly crawl onto his palm.

"You're a great man, Sebastian. You were made for greatness. I know that you are the best person to lead us into battle, powers or no powers. You're the one who will someday be remembered as the protector of Victory."

"How do you know that?"

"I know. I feel it."

I watched the firefly, still crawling around his palm.

"Is this firefly a metaphor? Are you passing the torch to me?" he asked, smirking.

"It was never mine to give." He may have been kidding, but I was entirely serious. He looked at me and smiled.

"Thank you," he said.

"I look forward to following you into battle," I replied, smiling back and giving him a lopsided salute. We both laughed and looked up at the sky.

Then we sat in silence. Sebastian pulled me up close to him and held me in his arms. I could feel his warm breath on my forehead. There we spent the next hour, staring at the sky, watching the fireflies and the stars fade together, so you could no longer tell which was which.

CHAPTER THIRTY-FOUR

While we waited for Alexandra to wake up, Penny and I spent our time baking, the classic unwinding activity for two perfectly normal, twenty-something girls. Not often did I get "normal girl" moments, so I surely didn't plan to take this time for granted. Besides, I loved spending one-on-one time with Penny.

She and I spent a lot of downtime together in my first few months at the house, but as things got busier, we didn't have time to connect like we did before. Maybe it was not the best time, seeing that there was an unconscious woman in the other room, but I wanted to take any opportunity I could get.

"So," I said, measuring out the flour, "you and Theo. What's that relationship?"

Penny blushed.

"It's complicated. We've always been close friends, and just friends, you know? But he's such a flirt! And he's so clever and strong and protective and—"

"So you're essentially in love with him?" I laughed, cutting right to the point.

"Well, no I'm not in love with him! I won't pretend like I haven't thought about it. A lot. I don't *think* I have a crush, but it's hard to tell sometimes." She sighed a little before continuing, wrinkling her nose as she looked up to the ceiling on the exhale.

"I can't decide if I'd be stupid to love him."

"What do you mean? Why would you be stupid to?"

I mixed the flour into the wet ingredients and glanced over at Penny. She had stopped mixing and leaned on the counter, looking out the window.

"I think he's got a naturally flirty personality. I don't think he's into me in particular. Don't want to emotionally invest myself when I'm not sure. I think he may be sister-zoning me." She sighed again. "But you, I think he's intrigued by you."

I stopped the electric mixer.

"Me? No, definitely not. Definitely, *definitely* not."

Penny laughed and said, "I'm not sure he still is, after Jasmine made the comments recently about you and Sebastian. We had no idea, but I think you intrigued him."

"So you think Theo is into me?" I couldn't believe the conversation we were having. This was the type of things a person did not want to be told.

"Well I'm not sure. Again, I couldn't tell if it was him being flirty or if he actually had feelings." Penny's inability to read men, or situations in general, put me at ease again.

"He's such a hard one to read, so naturally smooth and all," she said. "He attempts to be a ladies man, doesn't he?"

"Sebastian called him the same thing," I agreed.

"So is it true? What Jasmine said about you and Sebastian?"

I couldn't help it. I smiled.

"It *is*! Bianca!"

"Shhh," I hushed her, laughing. She sashayed across the kitchen and leaned on me, giggling.

"We spend a lot of time alone together. There's been some cuddling. And I guess you could say we've had some cute moments."

"So is it true? Have you kissed?"

"Maybe," I whispered, glancing around the house, not wanting anyone to hear. I didn't exactly want to discuss this, but it lightened the mood and clearly pleased Penny. She giggled and hugged me.

"Bianca! I'm so happy for you!" she exclaimed, a little too loudly. "When did this happen? How did I not know? You're literally my roommate!" I grabbed her arms and shushed her again.

"It's not a big deal. It's just been a few months."

"A few *months*?"

"Yes, since July or so."

She squealed again, and I rushed to quiet her.

"I'm sorry I didn't tell you," I whispered. "I didn't want things in the house to be weird, and it happened so fast. I didn't know what you all would think."

"Does Theo know? Has he been hiding it from me?"

I think Penny was more worried about Theo not telling her than she intended to let on.

"No, I don't think he knows," I lied, fully aware that Theo *did* know, but I didn't want to upset Penny more. "He might suspect, as you said, after Jasmine let it slip. I think he might have taken her seriously and suspected. And on that point, did you not believe her?"

"I mean, I kind of did but kind of didn't. I thought she may have suspected you liked him and for dramatic effect, exaggerated the story. But wow, Bianca, that's amazing. I'm so happy for you!"

"So that being said," I continued pouring the batter into cups. "Theo's available."

Penny smiled. "I'll leave that up to him," she said. "I'm going to keep doing my own thing and let him do his. I've got enough to worry about now. You know, the usual things a girl in her young twenties worries about: fighting gunmen, missing children, super villains who want you dead. That sort of stuff."

I laughed.

"Sounds like you're living the drea—"

A door creaked and opened and a weak voice said, "Hello? Is anyone there?"

Penny and I turned to each other, mouths wide open.

"I stayed with him for about four years," Alexandra said, sitting cross-legged on the couch.

This felt like *deja vu*—the day that I woke up in Sebastian's bed. But this time, I sat on the floor, looking up at Alexandra as she unraveled the story of how she got to be in our home. And to my satisfaction, I played a major character in that story. Already, I had learned so much about my past.

Alexandra explained that years ago, Dr. Fadel, formerly known to us as S, created a list of potential supers and tracked them. My name had been on that list since a time in high school when I apparently had a mental breakdown in a parking lot. She explained that someone must have seen and reported me. News of this sort of things gets around, and consequently, it eventually reached Fadel.

He had been tracking me for a while, and when I departed for Victory, he placed Alexandra in my way. She was the trap to lure me to him. However, at that time, she didn't know that she served a malicious purpose.

"Like, you, I genuinely believed we were the ones serving people, that we were the ones in the right. I saw it as an honor that the doctor chose me to intercept and encourage you. I saw that as my role in the story."

"So you don't have powers?" Jasmine asked.

"No, I don't. He recruited me through an application process. The questionnaire seemed vague but focused on philanthropy work, so I thought *why not?* I essentially acted as an administrative assistant. Much of my responsibility revolved around tracking supers, trying to determine which were potential allies and which were actually villains—no offense; I clearly know now that you all are the good guys.

"I did a lot of recruiting over those years. But Bianca! Bianca would be the crown jewel of my accomplishments. Fadel wanted her most."

I suddenly felt my skin prickle, not because of pride, but because of discomfort.

"Why was that?" I asked.

"Because of the fire. He wanted your fire."

"And he got it, unfortunately," Sebastian said as he flipped the page of his notebook. He quickly scribbled everything Alexandra said.

"He did," she replied. "He stole a lot powers from kids. But Bianca's were special. They could do so much damage, much more than teleportation or super strength."

"Hey, I take offense to that," Theo laughed. "But it's a fair point."

I shifted uncomfortably on the floor. It felt bizarre to hear things about myself, things about my past that didn't exist in my own mind. It felt like listening to someone else's story. I couldn't believe it was actually mine.

"So I still don't know why I left. How I ended up here. How much do you know?" I asked.

"I know some," she said. "Probably more than you do right now.

You had passed your final test, the one where he finally took your powers on as his own. From there, he essentially took you on as his assistant. The other supers ended up on the back burner. A lot of them got frustrated, since they had trained so long and hard to hit the streets. However, none of them got frustrated enough to leave—well one did—but the rest didn't. They continued to wait, biding their time until it was their moment. I guess a lot of them are having their moment now."

"So why did I leave?" I asked, getting really antsy.

"I think you started to realize the truth. You were promised a life of goodness and justice. You were told that you were going to help people. And I think you saw what the fire did, and it scared you. To be honest, I don't know exactly why you left. You told no one, not even me. Only *you* know. But I believe you ran away because he scared you."

"So maybe I was trying to go home?"

"Maybe. Maybe you were going home. Or maybe you were going to find them," she gestured around the room to the others.

"Regardless," she continued, "you ran. You packed all your things in the middle of the night, and you snuck out of your apartment. Fadel always made you park your car at the office, probably so you couldn't leave. He insisted it was the company car and that everyone had to walk to work. That night you left, you tried to get your car, but you couldn't find the keys anywhere in the office."

"I *knew* he had my car," I said, getting more fired up by the minute.

"You abandoned the idea of taking your car and took off on foot into the city. Unfortunately, that was the night that Fadel planned on speaking with you about a new assignment. He called you several times, but you didn't answer. The next morning, when you didn't come in, he went to your apartment and found it deserted."

"And he began the hunt," Sebastian said.

"Exactly," Alexandra replied. "And his rage got the best of him. You ran, and that made him furious. He attacked civilians, caught buildings and cars on fire. The police called your friends." She gestured to the others in the room.

"All of that to hunt down one person."

I found it hard to swallow.

"He finally found you, and you tried to fight back, but you got scared."

"And the fire didn't come," I whispered. "That's how I ended up in the road."

"And that's when we fought him off and took you home," Sebastian added.

I now knew for sure: My friends had saved my life.

"And when he returned, well, I'd never seen him more livid. He screamed and burned things. He smashed through the offices. He kept saying things like, 'We were so close' and 'I almost had it.' It seemed to me that there was more he still needed from you. I have no idea what he meant, but it scared me."

You don't know how powerful you are.

"I knew I didn't want to be around him anymore. His anger seemed constant. He cursed you all and talked of wanting you dead." She pointed to Sebastian who chuckled.

"Well, he can come and get me. I'll destroy him for what he's done to you two."

I looked over at him and smiled a little. He winked at me, and my heart fluttered.

"As I told you before, I continued to grow increasingly more skeptical and scared, and I didn't want to leave and have him hunt me down like he hunted you. But the Meadows kids were too much! I told him I wanted to leave, effective immediately."

"And then?" Penny asked with a shaking voice.

"He came at me. He beat me, called me a traitor, told me I deserved to be dead. I called him a villain."

Alexandra took a deep breath, trembled and continued with faltering breath. "He said that I was the true villain, the one fighting against the Good. He told me that I would die alone. And then he beat me unconscious. The next thing I knew, you rescued me."

Alexandra began to cry. Penny scooched over on the couch and hugged her.

"It's ok," she said. "You're so brave for what you did. You did the right thing. And you're safe now."

"I'm so scared of what he's doing to the others," Alexandra cried.

"Ok, so do you think you can tell us all of the supers he's collected? All of their powers and their names?" Jasmine asked. She glanced over at Sebastian, hinting that he should take notes.

"Yes, I think so," Alexandra replied, closing her eyes and rubbing her head. "I want to help them. I want to help them escape like Bianca did."

"And like you did," I said, reaching up and grabbing her hand. "You got out. You're free now."

"Unless he tries to find me, like he tried to find you."

"We won't let that happen," Sebastian said. "You're one of us now, and we will help you rescue them all. We will free every one of them."

Alexandra looked up, smiled at him, and wiped away a tear.

"The ending to your story hasn't been written yet," he continued. "Your character arc is still rising. You recruited these kids for Fadel, and now you'll recruit them for the good. And we will help you. If you're with Bianca, then we're with you. We're a team."

Alexandra wiped her tears, took a deep breath, and pushed herself off the couch.

"Well, when can we start? I'm ready to get some revenge and rescue my friends."

CHAPTER THIRTY-FIVE

MAY 7, 2019

"Bianca," I heard someone call in the distance. A man's voice. The doctor. I had to get away from him. Immediately.

I took another turn and suddenly halted, coming abruptly to an open street. I didn't want to be exposed, but I couldn't stop moving. I eyed a side street across the way. And taking a deep breath, I sprinted directly towards it.

Almost there ... almost there.

I needed to get inside, somewhere safe, where he couldn't find me.

Suddenly, an explosion to my left threw me off my feet. I turned to see a car on fire.

Did I light that one, or did he?

I could feel him closing in on me.

Keep moving ...

I began to crawl, trying to bring myself to my feet, but it was useless. Pain seized my body. I wasn't going to make it.

I inched towards a side street on my hands and knees, trying to block out the sound of screaming and the smell of smoke. I needed to focus on finding a hiding place. Out of the corner of my eye, I saw a shadow fly overhead. The flying super. Behind me, I heard screaming, the clashing of metal on metal, and a deep laugh.

Fadel now fought the other boy, the one with the baseball bat. My moment had come, the perfect distraction. I combat-crawled as fast as I could, but my arms started to give out, and I lost my focus. The pain overwhelmed me. The fear became unavoidable. I couldn't get up, and I was losing consciousness. I dropped to my stomach and tried to get air. Before I blacked out, I saw him. He had found me.

"Miss Williams, your time is up. You're a traitor, and I'm here to make you pay for your sins."

I heard two taps and a fireball appeared at the top of his staff. I lay on the ground, in so much pain I couldn't move.

"Please," I whimpered. "Please don't."

"I've come to save the world from evil people who want to see it destroyed. You, Miss Williams, have proven to be one of those people."

"No," I whispered. "I'm not. Please."

"You have two options, Miss Williams. Either you come back with me like this never happened, and we continue to work on what you've got in those hands of yours. Or, we end this now." He kept walking towards me with the fire glowing on his staff.

What you've got in those hands of yours.

I pushed myself up into a sitting position, screaming in pain.

I tried to light a fire, but I was too scared to spark a flame. He almost had me, but I couldn't run anymore.

Come on, Bianca, just light the fire. Please light the fire.

I couldn't do it. I was about to die.

"I see you've chosen the latter," Fadel said. His tone fell flat, and his face showed zero sign of emotion. "What a pity. You don't know how powerful you are. Such a shame to see a dying star fall from heaven."

He wound his staff back and prepared to end my life with a fireball. This was it. The fire-girl had been taken down by her own flames. I closed my eyes and prepared for the end. But the fire never came.

I heard more banging and grunting. Someone had attacked him. I opened my eyes, but before I could see who it was, I got dizzy.

Come on, Bee. Whatever you do, don't lose cons—

The only thing I was sure about was that *I wasn't dead.*

Somewhere in my subconscious, I realized this and suddenly jerked to life, gasping for air. I screamed from the pain. My temples thumped in tandem with my heart. I could barely open my eyes; the light stung them and caused my head to ache even more. I felt the hard asphalt under me, crumbled and broken, and I breathed in air that was thick and dusty.

Sitting up a little and leaning back on my hands, I glanced around and realized I was still in the middle of the road. On both sides of me, cars were upside down; some were on fire. The road had been destroyed.

Fadel was nowhere to be seen.

My body was numb, my senses weak. I felt the throbbing pain of the worst headache imaginable; the crumbling road under my hands bruised my palms, and there was strong pulsing in my left ankle.

I saw people running in the distance, all in different directions, panicked. Women with children scooped up in their arms sprinted and sobbed. The frightened people wore torn, dirty clothing. Even though I knew they were screaming, I couldn't hear it. In fact, I couldn't hear anything besides dull ringing. Focusing on it made my head hurt more.

Where was he? How was I still alive?

I tried pushing myself up, but my ankle couldn't bear the weight. I didn't have the strength to hoist myself off the ground. I was on my hands and knees and panting into the hot asphalt.

Then it hit me: I might die here.

I tried pushing up again, but this time, my arms gave out, and I collapsed onto my stomach. The air felt even hotter; the fire was closing in.

I was going to die.

I started slipping away, fighting to keep consciousness, but to no avail: I was going. Suddenly, I heard a voice. I felt scared at first, expecting to see Fadel. But it wasn't him. This sounded like the voice of a younger man.

I had no idea where it came from, but beyond it, I could finally hear the distant screaming. The voice spoke again; this time it shouted. "Keep breathing! Focus on breathing! We've got you!"

Without warning, someone rolled me over, scooped me up and cradled me. I opened my eyes as much as I could, but I didn't have the strength to turn my head and look up at the person who was carrying me. Instead, I faced forward with eyes barely open, and I saw a second person staring at me—a young man. I thought it looked like the super with the baseball bat. The one who fought Fadel. I couldn't be sure— all I could make out were brown eyes and a calm face.

My goodness, those eyes …

"I'll take it from here," I heard a woman say. "I'll remove everything we talked about."

"What's going on?" I whispered.

"Miss Bianca Williams? We're here to help you," the brown-eyed boy said. "You're safe now."

And that's when everything went black again.

CHAPTER THIRTY-SIX

A few days after we took Alexandra home with us, the crisp, fallen leaves began to pile up. Calendar pages flipped to October the first.

I had been free from Fadel since the first week of May. Officially six months. I felt like I'd known the people in the house for a lifetime, especially Sebastian. The days passed quickly and kept us on our toes.

Six months earlier, I woke up in the middle of the road, surrounded by burning cars. In those subsequent six months, I learned about my fire powers. I learned about the powers of my friends, and those of a mysterious man with a staff. I learned about my past as a supervillain. I learned that this man sucked the powers of supers, including mine. I quickly learned how to care about someone. I learned how to reign in my anger and use it for good. I learned how to fight.

And on that first day in October, I truly learned how to forgive.

Jasmine came outside and found me petting the cat. She gestured to the ground next to me and asked if she could sit. I said yes.

She wrapped her coat tighter around her shoulders and sat next to me. Like all one-on-one encounters with Jasmine, it started off quietly, unassuming. I felt uncomfortable, like I was walking on eggshells despite neither of us beginning to talk. Jasmine broke the silence.

"So have you named him?" she asked, stroking my small friend.

"Not formally, no."

She smiled and rubbed his tummy.

"He has such a nice, gray coat. He looks like a little elephant or a mouse. Ironically, in the case of the mouse," she laughed.

"Mouse is a good name," I said, not looking up at her.

I remained upset with Jasmine, and I knew she felt the same way towards me. I had caused her physical harm, and she had wiped my memory. We both had the right to be mad at each other.

"Bianca," she started. "I think we need to talk."

"Do you actually want to talk, or did Sebastian put you up to this?"

"It was Penny, actually. She told me we needed to talk. She said that otherwise, she'd have to find new friends. Apparently, this is exhausting for her," She used air quotes and rolled her eyes. "A little dramatic in my opinion."

"So, you still don't care?" I replied, frustrated.

"No, I do. I had thought about talking to you before Penny accosted me."

She pulled her knees to her chest. She looked so cold. I guess that being from Hawaii and then the West Coast, she wasn't used to the autumn weather. Winter would only be worse. I took off my jacket and handed it to her.

"Aren't you cold?" she asked, putting it over her shoulders.

"No, I'm much more used to this weather than you are. Just keep it."

She thanked me and we sat in silence for a moment. I found the silence deafening.

"Bianca, look—"

"No," I said. "I think I'm the one who needs to apologize. I've been holding a grudge for months now. I got so upset that you took my memories from me. I thought about it constantly after I found out. I couldn't understand why it was necessary. Why didn't you bring me home and explain the situation? Why didn't you use your Voice to persuade me to come to your side? Especially since I was already on the run from Fadel?"

"Because we couldn't be sure that you wouldn't turn back. Sebastian and I decided that it would be safest to have you only remember your life without powers. So, I cleared the two years with Fadel and any other memories you had about having powers. I don't know how many there were, but I cleared them."

I nodded.

"We wanted you to wake up fresh, knowing that we could bring you to health and then bring you home. Or at least I thought that was the plan. But then Sebastian had other ideas and decided he wanted to let you see your powers. He essentially erased our plan and therefore, our need to even have your memory wiped. But it was too late."

"Please don't blame Sebastian," I said, ready to flip the switch to anger if I needed to.

"No, that's not it. I don't blame him. I confronted him about it later, and I could tell that it was out of love, or something of that sort. He didn't feel right sending you home, not knowing. He felt that it was wrong to send you away with a massive memory gap. He felt guilt, regret."

"So then why did you stay mad at me? Why then did you keep antagonizing me? Why do you hate me?"

Jasmine's head snapped around to look at me. Her eyes were wet with tears, with hurt.

"I don't hate you. I never hated you, even when you burned me. But I kept that anger towards you because even as you were on our side, I still saw snippets of the old you. I continued to fear that you'd turn back. And I didn't feel safe. I didn't feel safe because I don't have a defense."

Time seemed to slow for a moment. I recalled the look on Jasmine's face, the fear as she ran from me. As she backpedaled and squirmed, scared for her life. Her fear was palpable, even when she was remembering.

"My Voice is great, powerful even. But it never seemed to work well enough. I never felt confident using it on villains. I had tried it a few times, even once on you before you attacked me. But it didn't work. So, the entire time we've now been together, I've been scared that you could hurt me again. And that I still wouldn't have a defense."

It all made sense now. Jasmine wasn't lying. She never hated me; she feared me. For the first time, I understood what it was like to be Jasmine. She grew up in a world that made her feel like the bad guy. She only saw how her powers manipulated and controlled people. But she took a risk, a huge one at that, by coming out here. She packed up her whole life and decided to dedicate it to goodness.

But that goodness came with consequences. Her risk yielded pain that was caused by me. Anyone hurt like that, especially after all their sacrifice, would never want to see their attacker again. But then I showed up. Her best friends, her only friends, welcomed me into her home against her wishes. They made her use her powers to manipulate things once again. Because of them, and because of me, she had to face her attacker every day.

All this, not to mention the comparison! Living with and being constantly surrounded by other heroes, she felt worthless regarding the one thing she sacrificed her normal life to do. She hated her own powers and how they made her feel weak. And compared to mine …

"Have you ever thought that maybe your powers are a lot like mine?" I asked.

She looked over at me again and released her legs from her chest. She reached up and wiped a tear from her cheek.

"What do you mean?" she asked.

"I mean that maybe your emotions, or your state of mind, affects your abilities as well." My thoughts were flowing together, and suddenly it made sense.

"For example," I continued. "When I get scared, I can't make fire. I'm completely helpless unless I'm feeling a certain, concentrated emotion. Unfortunately for me, that one emotion is anger."

"I don't think mine are emotionally related, though," she replied. "I don't think anything can help me trigger them."

"Right, but maybe it's not about what triggers them. Maybe it's the opposite. Maybe like mine, certain emotions or feelings fog your mind and make you unable to trigger them. What I'm trying to say is that I think fear affects you too."

She sat for a moment, thinking.

"You're right. Now that I reflect, I always have to be in the right state of mind." She took a moment to think. "But it's so hard. It's so, so hard to block out the fear. Especially when there are flames and gunshots, and people screaming. I want to run from it all."

Finally, Jasmine's tears began to fall. For the first time, I saw her really cry. We were so similar, in a multitude of ways, and I'd never realized it. The same thing motivated us to come to Victory. The same thing drove our emotions. The same thing held us back.

"I'm the same way, Jasmine. The fear is crippling. There are moments when I want to run away. To go back home and pretend like this never happened. In some moments my powers feel useless."

"Then why do you keep going out there? Why do you not leave? Have you ever thought about it?"

I remembered all the times I wanted to run. I recalled the nights I spent on the back porch, longing to be in some other place. Even now, part of me missed the life I used to have. My normal, safe life. But something held me here.

"I have thought about leaving. Many times, actually. But I always stayed because of my friends. Because you guys are surrounding me, protecting me. And I'm protecting you."

I thought back to that night, sitting with Sebastian, watching *The Avengers*.

"We fight as a team. We have each other's back. My life is in Penny's hands. In Theo's. In Sebastian's. And their lives are in mine. It's a game of trust. And it's scary! But if we want to stop Fadel, we need to trust one another. Defend one another."

"That's nice and all," she replied, "but I don't exactly have the best powers for defending you all. I'm not being modest when I say that I may be in the way. That's why I stay outside on evac."

"That's not true," I said, thinking back. "You saved my life in that bank. You saved Theo and Penny. Your powers came in the clutch at the perfect moment. And you didn't let the fear take hold of you."

"Because I wanted you all to be safe," she said, realizing what she was saying.

"Exactly. Care … love … It overpowers fear. Even if you don't want to admit that's what it is. It's true."

Tears poured down her face. I reached over and wrapped my arms around her. She wrapped her arms around me and we sat there, hugging each other tightly.

"Bianca," she sniffled, "I want you to teach me. Help me figure out how I can be a part of the team, like you did for Theo."

"I can't train you or lead you," I replied, thinking back to my conversation with Sebastian. "That's not my role or even my strength. But lucky for you, I know the perfect man for the job."

She kept hugging me, and I could hear a smile in her voice.

"Bianca?"

"Yes?"

"For the record, I left in a loophole."

"What do you mean?"

"When I cleared your memories, I said I wanted you to clear your mind of any memory indicating you had powers. For now."

For now.

"I don't know when *for now* will be over, but I think that someday, it will all come back to you. Not that you need those memories anymore, since the gaps have mostly been filled in. But I thought you should know."

It was such a little thing, funny even. But it mattered. My whole world depended on those two words. Jasmine had saved me. She was a hero.

"Thank you," I said, squeezing her.

It all might come back. Someday, I may know everything.

"I'm sorry that I tried to burn you to death."

Jasmine gave me an exaggerated side eye.

"Twice," she said.

"Yes, I'm sorry I tried to burn you to death *twice*."

She smiled at me. For the first time, she genuinely smiled at me with the face of a friend.

"It's all in the past. Just don't do it again, or I swear, I will join Fadel just to destroy you."

I let go of her and laughed.

"Deal. Now come on; let's go find our fearless leader."

CHAPTER THIRTY-SEVEN

With the gym doors locked tight behind us, we prepared to train.

It was finally time.

Jasmine looked nervous. She was wringing her hands and muttering. She tried to use her Voice to calm herself, but it didn't appear to be working.

I made eye contact with her across the room and smiled. She responded with a weak smile of her own. I hoped by the end of the night, her hesitation would change and once again, we would see the confident, powerful version of Jasmine that we all knew.

"Are we ready?" Sebastian yelled, looking around at each one of us.

Theo cracked his knuckles and affirmed. Penny jumped up and down a few times and yelled 'yes!' Jasmine muttered something and then slowly nodded. I closed my eyes, took a deep breath, and felt my hands grow warm.

"All set, Sebastian!" I yelled.

"Ok team, remember: *You* are the defenders of Victory."

He hopped up on one of the training blocks and crouched to meet us at eye level. In this moment, it became abundantly clear to all of us: Sebastian was our leader.

"You are the reason that this city's citizens will sleep safely tonight. You are Fadel's biggest fear. You are the reason that we will win this war. You are the reason that—"

"Are you trying to make us cry or pump us up, Caswell?" Jasmine said, rolling her eyes. I smiled, relieved to see this side of Jasmine again.

"That's the spirit! Ok team," Sebastian said, standing up on the block. He now towered above us like the commander of a major army. "Let's go!"

From the side of the room, Alexandra blew a whistle, and it began.

"Bianca! Flame!"

I tossed a ball of fire in Sebastian's direction. He hit it with the leg of a chair (one that Theo accidentally broke a minute or two earlier), nailing the tackle dummy anchored in the center of the room. Without hesitation, Alexandra sprayed it with the fire extinguisher.

Alexandra's experience with Fadel made her perfect for this job. Her entire career in Victory revolved around training and monitoring supers like us. In fact, she trained and monitored me. That being said, this definitely wasn't the first time she'd had to put out something I'd caught on fire while training.

While Sebastian and I tag-teamed with fire, Theo jumped in the air gripping two large dumbbells. The several box fans set up around the room perfectly simulated the gentle autumn breeze we would be dealing with now. Theo smacked full-force into the same dummy only seconds after Alexandra had finished extinguishing the flames. The moment Theo got out of the way, Penny roundhouse kicked it to the ground. And that's when Jasmine came in.

Before we started the training, Sebastian told her to practice as if the dummy were a real person. Nothing good would come from half-hearted attempts to use her Voice. She needed to give it the best of her ability.

After considering Sebastian's advice, Jasmine also decided to use a specific name or description when using her Voice. That way, her commands could be specifically aimed at her victim and wouldn't accidentally take over someone else. Despite the extra precaution, we all knew not to listen too carefully, as we didn't want to be put under the spell. We knew from the experience of evacuating crowds that she had the power to move many people at once.

"Hey dummy," she said and started walking slowly towards the beat-up, raggedy tackle dummy slumped on the floor in the middle of the room. Her eyes remained locked on the dummy as she approached. "You don't want to be here. You don't want to be in this room any-more."

She took slow, long strides. The glow in her eyes screamed confidence, maybe even a tinge of rage. Her tone could ensnare the most stubborn of listeners.

"You are done here. You no longer want to fight. You want to give in, to submit. You want to leave here, don't you?"

The scene was mesmerizing. After months without using her Voice, it came so naturally.

"You want to leave here," she said. "It will all be ok. I promise. You're going to be ok. But it's time. It's time for you to go."

Suddenly, the dummy on the ground moved slightly.

Standing next to me, Penny gasped and raised her hand to her mouth. Sebastian shushed her. Jasmine's eyes grew large and revealed her fear.

"Guys," she said, frozen in place. "Guys did you see that?"

"Keep going, Jasmine," Sebastian whispered. "Keep talking; keep concentrating."

Jasmine took a deep breath and continued with eyes still open wide.

"I—it's ok! You can leave. You have permission to leave. You want to leave. I know you do. So do it! Leave now."

Sliding across the floor like a limp ragdoll, the dummy slowly started to move towards the door. Jasmine kept her eyes locked on it and whispered to herself, muttering words I couldn't hear. The dummy inched closer and closer to the doorway.

"Now stop!"

The dummy halted. Jasmine fell to her knees, gasping.

"Oh my," she whispered to herself.

Penny ran across the room and hugged her tightly around the waist. Jasmine continued to pant on her hands and knees.

"Jasmine! You're amazing!" Penny yelled.

"Did you know you could do that?" Alexandra asked, kneeling and grabbing her hand. "That was spectacular."

"No," Jasmine said, still staring at the ground in shock. "I had no idea."

I sat down with the three of them. Sebastian paced around, smiling and running his hands through his hair like a madman.

"Jasmine," I said, "you have telekinesis. Well, kind of, since it's not with your mind. But you can move people *and* objects with your words."

"I don't know what to say," she replied, pushing herself off the floor to a standing position.

Sebastian finally snapped out of his shocked pacing, ran across the room, picked up Jasmine, and twirled her around.

"I know what to say and it's one word: *game-changing.* Jasmine, this is what we needed. This is the advantage we've been looking for!" he said.

She laughed and hugged him back. I noted this moment for the history books, definitely a first, at least since I had arrived.

It reminded me that no matter what happened between us, we were still a family. Our lives depended on each other every day. We fought as a team, meaning we won as a team and we lost as one. And Jasmine, for the first time, finally knew what it felt like to be a part of that.

"So what I'm thinking," Alexandra said, getting back to the practicalities of the situation, "is that Jasmine can throw objects to Seb and Theo with her Voice? And she can attack Fadel with inanimate objects from a distance? And maybe she could even control the wind for Theo and the fire for Bianca! Jasmine, you might be the connecting piece!"

Theo was leaning back on his hands with one leg over the other. "So what *I'm* thinking," he said, echoing Alexandra, "is that Jasmine has now surpassed my skills. Once again, Theodore Martin has the worst powers."

Jasmine smirked, "You've got that right, Theo."

She smiled at Sebastian, "Come on; let's go again. I'm just starting to see how this will work."

CHAPTER THIRTY-EIGHT

The call came two days later.

After two straight days of practice, we finally got the call we'd been waiting for. Fadel made an appearance outside the hotel again. "He's probably going back in to see if I'm still there. Or to dispose of evidence," Alexandra said, handing me a hair tie.

"I think you're right."

"And I hate to break it to you, Alexandra," Jasmine added. "If you're not dead, he probably wants you dead. You know too much."

"Which is why we are going to keep her here," Penny said and smiled. "Safe and sound!"

"Yes, we'll be back soon. I promise," I said, giving her a hug.

"I'll have dinner ready for your return," Alexandra half-joked. Thanks to this loyal and thoughtful friend, dinner would probably be ready by the time we returned, if not out of kindness, out of distraction.

We quickly said our goodbyes and Jasmine, Penny, and I left to meet the boys in the van.

"The plan is simple," Sebastian said as we approached Victory.

"We try to knock that staff out of his hands. I don't know if he has his goons with him today, but if he does, I want Penny and Theo to work on them while Jasmine, Bianca, and I work on Fadel. The goal will be for Bianca and I to knock him down or have him drop the staff. Jasmine will assist us, and then once the staff is down, she will lure it to either herself or to me. Without the staff, he's powerless—just a crazy dog with no bite. Jasmine will convince him to sleep or lock himself in a closet or something, and then we call him in. The police can take it from there."

Theo parked a block from the hotel. We got out and ran towards the sound of screaming. Unfortunately, it was a sound I was used to by now. When we got to the front entrance, it became clear that our man was already inside.

"Top floor, guys," Sebastian said, pointing to the stairs.

"How do we know he won't leave? That he won't teleport out while we're in the stairwell?" I asked.

"We don't know, but we might as well try the place we know he's headed to first."

We started towards the stairs, but before we could get there, we heard a cracking noise, and turned around sharply.

Fadel. Between us and the exit.

"Going somewhere?"

"What are you doing here, Fadel?" I asked, creating two small flames.

"Please, Miss Williams, call me *Dr.* Fadel. You should know that you never quite made it to that level of a personal relationship with me. You left … too soon."

"I'm about to call you dead if you don't shut up right now and answer her question," Theo said, cracking his knuckles.

"I came to retrieve something I left here," he smirked. "Maybe you know where it is."

"We don't know what you're talking about," Sebastian lied. "But your time's up, Fadel. You made a mistake by coming back here."

"Maybe *you* made the mistake and shouldn't have come back here. Had you thought of that, Mr. Caswell? Because if you haven't already noticed, I'm between you and the only exit. What a pity."

He surveyed us, and his gaze stopped on Jasmine.

"Oh look, your scared little friend decided to play superhero today. That's cute."

Jasmine cursed at him and cracked her knuckles, glaring with intensity I'd never seen.

He only smiled all the wider.

"What? Are you going to tell me to stop being a meanie and join forces with you? To go home and never return? Are you going to use that pretty little voice of yours to command me to forget who I am and act like this never happened?"

"No. I'm commanding you to come over here and hit him," Jasmine said.

Fadel frowned.

"Hit who?"

"You heard me," she smirked. "Hit him."

"Do you want me to hit Mr. Martin or Mr. Caswell because both prospects would be quite equally satisfying, Miss Kahale. Please elaborate."

"Hit him. Now," she said, determined. Fadel got angry and shouted. "Look at me when I'm talking to you—"

But her eyes weren't on him. They were locked on the lobby chair flying towards him. The chair smacked him to the ground, and he landed at our feet. Unfortunately, his hand still gripped the staff.

"Now!" Sebastian thundered and lunged for it. Fadel disappeared and reappeared across the lobby, still on the floor. The plan was back on. And luckily, without the goons, it was five on one. Penny and I ran in to attack.

Penny kicked and punched while Fadel dodged and countered with his staff. He worked at superspeed. While trying to avoid Penny, I threw flame after flame, but he continued to put them out with his own. He somehow countered her and dodged me simultaneously. Sebastian threw chairs, but every time one got close, Fadel disappeared and reappeared across the room. He had mastered so many powers that we could barely keep up or keep track. But one thing became increasingly more obvious during our fight: He was tiring.

We kept fighting, and he kept countering. Hit after hit, punch after punch, flame after flame, we kept going. He was getting worn out. But unfortunately, so were we. Thankfully, as if she knew the perfect moment to do so, Jasmine called a strong wind to come inside, and Theo rode it, carrying a chair. He smacked into Fadel, who fell once again.

This time, he let go of the staff, and it clattered to the floor. Jasmine commanded the wind to blow it across the room, to roll it away from him.

But he didn't look frightened.

Why didn't he look frightened?

"You think I'm weak," he said.

"Your time is up, Fadel. It's over," I said.

"I always have more tricks up my sleeve," he smirked.

How I hated that sadistic smirk. With rage, I attempted to blast him with a large fireball, but at the very last second, he dodged it. Regardless, I knew he stood at the end of the line. He was about to give in. I could feel it.

The staff would be ours.

"Penny, grab the staff!" Sebastian yelled.

But as she lunged for it, Fadel did too. He and Penny grasped it at the exact same time. Suddenly, sparks flew, and a loud zapping noise rang out across the lobby. Penny screamed and fell to the floor, writhing in pain.

The staff had electrocuted her.

"I told you I had more tricks up my sleeve," Fadel laughed maniacally.

The world slowed down.

I couldn't breathe. Penny screamed in pain, but I could only hear dull ringing. Theo ran over, dropped to his knees, and pulled her into his arms. Sebastian, armed with a lamp base, rushed in towards Fadel. Jasmine stood frozen, with her hand over her mouth.

Fadel smiled and teleported across the room. He taunted us popping up in a new place every second or so. Sebastian continued to rush at him, fighting the best he could. I knew he needed my help.

But my mind wasn't in the fight now. I was standing in the eye of the hurricane, and my heart stopped. My mind could only focus on one thing … the electrocution.

Molly and James.

He had taken Molly Meadows' power. It was over—he had it. He no longer needed them. And they were too young to be weapons for him. That must mean …

They could be dead. Those two, young, innocent children. They could be dead. And it was all our fault. We didn't get there fast enough to save them. We let them die.

A pain moved through my body, one stronger than I'd felt before. An overwhelming wave of immense sadness poured over me. I couldn't control it. I couldn't keep it bottled up. In the midst of the battle, at the peak of the fight, I screamed in sorrow and fell to my knees.

And in that moment, the ground around my body froze into a sheet of ice.

CHAPTER THIRTY-NINE

When I snapped out of it, I could see Sebastian and Jasmine staring at me. They were stunned. I turned to see Theo hugging Penny's unconscious body. I looked down and saw the ice under my body.

How did this happen?

I looked around again and saw that Fadel was gone. He had used the moment to escape.

"You have no idea how powerful you are," Fadel had told me. I finally understood what he meant. And then I gasped. I remembered.

I remembered everything…

MAY 5, 2019

Every once in a while, Fadel put us through random testing. These were opportunities for him to examine our skills—to see how they evolved and how they improved.

I couldn't believe I had been at Helping Hearts for two years. Time really flew by. My skills grew so much since the day I arrived. At first, I could make a flame or two at a time, which was only possible with intense concentration. Now, it came naturally. I produced little flames with almost no effort, fireballs of all sizes, and something I called "the heat wave," which was essentially a large blast of fire that I could throw and spray. It was very dangerous and absolutely fantastic.

Things had also changed around Helping Hearts over the last two years. Maggie, Alexandra, and I had grown closer, spending practically all of our time together when we weren't training.

But that was only because Eric left around Christmas. Life felt so different with Eric gone. No one ever left Helping Hearts, so it came as a shock to us when he departed. I leaned on my friendship with Maggie and Alexandra to cover the pain. I cried for days.

On a happier note, Maggie gained more and more speed, which hardly seemed possible. She was practically invisible while running. It was impressive to say the least. And Alexandra was always there to support us and cheer us on as we trained.

I hadn't had female friends since high school. I wondered how Kimmy was doing these days. I wondered if she ever thought of me and how I disappeared after college. I should have written to her, but I never did. In essence, I dropped off the face of the earth.

My focus had shifted to Helping Hearts, to Dr. Fadel, and to testing. Dr. Fadel had tested Maggie again a few days earlier, so I knew it was only a matter of time before I was called in as well.

When it was my turn, I made my way down to his office, as usual. But this time, when I came into the room, something felt different. Anxiety hung in the air. I suddenly felt on edge.

"Please, Miss Williams, come in."

The doctor looked frazzled, like he had lost sleep for days. He obviously wasn't in a good mood.

"Is everything ok, doctor?" I asked, hesitantly walking up on the testing platform.

He snapped out of his daze.

"Yes, yes of course. Now just be quiet for a moment while I program the computers."

I shut my mouth and looked around the room. There seemed to be more wires than ever. And his staff stood plugged into its stand. That was unusual. He hadn't hooked me up to machines or wires in months. And he certainly never had his staff plugged in while testing. Not since I passed my final training test years ago. But there it stood, hooked to wires and pulsing with a strange, blue glow.

I knew better than to ask about it. The doctor silently came over and began strapping the wired cuffs on my arms, as he did two years ago. "Now Miss Williams," he said, going back to his screen, "we are going to do things a bit differently today. I've been picking up on a few ... signs ... in the last couple of weeks, and I would like to test my theories. If you don't mind."

"Not at all," I said, stretching my arms a little.

"Fantastic. Today, instead of anger, I want you to focus on a different emotion entirely. Could you do that for me?"

I hesitated. "Yes, of course. Which emotion?"

"Sadness. Can you do that? Can you focus on a deep sorrow?"

"Yes, I can. But it won't produce fire. I can only get fire when I—"

"I know," he said, cutting me off. "I don't *want* you to produce fire right now. I want to see what happens when you focus on sadness. I need you to focus on sorrow like you focus on anger."

He clicked a few things, checked a few wires, and then started the machine. It hummed, and the wristbands tingled.

"Alright Miss Williams, whenever you're ready, please begin."

My mind raced. So did my heart. I didn't know what to focus on. What made me sad? Nothing immediately came to mind.

"I need you to *focus*, Miss Williams." He did not sound happy.

"I'm trying," I said, panicking. My heart pounded. What would happen if I failed?

"Try harder. Focus."

I closed my eyes and tried to think. *What could possibly make me sad enough?*

My family? I hadn't seen or spoken to my family in two years. For all I knew, they could have moved away. Or forgotten about me. For all they knew, I could be dead. Did they still think about me? Did they still love me? Would I ever see them again? These thoughts weren't doing anything. My hands, my body felt no different.

"Try harder, Miss Williams. This is not good enough. I demand that you think harder. Truly feel the pain. Let it spill over you."

Was my sister ok? She must be in college now. I wondered where she chose to go. I wondered if she followed in my footsteps. Does she miss me?

I started to get scared, but not the same scared as when Fadel got mad at me or when I was alone on the streets at night. It was a sad type of scared. I started to tear up a little.

"Good, good. Keep going; dig deeper."

Did she hate me for leaving her?

Leaving.

I thought of Eric.

Eric left. I didn't know where he was. I wasn't even sure why he left. That night, when he hugged me goodbye, he told me to protect myself. And then he left.

Would I ever see him again?

I started crying. My body shivered. Chills ripped up my spine. Why were all the people I loved so far away? Why did I come here? Should I go home?

I felt alone. Truly alone. I sobbed in excruciating pain and sadness.

Finally, Dr. Fadel got what he wanted. I moved my hands to my sides and tiny icicles clinked and shattered on the floor. I opened my eyes, and tears covered my face; when I tried to wipe them away, they immediately froze on my cheeks.

"What?" I whispered. "What did you do to me?"

"I didn't do anything, Miss Williams," the doctor said, fiddling with the machine.

"You have more in those hands than we originally thought," he said. He now moved over and checked his staff. Pulling it from the stand, he waved it around and struck the ground with the base. Nothing happened. He cursed and ran his hands through his hair.

"Miss Williams, I will need you back here for testing again next week. And by then, you must have this skill up to the same level as your fire skill. Do you understand?"

He was becoming more furious with each heavy breath. I hadn't seen him like this before.

"You will go through another final test, and you are expected to pass. Is that clear?"

I nodded, shocked, and let myself out. After I closed the door, I could hear something bang and then shatter. Dr. Fadel was in a rage. Alexandra found me in the hallway. "Hey, Bee! How are you? How did it go?"

For once, I felt void of emotion. Too many thoughts had merged to think of anything specific.

"I don't know," I replied.

"Did the test go ok?"

"No, I don't think it did. He was very angry."

"Oh no," she said, wrapping her arm around me. "But it usually goes so well! You have your skills mastered!"

"This time was different."

"You're so cold," she said, touching my arms with her warm hands. "Are you alright? Do you want to talk about it?"

I didn't want to talk about it. I didn't want to tell her about my other skills. I didn't want anyone to know.

I gave her a hug goodbye and walked home.

Two days later, I sat on the couch in my apartment with Maggie on one side and Alexandra on the other. I still hadn't told them about my new skills. I didn't plan to tell them, either. "I don't think this place is exactly what we think it is," I explained.

The last forty-eight hours had been emotional. I ran through the last two years in my mind, over and over again. I tried to think through each interaction, each test, each battle. It was so confusing, but at the same time, it was revealing. It wasn't what I had originally thought. Or what I had hoped.

My friends, however, didn't believe me when I insisted something was wrong.

"Bee," Maggie said, "we're helping so many people! We are doing a service for the city! Dr. Fadel is a good man."

"I don't know about that." I couldn't stop thinking about his anger, the way he obsessed over any new skill that came along. I had known for quite a while that he was collecting our skills in that staff. We had all known that. But none of us thought very much about what he was doing with them.

"Why do you think he collects our skills in his staff?" I asked my friends.

"I think he wants to use it as a testing device. It collects only when we hit a peak in our skills, so I think that's his way of determining whether we're performing at our best," Maggie replied.

"That's what he wants you to think. But it's not even logical! If that were true, why wouldn't he just test it with his computer? I think there's another reason. He's collecting them because he wants all of our skills."

Maggie shifted uncomfortably in her seat. "Well if that were the case, which it's not, why would he need us?" she asked. "If he wanted our skills, why does he not take them and dispose of us?"

My stomach churned. I didn't like the direction this conversation was headed.

"What if he thinks we're disposable? He can put us on the front lines because it causes him no harm?"

"Bianca! You're making him sound evil! That's very unkind," Alexandra said.

"I don't believe this operation is what I thought it was earlier. It's been on my mind for a while, but I think I understand more now."

"Bee," Alexandra said, taking my hand. "You're tired and stressed. You've been overwhelmed since you failed your last test, but you'll retest next week and you'll pass. And then everything will be ok, I promise."

"No, I mean it," I said, letting go of her hand, "I don't think what we're doing is right. I don't think we know what Dr. Fadel is doing here. None of it adds up! Think about it: the staff, the testing, the desire to destroy actual human lives just because they're deemed 'bad' by one man."

"Bianca, you need to stop this. You're overly tired. That's all." She smiled a smile of concern and stood up. "For now," she continued, "you need sleep."

She and Maggie made their way to the door, and I hugged each of them and said goodbye. They didn't know it then, but this would be the last time they would ever see me.

It hurt my heart to do it, but I knew what needed to happen. After they left, I quickly put as many things as possible into my backpack including a few items of clothing and my toiletries. I changed into my Helping Hearts wet suit-like uniform for maximum comfort and flexibility. I also packed my fanny pack, my wallet, and a few snacks, just in case. On my way out the door, I heard the landline ring. It didn't matter who was calling. I wasn't going to pick up. Ignoring the incessant ringing, I shut and locked the door behind me.

Where would I go?

I had no destination in mind. All I knew was that I needed to get away. I searched my pockets for my car keys, but realized that Dr. Fadel had my car at the office. I cursed. What a stupid rule, to have to leave vehicles there.

Probably so we couldn't run away.

My heart rate increased as my fears were once again confirmed. I left the building and started on foot in the direction of the airport. I wouldn't take a taxi. Couldn't risk being identified. Once at the airport, I could try to get a flight out west.

Yes, that made sense. I would find Eric. Wherever he was, I would find him and tell him he was right. Eric had told me that he was traveling west. He was originally from Utah, so maybe that's where he was going. I would catch a flight to Salt Lake and call him from a pay phone. I had both cash and a credit card in my wallet, so getting a flight would be no problem. I could do this.

After an hour of walking, I remained a good ways from the airport.

I was getting tired and starting to doubt my plan, but I didn't have much time to think about it.

Suddenly, I heard a piercing scream behind me. Then a bang and an explosion. Terrified, I started to run.

The noise only got louder, and closer. I kept running in full panic.

He was coming after me.

CHAPTER FORTY

"I remember *everything*," I said again. My pulse quickened, and my head filled with pressure. I felt dizzy, and I leaned on my arms, trying to control my breathing. My head was being blasted from all sides with memories of my past.

"Absolutely *everything*?" Sebastian came over and helped me up. I nodded. It all flooded back, every minute from the day I left home until now.

"Ok, let's get you home. You should talk to Alexandra about all of this. For now, we need to get Penny somewhere safe."

I nodded again and Sebastian walked me towards the van. Theo carried Penny in his arms, whispering to her as he walked. When he didn't think anyone was looking, I saw him gently kiss the top of her head.

When we got home, Alexandra let us in and quickly escorted Theo inside to put Penny in bed.

"She should be fine; she has a steady pulse. I think we should give it some time," Jasmine said, coming downstairs to join Sebastian and me on the couch. Alexandra followed her.

"I wanted to give Theo some alone time with her," Jasmine continued.

"That's kind of you," I said.

We sat in silence for a moment. We had already told Alexandra what happened, including the parts about electrocution and ice. She still seemed surprised by all of it. I could also tell that she wasn't too happy with me.

"Why didn't you tell us?" she asked. "Or did everyone know except me?"

"No," I said, "No one knew, not even me. I didn't know until it happened. Everything came back to me at once. I don't think I knew about it long before I lost my memory."

"But you knew while you were still at Helping Hearts?"

I sighed. There was no way to avoid conflict now.

"Yes, briefly. I figured it out during my final test."

"So why didn't you tell me back when we were in your apartment? The night you left, you never told me why."

"I guess I didn't want anyone to know. I didn't want him to find me, so I couldn't risk anyone telling him."

"So you didn't trust me?"

"No, that's not it. It's more that I had seen someone else leave without telling anyone why. And it worked. They got away. So I guess I wanted to do the same because I wanted the same result."

"But Eric *did* tell you he was leaving."

Alexandra's eyes welled up with tears. She bit her lip, and Sebastian cut in, "Who is this Eric?"

My heart skipped a beat. I filled him in on everything I could remember. At least, as much as I was willing to share.

"Eric was another of Fadel's goons, a teleporter."

"Wait," Jasmine asked, "was this the same teleporter that you faced in the school a while back?"

"No, actually," I replied, thinking back. "I think that was probably Fadel's replacement for Eric. Funny that he found another person with the same powers. I didn't think there were duplicates. But apparently, there are. Anyway, Eric left Fadel last December."

"And you knew he planned to leave," Alexandra said again.

"Yes," I said, thinking back to that night—the night whose memory first caused my cold powers to appear.

"But I didn't know exactly why," I said. "He wouldn't tell me where he was going. He just said that he was leaving—heading west, but I didn't know where—and he wanted me to cover his tracks, so Fadel wouldn't worry or go after him. And I did."

The thought of that night brought tears to my eyes again. I shivered.

"I wish you had told me," Alexandra said, softly.

"I know, I'm sorry."

I felt bad that I had hurt her since she hadn't done anything to deserve it, at least not intentionally. Luckily, I knew Alexandra wasn't one to hold grudges. She could remain hurt, but not mad. I knew it would still be painful for a while, but she wouldn't hold it against me forever.

"It's ok," she said. "We're together now. And we're both finally free."

"We're all free," Sebastian said. "We all got out safely today."

My heart leapt back to the hotel, to the Meadows kids.

"Sebastian, what about Molly and James? What do we do about them? Now that they might be—"

"We don't change a thing. We treat it like we did before. We will find them and rescue them."

"And if they really are dead?" The dreaded words finally tumbled out of my mouth.

"Then we'll worry about it when we get there. For now, we need to find a way to get them back."

"I wish you had your car. Then we could at least split up and try to find them that way," Jasmine said.

"Wait," Sebastian said. "The car! Bianca, is there any way you can remember your plate number?"

I laughed, "For real? No, I can't remember that!"

Alexandra smiled.

"But I can."

"You have my plate memorized? What are you, a psychopath?"

"No," she said, "but if I can tell you where he parked it at the hotel, we can try to get security cam footage."

I hugged her. "Alexandra, you're amazing!"

Inwardly, I hoped this would ease the tension between us. I wanted my friend to trust me again.

"It's settled then; first thing in the morning, we go to the hotel and ask them to check the footage," Sebastian said. "We then take that information to the police and see if they can check traffic cams and such to locate the vehicle. That may be our ticket to finding Fadel."

We all agreed and the girls went up to bed. Alexandra would sleep in my bed, and I would take the couch. It only felt right to rotate. And it did have its perks. For instance, this allowed Sebastian and me to remain behind on the couch, cuddling.

"You know we're going to need a bigger house if we keep rescuing women and bringing them back here," he said. I laughed and cozied up to him.

"Yeah, but you like some of the women you rescue. Especially one in particular."

"That's true," he said, leaning down and kissing me gently. I reached up to hold his face. His hands slid down around my waist and rested gently on my sides. I continued to kiss him. I moved my body closer to his.

Suddenly, we heard Theo coming down the stairs. We jumped and pulled apart as he rounded the corner, looked at us, and smirked.

"Please, don't let me interrupt your little make out."

"Too late," I muttered under my breath. Unfortunately, he heard me.

"Yeah, uh huh, anyway I am going to bed. Just left Penny with the girls."

"How is she doing?" I asked.

"The same. Hoping she wakes up in the morning. I'm worried about her."

"We are too. Get some rest. We're headed to bed in a minute," Sebastian said.

"Sounds good," Theo replied. "Goodnight, you lovebirds."

He went into his room and closed the door.

"A bigger house could mean more privacy," Sebastian whispered.

"Once we take down Fadel, finding a bigger house will be my first priority," I whispered back.

"Deal," he said and laughed.

We sat quietly for a moment. I cuddled up against Sebastian again, back the way we were before Theo interrupted. I looked up and smiled at him, and he smiled back. He leaned down and planted a kiss on my cheek. Slowly, he moved his kisses from my cheek to my lips. I had chills. Holding him tight, I breathed in his cologne, and the scent made me swoon.

"Bianca," he whispered in my ear between kisses, "I'm falling for you."

I moved my hands to his chin and pulled a little to make his lips meet mine. He was my everything in this moment. Nothing else mattered. There were no villains, no dangers, no worries. We weren't Victory supers. We were two normal people, falling in love.

CHAPTER FORTY-ONE

The next morning we arrived at the hotel by 8:00 a.m., and Jasmine "persuaded" the concierge to introduce us to the security officer. She then "persuaded" the officer to show us parking garage footage from the day Fadel left. The footage was choppy and silent, as expected, but clear enough to give us our answer.

Onto the screen walked Fadel, carrying his staff; the speedy girl—whom I now realized was actually Margaret Andrews, a former friend and colleague—Zeke, and the teleporter from the school. Zeke carried the two Meadows kids, one under each arm. They kicked and hit him, but he didn't flinch.

The party crossed the screen and unlocked a sedan. The teleporter popped open the trunk, and Zeke threw the Meadows kids in. Zeke then got into the driver's seat; Fadel took the passenger seat, and the other two got in the back. As they pulled out, I saw the plate.

"Freeze it," I said, and the security officer stopped the footage. I scribbled down the plate number, SQH 4829.

"Great," I answered, turning to the officer. "That's all we need. Thank you so much."

On the way to the police station, we picked up a weak but recovering Penny from the house. She felt much better in the morning. Physically exhausted but mentally and emotionally sharp, as always.

I proceeded to fill my friends in on everything I could remember about Fadel's operation, past and present. "Ok, so Margaret Andrews used to be one of my best friends. She was the speedy one in the bank. It's really unfortunate; that day she definitely seemed a lot crueler than I remembered, especially towards me."

"Yes," Alexandra replied from the passenger seat. "She was quite unhappy when you left. You know Maggie takes things quite personally. She probably saw that day in the bank as an opportunity to take her bottled-up anger out on you."

"Scary how fast she turned. I don't like the way she talked to us. She thinks we are the villains, doesn't she?"

Alexandra closed her eyes and leaned back into her seat.

"Yeah. They all do."

"Well, we will have to prove them wrong," Theo said, taking a hand off the wheel to pat Alexandra's shoulder.

"So who else do you have dirt on?" Jasmine asked from the back row.

"That's all I have. Zeke and I barely overlapped, and the teleporter showed up after I left. As I said before, Fadel used to have a different teleporter. Interesting that he even still wanted one, since he definitely sucked power from Eric. Maybe he never got it at its peak?"

"I think you're right. If my memory serves me correctly, I think that Eric only gave him the ability to teleport objects, not himself. I think Fadel pushed Eric pretty hard in order to get more from him, but he never succeeded. I think that's why he got Lawrence. Lawrence, for reference, is the new guy. Lawrence Garrison. I never got to know him well. He was quite closed off. I knew Zeke a little bit more since I recruited him."

"Anything worth reporting on Zeke?" Penny asked.

"Not much more than you already know. He's a strong guy, practically a brick wall. But I'll be honest; he's not a brick wall emotionally. He struggled when he first arrived. He talked to me a lot about his little sister and his parents. He really missed them. I'm not quite sure if he's past the emotions yet."

"Great," Jasmine said. "Emotionally weak is good for us. I can definitely work with that."

"Of the three of them, I think Zeke's the most likely to be persuaded. The only reason he came out to Victory at all was because Fadel had me tell him that anyone with skills that didn't join the cause was *against* the cause. And if they're against the cause, well, then they and all their loved ones become vulnerable. He came on board to protect his family. He's a really good guy—his heart is in the right place."

"So hopefully we get the chance to get him out of here and back to his family. Let's get him home," Sebastian said.

Alexandra nodded.

"Speaking of going home …" she said. "I've been thinking a lot about it." I knew what she was going to say before she even said it.

"You want to go home."

"Only when this is all over, when the Meadows kids are safe. But as much as I want to help you all, I need to go home. I'm not a superhero like you all. I'm someone who mistakenly got tangled up in all of this. I think I need to go home and start my new life, my *free* life."

"We will get you home, Alexandra, I promise," I said.

"You've already done such a service to us, to your friends, and to Victory," Sebastian said. "Once we are in the clear, when Molly and

James are safe, we will make sure you get home too."

"Thank you," Alexandra said. I could hear her sniff. I knew she had tears in her eyes.

Jasmine laughed a little. "Anyone else want us to take them home while we're at it? Make it a road trip?"

None of us replied. I think it had probably occurred to all of us at one time or another. We probably all longed for home to some extent. All of us except Sebastian, that is. Sebastian longed for a home that no longer existed. And so long as he didn't have a place to revisit, I knew that none of us would leave him alone.

Penny broke the silence. "My family is right here. And this family wouldn't be complete without all of us," she said, smiling.

"Agreed," Theo said. "We all miss our families, but we also have a duty. We have skills, blessings that other people don't have. It is our duty to use our skills for the good of those around us."

"Here, here," we all replied as Theo pulled up in front of the police station.

The police looked concerned to see us. It wasn't often that we showed up on their turf, asking for help. It was usually the other way around.

"Mr. Martin," the sheriff said, shaking Theo's hand. "Surprised to see you all here. What's going on?"

"We need your help tracking down our special friend."

"You know we've tried tracking him before. We've done searches of every location we can think of in the city. He just disappears, never leaves a trail."

"No, this time we need to track a plate. It's his," Theo replied.

"Well, it's actually Bianca's, but he stole it from her, and now we need to know where it is. If we've got the car, we've got him."

"And you're sure he still has this vehicle? How do you know he didn't abandon it somewhere and continue on without it?"

"We don't know for sure, but we at least want to track the plate and see where the car is," Sebastian said. "It's our best guess, if we want to find him."

"Alright, well if you leave us the plate number, we can do a search on it and get back to you in a few days." The sheriff extended his hand to me, wanting the paper with the plate number on it.

"No," I said, pulling the paper to my chest.

"No?" The sheriff crossed his arms.

"No, we need this information now. Right now," I replied.

"Sir, it's about the Meadows kids," Penny said. "We have reason to believe that their lives are in danger."

"Well we are really busy here, and we already have our best people on the case. And, no, I don't mean you all. We have a search team out right now. If you leave the number with us, we can get back to you tomorrow."

"Sir I don't mean to be rude, and I certainly don't mean to be morbid, but they may be dead by tomorrow," I said. "So we won't be leaving until you help us find this car. Right now."

The officer sighed and told us to follow him to the back office.

"This is Officer Thompson," the sheriff said, gesturing to a tall, dark-haired man at the desk. "Officer Thompson can help you run a search on the plate. James, just run a camera search. See if there are any hits in the city or the surrounding areas. Check Madison County as well if you can."

The sheriff left the room, and I handed Officer Thompson the number.

"It's a blue sedan. We know it left the parking garage at the Hotel Victory on the third of September. After that, we have no idea."

He typed the number into his system and hit *Enter*. A few results came up. "We have some hits," he said, clicking on the first one. "This one is from the third of September, as you said. It's parking garage footage and a few stoplight hits. Let me track which lights those were."

He began scribbling down intersection names: Maple and Fourth; Jefferson and Seventh; Beckworth Ave, and Madison Highway. He was heading towards Beckworth campus.

"Our last hit on that date was a traffic light on Beckworth Avenue. There's only one more date with hits, and that was four days later. We caught him once outside the Beckworth Library on Lionsdale Road, coming from the west and then going back the other way an hour later. We don't have anything after that."

"What's to the west of the library?" I asked. "Officer, could you pull up a map?"

The officer pulled up a city map in another tab. He traced his finger from the library westward. "We know he didn't turn at all from the county line to the library as we don't have any traffic camera hits."

"How far is it down Lionsdale from the county line to the library?" Jasmine asked, leaning forward to look at the screen.

"Not far at all, maybe only a mile and a half? The campus is on the west side of the county already."

"This is really useful, Officer," Sebastian said. "I think what we need to do is drive or walk down Lionsdale from the county line to the library and see what we can find. We know he's on that road somewhere since he drove from the west end and back. He was going out and then coming home."

"And did you notice," Theo said, pointing to the screen, "Lionsdale is only three streets from our house."

"Oh my gosh," Penny replied. "He's been hiding under our noses this entire time."

CHAPTER FORTY-TWO

W e drove up and down Lionsdale Road seven or eight times, trying to determine which house Fadel could possibly be hiding in. Lionsdale Road was an extension of our residential area; the tiny houses that lined the street were not much bigger than ours. Fadel's operations had really run the gamut when it came to headquarters locations. At least in my time, they had been in a high-rise office space, a hotel penthouse, and now a tiny house in the middle of nowhere.

The latest location was the perfect hiding spot. Never once did it cross our minds that Fadel could be in a house, just like us. I found it shocking that he had been so close to us for so long, that he could have discovered our location by simply taking a walk around the block. It was frightening to know how unsafe we actually were, even in the comfort of our home! That was the most shocking discovery of all. We'd been three streets from disaster for a while, and we didn't even know it.

"It makes me consider moving; that's for sure," Theo said as he pulled off St. John's Lane onto Lionsdale for the ninth time that day.

"I still don't know what we are looking for," Jasmine said. She pressed her forehead against the window and let her breath fog up the glass. "Are we seriously hoping he *happens* to emerge as we drive by so that we can pin down the exact location? Because otherwise, I'm not sure how we will be able to spot him."

"Well first of all," Sebastian said, "we need to find a house with a garage. We know he wouldn't risk leaving Bianca's car out in the open. So obviously he's got it hidden. Second, I'm looking for a house with closed blinds, probably dark."

"I'm also assuming it will be a house with a basement," Alexandra chipped in. "Because in order to load his staff with powers, which we know he has, he needs his fancy platform, his computers, and the stand for his staff. It's pretty big. What I'm not seeing is a house big enough to fit the darn thing."

We sat in silence for a few moments, looking at each house as Theo drove. I thought back to my time at Helping Hearts and the training days. I closed my eyes, imagining the hum of the machines as they roared to life. I remembered the wires covering the floors, the computers, and the padded walls. I couldn't imagine all of that in one of these little houses.

"Doesn't that machine require a lot of energy? I feel like these houses couldn't handle the amount of power to run it. Plus, anyone exhibiting powers like we all have would absolutely destroy the inside of a house that small. Think about it. We go to the gym because we need space. Not to mention padding. Combine that with his energy usage, and I don't think he's using the house, not even a basement. I think he's living in the house but working elsewhere."

Sebastian replied, "From what we gathered at the police station, we know he's only going out for short errands. Even if he's not doing it in the house, he must be doing it on the property."

I looked at the house coming up on our left. It was a small, blue, two-story with white shutters and dark curtains in the windows. The curtains were closed, despite it being an unusually warm and sunny fall day. Every other house we passed had open windows. Not only that. The driveway wrapped around behind the house. Back there, I could see part of what looked to be a car barn.

"Wait, Theo," I said, jumping to life and leaning forward to grab the shoulders of his seat. "Theo, pull over. It's going to be in a car barn. It's going to be in a car barn behind a house. It will be isolated from the road in its own building, like this on our left."

Theo slowly pulled over, and we all looked at the house on the left.

"Now I don't know if it's this one for sure, but it's gotta be one like this. And this is the only one I've seen with the driveway wrapped around back."

"But wouldn't he be using the barn for the car?" Penny asked. "Didn't we already determine that he's probably hiding the car?"

"But that's just it," I said, putting the pieces together. "That's why this house makes sense. Everything behind the house is hidden from the road. He doesn't have to put the car inside if it's not visible to drivers. I would bet anything that my car is behind the house."

"So what do we do now?" Jasmine asked. "We can't go in while he's there."

"No," I said. "I want to see if my car is out back. And if it is, I want to stake out the house. It might be our only opportunity to see if the Meadows kids are alive."

"She's right," Theo replied. "I think that one of us should try to get around to the back of the house to confirm we have the right place. Then I think we wait until he leaves to get inside. We need to find those kids."

"I'll get out and look," Alexandra said. "I'm the one who saw the car last, so I will know for sure if it's the right one."

We all agreed and Sebastian handed Alexandra his coat. Theo said he had a baseball cap in the trunk, and Jasmine dug it out. Alexandra put on her half-hearted disguise and slipped out of the van. We watched her walk down the street past the house, cutting a sharp left into the backyard of the neighboring one and disappearing behind it.

The next two or three minutes were agony.

Finally, she came around the other side, having completed a big loop. As she approached the van, she nodded. "I went back and snuck behind the barn. When I could finally get a good look at the back of the house, I saw it. Your car is there, Bianca. He's here."

"Great work, Alexandra," Sebastian said. "Now we need to wait until he decides to leave again."

"Not to be a downer, but what if it takes hours?" Jasmine asked. She frowned and leaned back in her seat. "What if it's days? We can't sit in the van for days on end. Besides, if his goons are home when we try to go in, Alexandra is unsafe. We at least need to get her home."

"It would be good to have a solid plan," Sebastian mused, looking through the window at the house again.

"Let's go home, reset, and come back tonight with a game plan. Alexandra can stay at home, and the rest of us can come back here."

While we were desperate to get the kids back as quickly as possible, we knew we needed a plan of action. Therefore, we all assented and Theo started the van.

CHAPTER FORTY-THREE

DECEMBER 20, 2018

"Bee, I need to tell you something."

Eric and I spent the evening walking around Helping Hearts' farm property. I told him it was too cold to do such a thing, but he insisted. He wrapped his scarf around my neck a few times and said, "There, now you're warm enough." And so we walked.

"What is it?"

Eric hadn't been acting like himself recently. He seemed quieter and jumpier. Not only that; he'd been failing his training sessions. Dr. Fadel lashed out at him with an unusual rage every day. He couldn't understand why Eric's powers were weakening. But I didn't think they had weakened at all. I thought Eric intentionally failed his tests.

"I'm leaving," Eric said.

I froze in place, and my hand shot up to my mouth. I was at a loss for words. No. No, he couldn't leave. Eric. He was talented; he was powerful. He was my best friend. He was …

"Eric, no," I said, my eyes filling with tears.

He looked back at me and sighed, "Yes."

"Please, no—you can't leave me."

"I have to."

"*Where* are you going?"

"I can't tell you that."

"Eric, please tell me why you're doing this to me. Have I done something wrong?"

His face turned away. He looked so dejected.

"No, of course not. You've done nothing wrong. I just need to go."

"Why then?" I sniffed. I put my head down so he couldn't see how hard I cried. I let the tears flow.

I was in hysterics. The tears fell, and my face stung as they froze on my cheeks. Eric pulled me into his chest and held me there.

"I have to. Something … something isn't right here, and I need to leave. I can't be here anymore."

"What do you mean?"

"I don't know how to explain it, but something doesn't feel right. It hasn't felt right for a while. I don't think I should be here."

I wanted to know what wasn't right. I wanted to understand what brought him to this decision. But mostly, I wanted to know how he could possibly leave me.

"I don't want you to go," I cried.

"I know," he said, stroking my hair. "But I need to. You need to trust me. I have to go."

"Take me with you," I gasped, pulling myself closer to him. I couldn't let him go. There was no way on earth I could let him leave me.

"No, Bianca. You need to stay here. If we both leave, he'll know something is wrong. No, I need you to stay here. I need you to be safe."

"No, I'm safe when I'm with you. Wherever that is! Don't you understand? We can protect each other from the supers! Together we can take them down and protect our world. Don't you want that?" I wiped my tears and looked up at him. "Don't you want to protect innocent people with me?" I asked.

"Bianca, you're the innocent person I want to protect. That's why you have to stay here. Where I'm going isn't safe."

"Where could you possibly be going that I can't come? Where are you going that is so dangerous you have to face it alone?"

My initially soft-spoken pleas turned to thunderous cries of pain and anger. This entire conversation infuriated me.

"Bianca, some people need protection. The people of Victory have protectors, but there are people out there who don't."

"Then let that be other peoples' problems! We have a job here! *You* have a job here!"

"That's the thing, Bee. I don't. What we are doing ... it's not the good we think it is. And to do good, I need to go. I can't be here any longer because I can't be with *him*."

"Dr. Fadel?"

"Yes, Fadel. I need to get away from him."

I was stunned. What could the doctor possibly have done to make Eric want to leave so badly?

"Has he hurt you?" I said in a hushed tone, looking him up and down.

"No, not physically," he replied. "But what he's doing isn't good. I can't say too much because I want you to be safe, but believe me when I say I need to go."

"Then I'm coming. End of story."

"Trust me when I say I need you to stay."

"That's the problem, Eric, you want me to trust you, but trusting you means being abandoned. Abandoned by the person I love most!

Do you not understand that?"

I was almost winded, still in shock from what was happening. Everything was boiling over. There was no going back now.

"Eric, I'm in love with you, and now that I have finally found the guts to say it back, you say you're leaving me forever. You told me you loved me. You call this love?"

"Bianca, it's because I love you that I need you to stay here. When Fadel discovers I'm gone, he's going to send someone after me, to hunt me down. I assure you, if you left with me, he would follow us—himself—because he can't lose you right now. I can't risk your safety like that."

"But he's not dangerous!"

"Bianca, I need you to trust me," he said, grabbing my hands. "I'm going to leave, and I need you to cover my trail."

"No. No way," I snapped, pulling my hands away. He grabbed them back.

"Bianca, I need you to cover for me. I need you to make sure he never finds me. You need to tell him that I've been spiraling for weeks now, talking about warmer weather. Tell him I've been dreaming about an island. I need you to make him think I went south, but I'm actually going west. Do you understand? I need you to make sure they can't find me when I leave."

Tears rolled down my cheeks again.

"But what about me?" I felt selfish saying it, but my selfishness seemed justified.

"I want you to come and find me. But only after the doctor has finished his work with you. I need to make sure that he no longer relies on you. Only then will you be able to slip away without him following. Do you understand?"

I nodded.

"How will I find you?"

"You'll know," he smiled. "I'm heading west, and I'm going to help some particular people. I'm going to make sure he never does to them what he's doing to the people of Victory. I know you don't understand what that means right now, but you will, I promise. You have a heart of gold, Bianca. Soon you'll understand everything because with your capacity to love, you're bound to see things the right way. And when you do and Fadel has finished his tests, you can come find me. Ok?"

I sat in silence for a moment, unsure what to say in return. Eric hung onto my silence, waiting desperately for my reply. No matter how badly I wanted to say *no*, I knew I couldn't.

"Ok."

He wiped a frozen tear from my cheek and pulled me into his arms. With his soft, gentle hand, he tilted my face up towards his, giving me the longest, most soul-crushing kiss I'd ever had. He pulled away, smiled at me, and whispered softly.

"I love you, Bianca."

And then he was gone. He had teleported away. I fell on my knees, crying icy tears into my shaking hands.

Later that week, Dr. Fadel asked me if I had seen Eric recently. I put on a brave face, acted as though I didn't know he had left, and told him that Eric had been dreaming of an island...

CHAPTER FORTY-FOUR

I heard my car start. A few days earlier, I didn't even know I had a car, but now, hearing its engine rev, I instinctively knew that it was my car.

"He's leaving," I said and we all ducked down below the dashboard. My heart pounded in my throat.

"I'm trying to see if there's anyone else inside," Penny said.

We sat in silence as the car pulled out and turned left onto Lionsdale Road. The headlights lit up the inside of the van, and we froze in place. My heart kept pounding. After a few seconds, the sound of the engine was gone, and we once again sat in darkness.

"He was alone," Penny said. "I'm positive."

"Alright guys," Sebastian finally said, sitting up and pulling his sweatshirt hood over his head. "It's time to go. You all know the plan. We're going around the right side of the house, along the back wall. Then, Jasmine, Bianca, and I will continue to the right side of the car barn. If what Alexandra said was correct, there should be a door on the left side. Bianca will try to melt the handle, and we will enter. Meanwhile, Penny and Theo will enter the house through the back door."

"Have we thought at all about cameras?" Jasmine asked. "Or motion sensors?"

"Good question," Theo replied. "Alexandra didn't see any, but we should still move carefully and look ahead. And if there are cameras, they'd likely be too high up for Jasmine to manipulate without ending up on the footage herself. If we can't avoid them and if we can't control them, we might as well keep moving with purpose. Besides, if he has cameras, Alexandra is already on tape. Might as well embrace it by finding the kids and getting out of there unscathed. Dividing and conquering should help us get in and out a lot quicker."

Sebastian nodded and said, "Agreed, forget the cameras. We move quickly. Get in; get out. Our primary mission is to find the Meadows kids."

I saw one major flaw in Sebastian's logic, but I didn't say anything. I worried that it was too late for the children. My biggest fear was finding that they *were* in there, but that they were no longer alive. I didn't know what we would do if we found them dead. We made our way across the lawn and around to the back of the house. I could see the spot where my car had been—the dry oval in the wet pavement.

"Ok, I don't see any cameras. Around here to the left," Sebastian whispered, waving us onward.

When we reached the back wall of the house, Penny tried a few of the windows. Miraculously, one slid open. Theo boosted her inside, wishing us luck before disappearing himself. We kept moving towards the barn.

Just as Alexandra had said, there was a door on the left side of the car barn. Jasmine tried the handle, but unlike the house window, it didn't budge. I heated up my hands, made a little flame, and melted off the handle.

As it clattered on the ground, I smirked and crowed, "Well, I guess he's gonna know we've been here now."

Jasmine and I stepped back and Sebastian gently pushed the door open. He slipped inside, and we slowly trickled in after him. The inside of the barn was pitch-black. The whole room hummed with the sound of computers. Before Jasmine even hit the light switch, I knew exactly what I was about to see.

As the lights came on, I looked around the room. Instantly, an overwhelming tsunami of emotions flooded back to me. I walked around the machine in silence, examining each wire, each outlet, each rivet.

On this platform, my life had changed forever. I'd discovered a power I wasn't sure I really had. All those years after my school dance, I convinced myself it was a dream. I blocked it out, told myself it wasn't real. I created a false persona: normal, harmless Bianca Williams. I believed I'd never be anything more than that. But then I saw those people on television. And I wondered if it was possible to go back in time and embrace what I had hidden. To let the dream become reality.

This machine allowed me the opportunity to do so. With it, I could finally understand my strength, my power. I became more myself than I had ever been, but it wasn't a good version of myself. In this machine, I became a villain. All because of this hunk of metal.

But it didn't end there. Hooked to these wires, I also happened to give the most dangerous villain imaginable the power to murder innocent people. While I became more myself, so did he. There were consequences to my actions and ambitions, and I would never be able to escape that fact. This machine signified both change and pain. And I wanted it gone.

"I'm going to destroy the machine," I said aloud. I didn't know whether my comment was meant for Jasmine and Sebastian or myself, but it didn't matter. I wanted the machine destroyed.

"Seriously?" Jasmine cursed and ran her hands through her hair, "What are you talking about?"

"You can't do that, Bianca," Sebastian said. "We're going to need that for evidence. The police will need to investigate what's in those computers. They'll need to pull data or something!"

My anger overrode my ability to listen. My head pulsed hot with rage, and my eyes saw red. I lit a fire ball in my left hand and kindled it with my right.

"I don't care. I want it gone. This thing ruined me. I lost every sense of myself in it—I became an evil person."

I grew the fireball slowly, and the little flames wove between my fingers, in and out. I looked Sebastian in the eyes and continued.

"I literally gave him the power to *murder* people. Do you not understand that? I need to see this machine destroyed. I need to see it burn."

Before I could do anything, Jasmine rushed forward, grabbed my wrists and lowered them. It forced me to extinguish my flame.

"Bianca that only feels true right now. But it's not. In fact, it's so very far from the truth. You didn't just give Fadel your powers; you found your own."

"Yes," I said. "And at the core, they're evil. You should know better than anyone, Jasmine! My powers have hurt people, innocent people! In this machine I became someone I shouldn't have."

"Your powers aren't evil. You didn't become evil. You were misguided!" said Jasmine, "You were tricked into thinking what you were doing was right. You were genuinely trying to do the right thing. And look where that led you!"

"That's right, Bianca," Sebastian added, approaching me slowly. "Your time with Fadel was only one leg of the journey. I know it may feel like it sometimes, but it's not like you've lived two different lives. You've lived one single life and been dragged on an adventure. When you're on an adventure, sometimes you go through hell before it's over. You need to traverse mountains and crawl through caverns to finally see clear skies. Your time with Fadel was dark, yes, but it helped you see the light. It was brief, Bianca. It wasn't the full story. You still have so much more to experience."

"But this machine …" I whispered. "This machine is evil. It sucked out our powers and gave them to *him*. I don't want him to do that to anyone else. I don't want people to hurt like I'm hurting."

"We won't let him, Bianca. We will put Fadel behind bars where he won't be able to hurt anyone else."

I breathed heavily, unsure of what to do. I wanted to collapse in tears. I also wanted to blow up the machine.

"Please, Bianca," Sebastian said softly. "You can't destroy the machine. The police need it. We all need it. It's the way that we can find out exactly what he did to you all. With it, we can fix things."

I sighed deeply and fought back tears.

"Ok," I whispered. "Where do we find the Meadows kids?"

Wordlessly, Sebastian crossed the room and pulled me into his arms. He tenderly kissed the top of my head.

"Let's go find them," he whispered.

We pulled apart, and the three of us began looking around the barn. There were two closets, both empty. Other than that, we couldn't find anywhere else to hide children. They must be in the house.

We turned off the lights and shut the door behind us. Despite the handle being broken, it seemed like the best approach was to make things look as "normal" as possible, to buy time upon Fadel's return.

Crossing over to the house, Sebastian helped Jasmine and me through the window, and then he climbed in himself. The window led to a surprisingly bare living room. I could only make out a couch and a small chair against the wall. As we made our way around the corner into the kitchen, I noticed the same thing: The house was practically empty. Fadel lived in a bare-bones structure. Instead of a dining table, there was a plastic folding table and two folding chairs. On the table were a stack of bills and two drivers' licenses: a Florida license for Margaret Andrews and an Alabama license for Zeke Nicholson. I pocketed both. We made our way around the ground floor, finding nothing else of note.

"Penny and Theo must still be upstairs," Jasmine whispered. "Let's hope the minions aren't up there too."

"I wonder what's taking them so long," I whispered. My heart was racing imagining Theo and Penny knocked out with Zeke standing over them.

"Get behind me, and we will move up the stairs slowly," Sebastian said. I knew it wasn't smart to put the powerless guy in front, but I sure didn't want to lead either. Grabbing Jasmine's shoulders, I maneuvered her between Sebastian and me. She shook with terror.

Even after her breakthrough, it was still rare for Jasmine to be on the front lines with us. This kind of mission was not one that she would have ordinarily signed up for. But we needed her. Our team wasn't complete without each member.

We moved slowly and silently, trying to prevent the stairs from creaking. As we got to the top, we looked down the hallway in both directions. There were three doors, one to our right at the end of the hallway and two to our left. Sebastian gestured, and we turned to search the one on the right. Leading the way, Sebastian entered the first room; Jasmine followed him closely. But before I could cross the threshold, I felt a hand grab my shoulder.

"Holy s—" I jumped and whipped around just in time for Theo to clamp his hand over my mouth. My whole body flushed with relief. He pulled his hand back and shushed me.

"Theo, what are you doing?"

"We need to be quiet; the three lesser villains are in the middle bedroom. We took care of them, but they could wake up any second, so we need to move quickly."

"What do you mean you took care of them?"

"Knocked 'em out and threw 'em on the bed. They're bound to wake up soon, so you better follow me quickly." I went into the bedroom Jasmine and Sebastian had entered and whispered to them that we needed to follow Theo.

"You aren't gonna believe this," Theo whispered as he took us back down the hall and opened the door on the far left.

There on the floor sat Penny with a young boy in her arms, and a young girl, about ten years old, lay curled up next to them. Both children looked ragged and sleep-deprived. They were bone-thin. The girl looked up and smiled at me. "Miss Penny says you're the girl with the fire. The one who's here to save us."

CHAPTER FORTY-FIVE

M olly and James. Alive. I almost couldn't believe it.

"That's right, Molly," I said. "We're going to get you out of here, so we need to move. Now."

"James is really tired," the girl said. "The doctor put him on the machine and told him to do the magic."

"He wanted James to demonstrate his powers?"

Molly nodded.

"Yes, he did it to me too. He wanted me to show him my lightning, so I did. Now his stick can make lightning too. But it's James' magic he really wanted to see. He puts James on the machine every day."

"Molly, what's James' magic?"

"He can stop time."

My mouth hung open in confusion and awe.

"What do you mean when you say he can stop time?" Jasmine asked.

"The whole world goes frozen, but he can keep moving around! Sometimes I can do it with him, when he holds my hand, but we didn't want the doctor to know that part because it's our special game we play together. It's called Time Freeze."

Sebastian squatted down and whispered to them, "Did the doctor get the magic? Can he do Time Freeze now, too?"

"No," Molly said, shaking her head. "He can only do the lightning. That's why he keeps making James do the machine. He hasn't learned how to do Time Freeze yet. I think the machine teaches him how to do our magic. Time Freeze must be really hard to learn." That explained why they were still alive. Fadel couldn't get James' power.

I looked up at Theo and Jasmine. "It's important we get them out of here right now. We can't let Fadel get James' power. Can you imagine what he would be capable of if he could freeze time and move through it?"

"Agreed," Sebastian said, taking James out of Penny's arms. "Let's get out of here. Theo, can you carry Molly?"

Molly reached out towards Theo, and he picked her up. She looked so small, so delicate in his arms.

"Let's go," Theo said, "and fast."

But downstairs, the front door opened and footsteps entered the house.

Fadel was home…

"We're trapped," Molly gasped, tears in her eyes.

"Shh," Theo said, hushing her. "It's going to be ok."

"How are we going to get out now?" I whispered. "There's no way we can get out the front door.

Theo nodded towards the window.

"You've got to be kidding me," Jasmine whispered back.

"I can't think of any other option right now. Can you?" Theo shuddered and pushed Molly's head to his chest. "Molly, keep your head right here. We're about to get you out of here, but I don't want you to be scared."

She obediently curled up against his chest and shut her eyes tight.

Sebastian opened the window and put James under Theo's other arm. He clutched both kids and stuck his head out the window to feel for the wind.

Once he confirmed that the kids' heads were properly buried in his chest, he leapt out the window into the air. Slowly, he floated to the ground. He and the children were out of the house.

"Go to the van," Sebastian mouthed, pointing in that direction. Theo put the kids on the ground and gestured for them to run to the van. They took off at a sprint.

Theo jumped into the wind and rode it back up to the window. We could suddenly hear movement in the other bedroom. The minions had awakened. Jasmine rushed over and shut the bedroom door. She began whispering to it that it should lock and not open under any circumstances. Thank goodness for her new-found power.

Theo floated both Penny and Sebastian down to the ground and came back up once again for Jasmine and me. Fists pounded at the door. "Williams, we know you're in there! Come out and face us, you coward!"

"Theo, hurry!" I yelled, since there was no point in being silent anymore. Everyone had made it to the ground now except me. As I turned to move towards the window, I heard a cracking noise. I smacked right into someone and fell.

It was the teleporter, Lawrence. He stood between me and the window.

"Going somewhere?"

My throat felt dry.

Miraculously, Theo flew up through the window and punched Lawrence in the back of the head, sending him to the floor.

"Thanks," I said, as Theo picked me up and moved to the window. As we jumped out, I saw Fadel teleport into the room. But by the time our feet reached the ground, he was outside. I scrambled out of Theo's arms, and the two of us stood firm next to each other, ready to face off against Fadel. None of our friends were in sight, having all taken off towards the van.

"Miss Williams, you never seem to listen when I tell you to give up."

"And I never will," I said, hurling a fireball at his head. He dodged it without hesitation.

"I know you took the children and by standing here now, you're merely stalling so that your little friends can help them get away," he replied.

I threw two more fireballs at him and once again, he dodged both.

"In case you wondered, I'm actually done with them. So there's no need to hide them from me now." He smiled a wicked smile that shook me to the core.

"That's not true and you know it. You're not done with them because you never got what you wanted from James."

"That may be so," he replied, circling around Theo and me, "but I've found better prospects elsewhere."

I scowled at him. "What are you talking about?"

Fadel laughed and threw his arms in the air, gesturing around himself. "Haven't you heard? I'm moving! I should have told you sooner. Maybe you ladies could have thrown me a little goodbye party."

"Where are you going?" Theo spat out. He was stalling for time, hoping that the others would notice our absence and come back to assist us.

"Oh tsk. You think I would tell you? Wouldn't want you following me, now would I? All you need to know is what I said before; there are better prospects elsewhere."

Finally, Sebastian came running around the corner, stopping dead in his tracks when he saw Fadel. At the same time, the three minions emerged from the house. Maggie and Zeke blocked our only exit. Lawrence teleported next to Sebastian and seized him, pulling his head back by the hair with one hand and pinning his arm behind his back with the other. Sebastian squirmed but couldn't break free. So much for our knight in shining armor.

"So from where I stand, I see two options," Fadel said, smiling at us.

"And what are those?" I asked and glanced around, trying to find a viable escape route.

"You let us leave here right now, and that makes you the heroes of Victory. The champions you've been fighting for years to become," Fadel said with a smile, "You'll have finally driven out the so-called villains you've been 'protecting' your precious city from. You stay here and live in bliss."

"You know we aren't going to let you leave, Fadel," I said. "We won't rest until you're behind bars."

"We've already called the police," Sebastian said and gasped. "They're on the way."

"You still haven't heard the other option."

"Which is?"

"I kill you all right now, and we leave anyway."

My heart started pounding again. With Sebastian trapped and our only exit blocked, I knew escape was impossible. Or was it? I suddenly saw Jasmine sneaking up behind Maggie and Zeke. She whispered something, and both instantly fell to the ground, asleep.

As Fadel turned around to look, I seized the opportunity and struck. My fireball burned through his coat, and he gripped his side in pain and screamed.

Theo charged and we continued to fight Fadel by hand. Out of the corner of my eye, I saw Penny come running and take down Law-rence, who let go of Sebastian. Penny and Sebastian squared off with Lawrence, two-on-one, the same as Theo and my situation with Fadel.

Fadel shocked Theo with an electric current and hit me hard in the ribcage with his staff, but neither of us collapsed as he intended.

We weren't playing games, and we certainly weren't going down without a fight.

I grew a fireball the size of a cantaloupe and screamed as I threw it at Fadel. "That's for kidnapping innocent children!" I kept making fireballs and throwing them, one after the other, each one bigger than the last.

"That's for trying to kill my friends!"

I pressed my wrists together and sprayed a beam of fire at Fadel, knocking him to the ground. He screamed in pain. His body was now covered in burns.

"And that's for trying to make me a villain."

He looked up at Theo and me as we approached. For the first time, I saw fear in his eyes.

"It's over Fadel. You've lost."

He panted and looked around wildly. This was it. We finally had him on the ground ready to give in. And then he smirked.

"You forgot about my staff," he said and wound his arm back.

Before I could react, a wave of molten lava blasted right at us, straight from his staff.

Taken down by my own flames, I thought.

I closed my eyes and braced myself for the end. But the fire never hit us. As I opened my eyes, I saw the world frozen around me. The lava wave hovered less than a foot from my body, sizzling like a flam-ing wall. A frozen Theo floated next to me, falling backwards in fear. Fadel was still on the ground, laughing at us as his staff burst forth what would be the cause of our deaths. He, too, remained frozen in place.

Looking down, I saw six-year-old James Meadows holding my hand.

CHAPTER FORTY-SIX

"James!"

I gasped and stumbled backwards, adjusting my hand to grip his hand more tightly. "James, you saved us!" I said. "Whatever you do, don't stop concentrating. We need time to stay frozen, ok?"

"Ok," he said and smiled.

"Also, don't let go of my hand," I said, not wanting to freeze myself.

He nodded. I dragged him over to Theo and used my free arm to pull him out of the blast zone. He instantly thawed as we touched him. James' power passed through me.

"Bianca, what happened?" he said, frantically looking around.

"James froze time, and so long as we are connected to him, we remain unfrozen.

"Fantastic," he said, sizing up the situation. "So what do we do now?"

What could we do? The only thing we *couldn't* do was touch Fadel or the minions, since it would unfreeze them as well.

"Could we call the police?" I asked.

"No, the police are frozen. The whole world is frozen," James replied matter-of-factly.

"Right," I sighed, thinking aloud. "Ok, so we can't do anything to him unless I scorch him alive. But I don't want to resort to that if I can help it. If Fadel is dead, we have no hope of converting back Zeke and Maggie and Lawrence. They would seek revenge and I'm not killing them. They're misguided."

"Well for one thing, we could escape," Theo said, gesturing to my car which was parked out front.

"We could do that," I replied. "But then what do we do about Fadel?"

"Do you think we can at least take the staff?" Theo asked me.

"No, probably not, since it's practically a part of him," I replied, "I'm scared to touch him or anything he's holding, as I fear that would snap him out of it."

After thinking for a second, I came up with a plan. "I say I freeze-blast the lava wave to counter it. After that, I can freeze the minions in place. Then we move everyone around Fadel and unfreeze time. At that point, it's back to five-on-one."

"Is that the best solution we have? Other than literally murdering them all?" Theo asked me, a glint of fear in his eyes.

I sighed, "I think this is the best we can do with the moment we have. And I'm not sure how much longer James can hold out."

We went to work, remaining linked together by our hands. As we moved each person, they woke up, and we explained the plan. Once we were all in place, James let go of Theo and me and stopped the freeze.

As the world began to move again, the ice blast hit the lava wall and collapsed it. Fadel's smile faded.

"Well, well, well. I should have known."

"It's all against one, Fadel," Sebastian said. "Hand over the staff if you want to leave here alive."

"You say that now," Fadel laughed weakly. "But clearly some of you don't want me dead, since I'm still here." He half-heartedly sent a blast of lightning, which hit no one. His powers were weak and so was his body.

"You're not strong enough, Fadel. It's over. You can't beat us now," Theo said, approaching him slowly.

"No," Fadel said and gripped his side. "But I don't need to beat you." He adjusted his body slightly and angled the bottom of the staff towards the ground. I knew what he was about to do.

"I need to get away." He hit his staff on the ground and with a crack, and he was gone.

Three consecutive cracks followed and with each crack, one of his followers disappeared. He had teleported to each one and collected them.

"You've gotta be kidding me!" Jasmine yelled. "Where did he go?"

"I don't know, but I'm pretty sure he's not coming back," I replied. "Like he said earlier, he's moving on."

"Well what do we do now?" Penny asked with tears flooding her eyes.

"I don't know," Sebastian said. In a dazed state, he stared at the ground, and then he stared into the horizon. "I never thought he would leave Victory. And I certainly never thought he would get away. I truly don't know what to do. It feels like we lost."

CHAPTER FORTY-SEVEN

Two weeks later, we were positive: Fadel was gone. He never returned to the house on Lionsdale Road; nor was he spotted anywhere around Victory.

We were praised as heroes. All of Victory celebrated their liberation from the clutches of Dr. Fadel and his followers. I was no longer seen as a reformed Fadel minion, but rather as one of the core Victory Supers. It was as if the world had forgotten my past entirely. This sudden change convinced me to move on as well.

My friends and I lived together in our little house, unsure of what to do next. We knew that Fadel was out there somewhere; we just didn't know where. Furthermore, we didn't know what was to be done if we did discover his new location. We were settled here, in Victory. However, it felt like it was our duty to stop him, wherever he might be. But until we figured out where that was, we remained in a holding pattern.

The night we left Fadel's house, we brought the Meadows kids to the police station, where the officers called their parents. As one would expect, they immediately rushed the children to the hospital, hoping that no permanent damage had been done. Luckily, the tests came back negative. Molly and James were perfectly fine, just dirty and underfed.

The next morning the police returned to the house, where they began investigating the machine. The officers thanked us for not destroying it, and I politely nodded my head; a part of me secretly wished I had.

Now, two weeks later, they were still running tests and studying the computer data. The results? Inconclusive. The machine was worthless without the staff. But luckily, the staff wouldn't be able to gain more power without the machine.

"Unless he miraculously has the blueprints, I don't know how he would be able to recreate the machine," Sebastian said, as we sat around the living room on a blustery Wednesday evening.

"This isn't the first machine he's built," Alexandra replied, curling up on the couch.

"He had one in Durango too. To be honest, I'm not sure if it was an entirely different machine or if he transported the one from Durango to Victory. Regardless, he knows how to build it."

"So we assume he's moved on to another city with people like us, ready to rebuild his machine and collect more followers?" Jasmine asked.

"More followers and therefore, more powers," Theo replied.

Penny shifted uncomfortably on the floor, and asked, "So what's the next step for us?" We had been asking ourselves that question for two weeks.

"I guess we need to find where he's going and stop him before he succeeds," I replied.

I didn't want to—none of us wanted to—but we knew that it was our responsibility to stop him. We couldn't remain the Victory Supers. We had to be more than that.

"I agree," Sebastian said. "I think we need to find him and take him down. For real."

"And save the others while we are at it," I added. "You know, Zeke and Maggie and Lawrence. We need to help them, like you all helped me."

"Do you think we could persuade them?" Jasmine asked, worried that her Voice wouldn't be enough to convert a villain to a hero.

"I think between your power and Bianca's story, they will be won over," Alexandra answered. "I mean, think about it. You persuaded me to understand and come around, and you weren't even trying. It was the combination of you and Eric leaving."

Eric.

My gut twisted.

"Eric would persuade them," Alexandra continued. "Not only that. He's already on our side. If only we could find him, he could help us!"

"Yeah but you guys don't know where he is," Penny said and sighed.

"I know he went west," I said softly.

Alexandra suddenly sat up. "How do you know that?" she asked.

"The night he left, he told me that he was heading west, not south like the doctor thought. He told me that I couldn't understand then, but I would soon. He said that he was going to help people."

"Do you think he knew about another pod of supers in a city out west?" Sebastian asked.

"I think so," I replied. All the details of that night suddenly made sense. "I think he found another group, another city and wanted to beat Fadel to the punch. To win them over and train them."

"Oh my gosh," Penny gasped. "Do you think that's where Fadel is going now?"

"I'm not sure. It's possible, if he discovered the same place Eric did. Either that, or he's heading to a different city entirely, and there's more than one group out there. I mean, there was Durango and then Victory. Who knows how many people like us exist!"

Sebastian's phone rang, and he left the room to take the call. We waited in silence for his return, eager to find out what was going on. When he returned, he stood in the doorway and slid both hands into his pockets.

"That was Officer Thompson at the station. He's been running security footage from around town for the night that Fadel disappeared. He spotted him stealing a rental car from the airport and tracked his route out of town."

"Really?" Penny exclaimed. "Could he tell where they were going?"

"He couldn't be sure because it's possible he switched interchanges, but it appeared that he was initially on a highway going south."

"So he's not traveling west," I remarked. I was disappointed. "Which means that he's not going where Eric went."

"Probably not," Sebastian replied. "But that does mean that we have a lead. And there are at least two more cities out there that need our help."

"So how do we go after him?" Theo asked. "What's the plan, Captain?"

"I think we try and do some digging online, to see if we get any media hits down south. Any place where supers may have been spotted. If Fadel is heading somewhere, there must be a reason. He must have gotten a lead somehow."

"Great, so we find out where he's going, pack up the car, and then what? We can't all live in the van," Jasmine said. She was clearly not interested in playing cat and mouse with an invisible mouse.

"Well for one thing," Alexandra said, "you won't need to worry about me taking up space because I made up my mind. I'm going home. I think it's time for me to go back to my family and live a normal life."

Penny climbed onto the couch to hug Alexandra, and Sebastian nodded slowly. We all knew that this was bound to happen eventually, but it still felt bittersweet. Alexandra had been my friend, even in the darkest moments of my life. Our lives had followed a similar pattern: We wanted to do something great; we pursued greatness; we fell into a trap of evil; and we came out of it, choosing to fight for the good. We were so similar. But without powers herself, it wasn't worth it for her to stay away from home any longer. I sat on the couch and hugged her too.

"You'll stay in contact with us and let us know anything you find, right?"

"Of course," Alexandra smiled. "And you'll continue to update me too, yeah? I want to know you're all safe."

"Yes, of course."

"Promise me when you free Maggie, you'll tell her to call me. I miss her a lot."

I could see tears in her eyes as she smiled at the thought.

"I promise. We will free her, and then we can all reunite properly."

"I'd like that very much."

I pulled her in close. She told us that she would leave in the morning and needed to get some rest.

Jasmine and Penny went upstairs to get ready for bed, and Theo moved to the kitchen table to begin researching Fadel's possible target locations. That left Sebastian and me alone. "Can we go outside and talk?" I asked. He nodded and we moved out to the back porch. The sky was cloudy, not like all those nights when we sat together and looked up at the stars.

"Sebastian, I'm conflicted." He reached over and grabbed my hands.

"What about?"

"Part of me thinks I need to go west to find Eric."

He didn't react as strongly as I expected he would. In fact, he barely reacted at all. He just rubbed my hands with his thumbs. "Why do you need to find him?"

"I think he could help us. I think he's the key to convincing the others to leave Fadel. Convince them for the long term, I mean. Not like Jasmine's type of convincing. I think I could find him and bring him to wherever Fadel is, and Eric could help us."

"What makes you think he would come? Or that he wants to be found? Didn't he run away?"

"Because he told me to come find him. He said I would know where to go when the time came. I think he's in Utah. Back when we were training together, he mentioned people like him out near the place where he grew up. It would make sense for him to return to the community he most wants to protect. He would go home and prepare it so that Fadel could never come in and destroy it."

Sebastian looked at our hands and thought about this for a moment. "I think it makes perfect sense. But I don't know how I feel about you driving across the country alone to convince your ex-boyfriend to join us on our quest."

I blushed. I had told Sebastian a little about Eric. He knew that we had dated, but he didn't know everything.

"What if he's still in love with you?"

"He's not. I can say that for certain. *He* left me, not the other way around."

"Then why did he want you to come for him?"

I wasn't sure why. I wasn't even sure he meant it. I mean, did Eric really have enough faith in me to believe that I would figure Fadel out, escape, and happen to know where to find him?

"I don't know," I said, honestly. "But that reason doesn't matter now. All that matters is that he might be able to help us. I think Alexandra's right. If he really did what he said he would do, then he's been training supers to go against Fadel. And he could help us rescue the others. I think it's worth a shot."

Sebastian thought about this, too. After a few moments, he squeezed my hands and spoke, "Ok, but I don't want you going alone."

"You should come with me. We could go together and the others could go south."

"Bianca, you and I both know that I need to be the one to follow Fadel. It's my life's mission to make him pay for what he did to my family … for what he did to you. Truthfully, I want you to get your payback. I want you to have the chance to defend yourself after how he hurt you."

I opened my mouth to reply, but he cut me off.

"I also understand why you need to go west."

We sat in silence again, both of us trying our best to decide the right move. My heart wanted to go with Sebastian, but my gut knew that there was still an unsolved mystery, another piece of this ever-evolving puzzle, out west. Sebastian seemed to read my mind, or at least my face, and he made the decision for me.

"I think you should take Theo. I think he would be good protection for you. You two can leave tomorrow morning when Alexandra leaves. It will give you a head start to get out there and back. And meanwhile, the rest of us can make a game plan and start heading south. You can meet us there, hopefully with Eric in tow."

"Do you think the others will be fine with this plan?"

Sebastian smirked. "They'll do whatever I tell them to. I'm the leader."

I laughed and pulled myself into his arms. "Thank you for under-standing me. I promise, we will get there, grab Eric, and come to you as quickly as possible."

"You'd better," he said, squeezing me tighter.

"Sebastian?"

"Yes?"

I breathed heavily. There were butterflies in my stomach.

"I think I love you."

He smiled.

"I know I love you," he replied, softly.

My heart flipped in my chest, but it also ached. I felt hollow inside, knowing what I just gained, I was about to lose. The whiplash of it all caused cold tears to spring to my eyes and my throat to tighten as I whispered, "I don't want to be away from you."

"But you're coming back to me. It's only temporary. You'll come back to me."

I knew in my heart it was only temporary, but it still stung. The moment I had held in my heart, the one that caused me enough grief to bring my ice powers to life, had finally been surpassed.

I may be going back to find Eric, whom I had loved, but I loved a new man now. And leaving him pained me more than being left alone. My heart screamed out in agony, and my tears froze as they fell down my cheeks.

But in this moment, in his arms, I knew I would find my way back home. For tonight, everything was ok.

CHAPTER FORTY-EIGHT

The next morning, we all agreed to the plan. We said farewell to Alexandra, who took a taxi to the airport. She hugged us goodbye and promised to text everyone when she was home safe.

Once she was gone, I went upstairs to pack a bag. I owned very little; in fact, I didn't even own a suitcase. Sebastian had given me an old backpack, and I filled it with my toiletries, my pajamas, and the few pairs of clothes I had. I tucked the two IDs, Maggie's and Zeke's, in the front pouch, along with the phone and charger that we had purchased last week. I used a canvas grocery tote to carry my two pairs of shoes, my pillow, and my jacket. Everything I owned was now in two bags at my feet.

"How do you feel?" Penny asked me, perching on my bed. She folded the quilt and added it to my pile of things.

"I feel ok," I replied. "To be honest, I'm still not sure I'm doing the right thing."

"You are," she replied, without hesitation. "Alexandra said it herself, if anyone can save Zeke, Maggie, and Lawrence, it's Eric. And for him to do that, someone needs to find him and bring him here. It makes perfect sense to me. And it would be nice to have a teleporter on our team, honestly."

"I wish Sebastian could come with me."

"We're in the same boat. I kind of wish we could trade places."

"Yeah, how are you doing with that? That Theo will be going west with me and you'll be going south? I know it must be hard, knowing you'll be away from him."

"I know it will all be fine because he's with you."

I looked up, right into Penny's gentle eyes.

"You'll keep him safe, Bee. You know how to love better than anyone I've ever met, so I know he's safe with you. That's your true power. It's not the fire or the ice. It's your ability to love."

I rushed to the bed and hugged Penny.

"That's the nicest thing anyone's ever said to me. Thank you."

"And of course, Theo will keep you safe. You might be the most loving person I know, but he's the strongest. And the bravest. And did I mention he's the most attractive?"

She smiled at me and fell back on the bed laughing.

"Don't tell me that I will need to text you photo updates," I said and laughed.

"Only occasionally. Maybe when he looks particularly good. But honestly, I would never say no!"

We lay there laughing for a few minutes, but eventually, I helped pull Penny up so we could return downstairs.

After Theo and I had loaded the van with our bags and the over-the-top bag of snacks that Jasmine and Penny had packed for us, we prepared to say our goodbyes.

"Remember the plan," Sebastian said. "You two drive out to Utah, find Eric, and convince him to return with you. Then you two and

Eric will drive back east and meet us at the location we text you. By the time you've hit the road back, we should already be on our way. If Theo's research is correct, the location should be close to New Orleans."

We nodded.

"It should take you four days to get out to Utah. We are budgeting two days to get back on the road and then three days to New Orleans. If all goes according to plan, we should be together again in nine days, ten at most."

Ten days. We could do ten days.

"And while you're driving out there, I'm going to 'talk' the landlord into keeping the rent for the house at our current rate while we're gone," Jasmine smiled, mischievously. "I've already set up direct deposit with the bank. Man, I love my powers!"

We laughed.

"Never thought you'd say that," Theo said, hugging her goodbye.

"In about a week, we will begin our journey south, confirming that we are heading to the right location," Sebastian said, finalizing the plan. "Everything else, including all communication and specific timing will be worked out as we go. We all have phones now, so anything we need to do can be communicated that way."

We exchanged hugs all around and wished each other safe travel. The last person I hugged was Sebastian. It took everything in me not to begin crying again.

"Ten days," he whispered into my ear. "Only ten days."

"I love you," I whispered back.

"I love you too," he squeezed me tight and kissed me gently. As we broke apart, I bit back tears. Penny cried as she pulled apart from Theo.

Jasmine rolled her eyes.

"Thank goodness I get a vacation from all this lovey-dovey non-sense. Ten days of absolute bliss!" We laughed and Penny wiped her tears. Theo and I opened the car doors and prepared to get in.

"You all know the plan!" Sebastian yelled, saluting us. "Travel safe, and we'll see you soon."

"Ten days!" I shouted.

"Ten days!" the three of them yelled in return.

Theo and I got in the car, he in the driver's seat and me in the passenger's seat. I typed Salt Lake City into the GPS. We waved goodbye and pulled out of the driveway.

"Off on a new adventure," Theo said, smiling over at me. "Never thought I would experience, 'Go west, young man' myself, but here we are."

We rode in silence for a little while, mentally processing what an unexpected turn our lives had taken. After a few minutes, Theo turned the radio to a classical channel.

As the orchestra began to build, I thought ahead to all that was to come. And when the building melody of the symphony finally hit that long-awaited moment of breathless, suspended silence, I looked in the rearview mirror in time to see our home and Victory City fading in the distance.

ACKNOWLEDGEMENTS

First and foremost, I feel compelled to exclaim "Deo Gratias!" I give thanks to the Lord for everything He has done for me in my writing journey and all other aspects of my life. He has blessed me beyond words.

The biggest blessing He has given me also happens to be the person to whom my greatest earthly thanks is owed: my husband, Joshua. My patient, brilliant, and kind husband pushed me through my imposter syndrome and encouraged me to follow through with publishing this novel, even when I felt terrified of failure. Each step of the way, he's been my rock and my reason. Thank you, Joshua, for being so gracious and loving. Our love story is better than anything I could ever write.

Ever my inspiration, thank you to Olivia and Hannah for being the dearest friends. Each time I think about this book, my mind drifts to my sisters. I'll never forget that night in a Florida pool when we decided to play superheroes. Who knew there was more to that story than just an hour or two of splashing around?

I want to thank my first reader, OG editor, and friend, Sara. I wouldn't have had the confidence to pursue this dream without her talent and encouragement. A huge thank you to my dear friend, Madeline, for her steadfast friendship and headshot photography skills. It didn't really feel official until I saw the photo on the back cover.

Thank you to many other friends who have supported me from start to finish. I couldn't possibly list them all, but the love, support, and prayers from Mary-Grace, Ria and David, Vince, Ben, Carrie, Peter,

Hannah and Paul, Juan, Christina, Ari, Mikayla, Elise, and Abigail have not gone unnoticed.

Thank you to Paulie for being unknowingly present on three separate monumental occasions (when I finished the manuscript, submitted to Defiance, and accepted my publishing offer). He's been a big part of this and didn't even know it.

Thank you to my parents, and grandparents for listening to my stories for twenty-six years. They've also been the main source of my childhood reading materials. Thank you to my in-laws, professors, and everyone else who's encouraged me in my vocation of writing.

Thank you to my colleagues for not just cheering me on, but for being some of the most enthusiastic supporters. The joy I've felt from them has been overwhelming. Thank you to Jason for calling me a 'writer' before he even knew about my book.

Thank you to everyone at the Pinckney library for the best high school/early college job in the world. Nothing brought me more joy in those years than being entirely surrounded by books. Thank you to my fourth-grade teacher, Mrs. Houk, for reading and reviewing one of my first "books" so long ago. I wish she could be here to see the real thing.

Thank you to David, Mark, Cassandra, Kelly, and everyone on the Defiance team for making my dream a reality. Thank you to my Defiance editor for her patience, kindness, and talent. I'm sorry for my overuse of commas, I know that must have been super annoying.

Thank you to everyone who has encouraged my education and imagination. Thank you to each and every one of the authors I grew up with. I still find their stories enchanting and am honored to join their ranks among the shelves.

Finally, thank you, dear reader. I've waited my entire life to put a book in your hands. The day has finally arrived, and I couldn't be more excited, so thank you.

ABOUT THE AUTHOR

Starting around the age of six, Rachael Waechter would leave handwritten "books" around her parent's house, hoping to find a willing audience to read them. Now, twenty years later, she's releasing her first novel, *Playing with Fire*, still hoping to find a willing audience to read her work.

Having entered the world the same year J.K. Rowling released *Harry Potter and the Philosopher's Stone,* Rachael is, naturally, a lover of young adult fiction. The stories she embraced as a child were full of adventure, whimsy, romance, and bravery. She now hopes to build worlds and crafts characters reminiscent of those books which she read growing up. In her opinion, there is nothing more exciting than a book full of twists and turns, so that's what she's created with her first novel.

Rachael is a proud graduate of Hillsdale College, where she studied History and Rhetoric and Public Address. Rachael now spends each day strengthening civil society by helping mission-driven schools, churches, and nonprofits flourish in their fundraising. Outside of work and writing her next novel, you can find her reading, sewing, baking a variety of treats, or practicing Highland dance.

After a brief stint across the pond, she returned to her home state of Michigan, where she now lives with her incredible husband, Joshua.

www.ingramcontent.com/pod-product-compliance
Lightning Source LLC
Chambersburg PA
CBHW051102030726
47504CB00006B/1744